--- ★ ---

There was a big dent in the door on the driver's side of the van as though someone strong had hit it with his fist. Damn, I thought, for the second time that day. It had to be Tom—my shower had given him time to do it—but proving that would be time-consuming and troublesome. Thinking of ways to get even, I climbed in and tossed the gym bag on the passenger seat. A crumpled white envelope blew onto the floor. I picked it up and read the typewritten note inside.

"Stay away from Martha Iavello," it read. "Go back to Franklin. This is your only warning."

"Great."

--- ★ ---

SECOND ADVENT

TONY PERONA

WORLDWIDE®

TORONTO • NEW YORK • LONDON
AMSTERDAM • PARIS • SYDNEY • HAMBURG
STOCKHOLM • ATHENS • TOKYO • MILAN
MADRID • WARSAW • BUDAPEST • AUCKLAND

SECOND ADVENT

A Worldwide Mystery/December 2004

First published by Five Star.

ISBN 0-373-26514-X

Printed in U.S.A.

To Debbie, thank you for being the love of my life

And to my mom and dad,
Frances Catherine Bonte Perona (1929–1992) and
John Anthony Perona. Thank you for the love and
(especially) the patience that it took to raise me

ONE

FATHER SKIP WAS talking murder and I was thinking "oatmeal."

It's not as odd as it sounds. After all, I'd suspected something was up when he'd phoned me in Franklin, badgering me to return to my hometown of Clinton, Indiana yesterday for the funeral of the town patriarch, Gregorio Iavello. But it wasn't until this morning, Tuesday, that Father Skip had lured me into his spacious office to give me the reason—he was certain Gregorio was murdered and wanted me to look into it, something I had absolutely no intention of doing. So I checked my watch. Ten o'clock—the time my weight-gaining diet called for a bowl of oatmeal. What I needed was a graceful way to exit. Which would be difficult since Martha Iavello, granddaughter of the deceased, was blocking the door.

"So can you help us out, Nick?" Father Skip asked, his gray-streaked eyebrows knitted together. He leaned over his sturdy oak desk and looked me in the eyes.

I took a deep breath and studied my captors. Father Scipiannini, looking older than his seventy years, had declined considerably since he presided over my mother's funeral, the last time I'd seen him. His eyes, distorted by thick glasses, looked troubled, and his neck appeared to be thin as it jutted out of his stiff white collar. His hand shook a little and I wondered if he had developed Parkinson's; however, his mind was still sharp.

Martha's finely tailored plain black skirt and white, high-collared blouse gave her a severe, conservative look out of place for someone in her late twenties. Her strong jawline and prominent nose called to mind her two older brothers, closer to my age, with whom I had gone to Holy Family grade school. As she gave me a penetrating glance, I couldn't help but assume she could checkmate her brothers' egos.

"Father," I said, turning back to the priest, "I'd like to help, but I'm not that kind of reporter anymore. I don't investigate things. The only writing I do now is an occasional freelance piece, mostly fluff stuff. If you want me to place a feature in the Terre Haute paper about Holy Family's oldest living member and how she still says the rosary every day, I'm your man. But this…" I let my voice trail off as I shook my head.

The priest tapped his arthritic fingers on the desk blotter and glared at me. He obviously expected this to be easier than I was making it. "I know you don't attend Mass anymore, but that doesn't change the fact your skills are God-given and you should be using them. We need you to use them."

There's a reason Nick Bertetto doesn't use those skills anymore, I thought, but I wasn't sure saying it would get me home any faster. Father Skip was a man of faith, and he still had some in me, despite having learned I had become a lapsed Catholic. I decided to try another tactic. "If you're so sure Signor Iavello was murdered, why on earth didn't you tell the police?" I asked.

"Oh, we did," he replied. "Or rather, Martha did." He nodded toward the door.

"My grandfather wouldn't have tried to kill himself with antidepressants," Martha said, dismay in her voice. "He suffered through four years of depression, but he was cured. Only days before his death, we celebrated his cure, and he poured the rest of the tablets down the drain. I know, I watched him.''

What was she talking about? ''Antidepressants? He shot himself in the head, and his fingerprints were the only ones on the gun,'' I exclaimed. ''At least, that's what all the newspapers reported.''

Martha and Father Skip exchanged a look that I couldn't read, but then I was hungry and having trouble concentrating. Father Skip cleared his throat. ''Well, Martha wanted to keep that part from the press. The police went along with it since the overdose hadn't killed him. It was the gunshot.''

''Papá had guarded his depression from everyone, and I didn't think people needed to know about it now,'' Martha added.

Martha's calling her grandfather 'Papá' reminded me of how he and her grandmother had raised the children after her parents had died. She must have been very close to him.

''What did the police do when you told them he couldn't have taken the medicine because you had seen him get rid of the tablets several days before?''

Martha's lips tightened. ''They gave me the same look of disbelief you're giving me now.''

Ouch.

''What we'd like to know is where the medicine came from that was in Gregorio's body,'' Father Skip interjected. ''If we could do that, it would give us a clue as to who really killed him.''

I ran my fingers through my hair. ''Look, don't misunderstand what I'm going to say. I'm very sorry he died. Since my mom passed away a year and a half ago, I know how hard it is to lose someone you love. But wouldn't Signor Iavello's being treated for depression mean he was more likely to commit suicide?''

Martha and Father Skip exchanged glances again. I wondered if they had some kind of telepathy going.

Gunshots and overdoses. What was I doing here?

"Even if an investigation is needed, why me?" I asked as gently as I could. "I haven't lived here for nearly ten years, and I didn't know Signor Iavello very well. And I'm not a detective."

Father Skip answered. "Maybe not a detective, Nick, but you were an investigative reporter once, and a good one. You solved the murder of that young woman who lived across the street from you. The police couldn't find the body, but you did."

I had learned to confront this head-on. "Father," I explained, "it's because of that young woman I don't do investigations anymore. I don't want responsibility for the repercussions. If you had been through it, you would understand." Disturbing images I had tried to bury came rushing back—my nightly vigil watching the two men whom I suspected, their discovery of my activities, my wife's disappearance later. Then I saw myself frantically searching the house for her, praying she was there. "It was my fault they took Joan," I said.

"But you saved her."

My voice turned bitter. "I didn't save her. A friend did. Someone stronger. I'd failed and was desperate."

"I read your account in the papers. You planned Joan's rescue and helped your friend. That was heroic."

"I wish that were true."

Father Skip shook his head. "It is true. Don't give me that look, Nick. We're not asking you to be a hero, we just want you to look into this case. You know you can do it. The question is, why won't you?"

I glanced around the dark paneled office, trying to find a way to articulate my situation. What I found instead was a crucifix on the wall behind him. The eyes of Jesus stared down at me. I looked away. "Father, you're right. I could do this. I'm flattered you think so. But taking on something like this is a family issue, and Joan is not ready for me to go back to investigative reporting. She's making progress, but she still has fears she hasn't worked through yet. And I'm enjoying being a stay-at-home dad to Stephanie. So I'm not the right person to help you now."

The priest grunted and rose awkwardly from his chair, shuffling to an overstocked bookcase. He reached for a small statue of the Blessed Virgin Mary standing on one of the shelves. "I assure you," he said, picking up the figurine, "I know you are the right person."

The statue caught my attention. It didn't look like any other statue I'd seen of the mother of Jesus because—well, Mary looked pregnant. I started to say something but there was a knock at the door.

Rose, who'd been the church secretary since I was a boy, stuck her coifed, blue-haired head in. "Sorry to interrupt you, Father, but there's someone here who needs to see you right away."

Father glanced over at me. "Please excuse me. I'll try to be only a minute." Martha excused herself at the same time.

I was half-tempted to leave, but my upbringing wouldn't let me. Instead, I wandered over to the bookshelf to get a better look at the strange statue of Mary.

It was made of gritty plaster and felt a little rough, like fine grain sandpaper. Mary's hands were held out by her sides away from her body, as though offering motherly affection. I checked the profile and then turned it to the front again. Sure enough, Mary's robe had a bulge under it.

The statue had been in front of a large group of books, and I glanced at a few titles. With surprise, I noticed there were thirty or more books on apparitions of Mary. I recognized a couple of places in the titles—Guadalupe, Mexico and Lourdes, France. I was flipping through *The Sun Danced at Fatima,* when Father Skip re-entered the room. He carried a small wooden plaque with a paintbrush mounted on it. I knew the inscription read, "Thanks, Nick Bertetto." I had made it for him many years ago. He held out the plaque to me and I reached for it, setting the Fatima book down on the desk.

"Sometimes I know what's best for you," Father Skip said.

"Maybe then," I said, fingering the mounted paintbrush. "I was just a kid. But not now."

"It's no different. Just like the painting episode, I'm right, but you won't understand until it's over."

I shook my head. The circumstances didn't compare. The plaque I'd made at 17, when Father Skip had prevented me and a couple of friends from going to a wild party held by a group of seniors whose parents had left them alone while they went on a cruise. It was a time when raging hormones were more coercive than sense. The party was supposed to have featured prostitutes from Terre Haute, and having been invited, I thought I'd bought my boarding card on the rite-of-passage express. Instead, the party had featured drugs and been raided by the police, and everyone there ended up in jail overnight. Fortunately, Father Skip, having found out about the party, had created a basement-painting project for the youth of the church. My parents had forced me to go. In retrospect, of course, I'd been relieved.

But I was not relieved to think about another murder investigation.

"Remember, we're not asking you to do anything dangerous," Father Skip said, pressing. "We just want you to poke around and see if you can round up any evidence that Gregorio was murdered." He made it sound like shooting fish in a barrel, although that's probably not the best choice of analogies.

"I don't know how Joan would react."

Father Skip stroked his mustache, frowning. "Do you think your wife would really believe she was in any danger in Franklin, when you would be doing the work here, two hours away? And your dad could look after your daughter."

I was silent. Although he was correct in an abstract sense, I still worried about Joan having a setback.

"Look, let's assume for a moment you're right about it being a murder. Who would want to kill Signor Iavello? Robbery couldn't have been the motive. The police found nothing missing."

"Martha can fill you in on those kinds of details," he said, brightening as I changed my line of questioning. "She took care of him the last couple of years." As if on cue, Martha re-entered.

"Nick would like more background on your grandfather," Father told Martha. "Wouldn't you, Nick?"

I didn't, but that's not what I said. "Sure," I replied, through gritted teeth. Then my stomach rumbled noisily.

Father gave my shoulder a squeeze and evaluated me. "You look more, uh, solid, than I remember," he said.

"Weight-lifting," I answered. "I took it up to get stronger." I looked at my watch. "In fact, the last couple of months I've been doing some bodybuilding, and it's time for me to eat again. So I'll just get out of your hair and…"

"Why don't we take Nick over to the coffeehouse and get him something to eat?" Martha said. "We can talk more there."

"You don't have to do that," I protested.

"It's no problem," Martha said. "We own the place."

What could I do? My dad was making the rounds of relatives with Stephanie, showing off his 3-year-old granddaughter, so there was no reason to go back to the house. Plus, I *really* wanted a big bowl of oatmeal. I nodded.

Father Skip put the plaque I'd given him on his desk next to the Fatima book. "You'll have to go without me," he said, then noticed for the first time what book I'd been flipping through. "What do you know about Marian apparitions?" he asked.

"Not much. Fatima was the last, wasn't it?"

"Oh, you'd be surprised," he said, smiling.

Martha ushered me out the door. "I'll fill him in on everything," she told Father Skip. I said a hasty goodbye to my former guardian angel.

Martha's car was not at the rectory so I offered to drive us over to the coffeehouse. I retrieved my windbreaker from the closet and slipped it on. A soft spring rain fell as we left the rectory, and I took a moment to sniff the fresh, sweet smell of the air, a smell that had not changed since I was a boy. Passing the front doors of the church, I looked up at the Italian-style cathedral that stood out from its working class neighborhood.

Gunshots. Overdoses. What a strange day. At least, I thought, it can't get any stranger.

TWO

WE HAD NO SOONER shut the van doors behind us when the light rain turned into a deluge. Pulling out onto Fifth Street from Nebeker, I reluctantly set the windshield wipers on high, embarrassed about the loud "grink, groink" of the old wiper mechanism. Oh, for a new van.

Martha was quiet, perhaps sensing it would be difficult to compete with the rain and the wipers. She did provide directions, though. By the time we reached the corner of Elm and Main, I was aware that something big had happened to downtown Clinton. New shops had opened behind doors and windows that had been shuttered for years; empty parking spaces along the street were hard to find. If not for the modern cars, one might have thought we had returned to Clinton's heydays of the 1920s, when coal mining was hot and the jobs so plentiful wave after wave of Italian immigrants, including my ancestors, settled the area.

Martha guided me to the employee parking section behind The Saints & Angels Coffeehouse ("Where Dining is a Heavenly Experience" read the changeable marquee out front) on Main. We dashed into the restaurant from a door at the rear.

I didn't know about the dining, but the smells were certainly heavenly. The scents of freshly baked breads, cinnamon rolls and coffee hit me the moment we entered. And to think I was here for dull, low-fat oatmeal.

The building was amazing. The old bank that had been

there previously couldn't have fit it any better than The Saints & Angels Coffeehouse. With high molded ceilings and a mosaic floor, the place had a religious feel I hadn't noticed before the coffeehouse filled out. Carved wooden pedestals had been attached to the walls at key places and now held statues of either saints or angels. At the front of the coffeehouse, flanking a crucifix against the wall, stood life-size statues of Mary and Jesus on pedestals anchored to the floor. The statue of Mary was a bigger version of the one I'd just seen in Father Skip's office, and sure enough, Mary was visibly pregnant. It was unnerving.

Martha ushered me over to a table, waving to a waitress as we sat. The waitress obviously knew who was boss, because she hustled over even though the other fifteen tables were occupied. She offered coffee, poured it when we both said 'yes,' and handed us menus. While the waitress scurried on to other tables, I checked the menu for oatmeal and eggs, then looked up at Martha. She swept her thick, nearly straight black hair behind her shoulders and leaned forward. Martha wasn't beautiful, but she was striking and she knew it.

"I'm sorry I didn't have a chance yesterday to thank you for coming to the funeral," she said. She seemed more composed now that we were away from the rectory. Seated close to her, I noticed her perfume for the first time. *Giorgio,* I thought.

"I am sorry about your grandfather," I said.

She looked down at the table. "He was more like a father to me. I even called him Papá." She paused. "It wasn't suicide, Nick. Someone murdered him." Her voice cracked at the word "murder," and she cleared her throat.

"Papá wouldn't have committed suicide. Especially now, when he had finally put my grandmother's death behind him. It took four years, but people had begun to notice the change in him. He wouldn't have shot himself."

The waitress zipped by with cream. Martha added some to her coffee. I did likewise and added a little sugar.

She pulled a tissue from the pocket of her skirt and wiped her eyes. In a lowered voice, she said, "My grandfather was cured."

I matched her volume level. "You said you saw your grandfather get rid of the antidepressants. Do you know for certain he didn't have another bottle somewhere?"

Her eyes turned cold. "You don't believe me, just like the police."

"That's not it," I said. "I want to believe you. Is there a way you can prove to the police he was cured? Perhaps if you had his psychiatrist talk to them…"

"Absolutely not," she said, fighting tears. She reached into her pocket for another tissue as the waitress returned to the table. Martha cleared her throat. "I'll just have the coffee," she said. "Nick?"

"Oatmeal, an omelet with egg whites only, and a glass of skim milk." The waitress jotted it down and left.

Martha reverted to her softened voice. "You have to understand, the police department isn't like it used to be. I don't necessarily trust them to keep quiet about Papá's depression, and getting the psychiatrist involved will only bring on more questions. Then a wider circle will know. Pretty soon, so will everyone else."

"It's that important to you to keep it a secret?"

"Yes. Papá was very sensitive about his depression. He even went to a doctor way out in Greencastle to avoid having anyone suspect. No one needs to know now." She blotted her eyes.

I looked around. There was something creepy about the coffeehouse with its religious theme and the odd statue of Mary. Religious art generally avoided the issue of pregnancy, especially Mary's. With the statue in my line of sight, rising behind Martha's head, I found it difficult to ignore. I turned back to Martha, and, surprisingly, found myself in reporter mode. "Maybe I don't understand the facts," I said. "What do you remember about the night he died?"

She frowned a moment. "It was last Friday. I was Papá's secretary, and as usual, I'd worked with him all day. Papá was so happy and relaxed that I stayed and had dinner with him, something I didn't always do. We talked, just about things. Then we played cards until I left at quarter to ten." Her recounting seemed very smooth. But then she'd probably told the story many times.

"When you left, was your grandfather still in a good frame of mind?"

"Oh, yes, he said he was going right to bed and thought he'd sleep peacefully." Martha choked on the words. "The police say he died around midnight."

"When you left, did you see any other cars around or have the impression anyone else was there?"

"No."

"Who found him the next day?"

"I did," she said, her voice squeaking again as it had in Father Skip's office. "Sprawled on the floor of his study. I called the police immediately." She blew her nose.

I looked at Martha, used tissues in hand, sleepless eyes framed by dark circles. Maybe she was right. Maybe someone had gone to a lot of trouble to make Signor Iavello's death look like suicide. I puffed my cheeks and exhaled.

"But who would want to kill your grandfather?" I asked. I didn't want to get involved, but I wasn't to offering advice if I knew the full story.

Martha gave me a slight smile as if she could tell my instincts were kicking in. "Papá helped a lot of people in this town, but not everyone liked him. You don't get to be a successful businessman without stepping on a few toes."

"Can you give me names?"

Martha put her head down and spoke toward her lap. "Well, two farmers are unhappy because Papá owned the mineral rights to their farms, which would have made him rich and threatened their farms if Papá had struck a deal with a coal company. You might remember the farmers, Bill Blazevich and Angelo Ronchi."

I vaguely remembered them as also being members of Holy Family church. As I recalled, their farms were west of Clinton. "Killing your grandfather wouldn't solve anything, would it?" I asked. "The mineral rights would become part of the inheritance."

She nodded. "The deal hasn't been signed with the coal company, though. Mining has gotten a bad name. The vibrations from the blasting has ruined crops and damaged houses. Maybe the farmers think they have a better chance of stopping the mine if they deal with Papá's heirs."

Martha glanced up at me as though she were checking my reaction. Was I being manipulated?

"Okay," I said, "there's two names. Are there any others?"

"My brothers," she said matter-of-factly.

"Tom and Jimmy?" While I didn't know her brothers well, I couldn't picture them as murderers.

"They've both fought with Papá at one time or another. Jimmy works as a securities trader in New York and wanted Papá to turn over financial control of the family holdings to him. Papá said he could have control over his share only after Papá died. Jimmy was angry, really out of proportion. All he and his wife care about is money. They don't have any children, you know." Martha leaned forward as if she were going to reveal a secret. "If Jimmy was doing that well," she said, "why would he need Papá's money?"

I didn't answer. She continued. "Tom has never been married. He's spent all his time trying to get some kind of athletic career going—he's tried everything from triathlons to bodybuilding. He does well in those things, but not well enough to make any money from them.

"He was always asking Papá for money to continue training. For awhile, Papá believed he would succeed and gave him enough to keep going. But about two years ago he decided Tom needed to grow up. If he couldn't make it in the sports world, Papá reasoned, be done with it. Papá even offered to let him manage the grocery business. Tom didn't want it."

"What's Tom doing now?"

"We don't talk anymore," she said in a deliberate manner, "although we had to talk at the funeral. He has an apartment here in town. I've heard through friends that he's working as a personal trainer in Terre Haute. Supposedly he's preparing for a big bodybuilding contest. You saw him at the funeral. He's huge."

She cleared her throat. "Personally I don't like it. I wish he would have listened to Papá. But maybe he'll get the money now to back his ambitions." Martha closed her eyes dramatically.

A bit too dramatic, I thought. Still, I tried to give her the benefit of the doubt. She'd been through a lot in the last few days. And the talk of names and motives heightened my curiosity.

"Do you really think either of your brothers would do it?" I asked.

"No," she replied, "but then I can't imagine how anyone can commit murder."

"Any other people you can think of?"

She kept her voice lowered. "Nick, there are many who didn't like Papá."

"Have the police been over your grandfather's business records?"

"No. No reason to."

"There may be something there," I said.

"I don't see how. I've been his secretary for more than a year now. It would have been difficult to slip anything past me."

I shrugged. "It was just a thought."

Martha caught herself. "I'm sorry. Of course, you might be right. Perhaps if you looked at them…"

"I'm not an expert or anything," I cautioned.

"More than I am, or Father Skip. Please say you'll help us."

I thought of Joan. "I keep telling you and Father Skip, it's not that simple."

"Forgive me, I'm just not thinking right today," she said. "You'd probably have to put aside some of your freelance assignments to do this, wouldn't you? Let me pay you some money. Would a thousand dollars be enough to investigate it for a few days?"

I tried not to let my mouth drop. A thousand dollars for less than a week's work. The truth was, I was lucky to get a couple hundred dollars a week, squeezing in some articles while taking care of Stephanie. And since I had been concentrating on potty-training her the last two weeks, I hadn't taken on anything new. "A few days?" I croaked.

The corners of her mouth drew back into a slight smile. "Just through Thursday. If you would give me a report of what you find by first thing Friday, it would really help."

The waitress chose that moment to bring my food and refill Martha's coffee. It gave me a chance to think, especially about the money.

Damn. I hated to make the choice. I wondered if perhaps Father Skip weren't right—as long as Joan was back in Franklin, she wouldn't have anything to fear. Dad could look after Stephanie. And we could really use the money. Maybe Joan wouldn't even have to find out.

"I'll look into it," I said, "but I can't promise I'll turn up proof he was murdered. The police have already investigated it, and since they think it's a suicide, more than likely it is. I'm sorry—I know you don't want to hear that. But it's been my experience police departments know what they're doing."

"You'll turn up the evidence," she said.

I kept marveling at how much confidence Martha and Father Skip had in me. I almost asked Martha why she was so sure, but the statue of Mary behind her finally got the better of me. "Is that a special statue of Mary?" I asked, pointing. "I don't think I've seen anything quite like it before."

Martha raised her eyebrows. "Then you don't know?"

"Know what?"

"We have a person in this area who is receiving messages from the Blessed Virgin Mary. She has come to us as 'Our Mother of the Second Advent.' That's how she appears."

"Oh." I tried to keep the disbelief out of my voice. Still, I felt the hairs on the back of my neck rise. The apparition must have been what Father Skip meant when he said I would be surprised about Mary's appearances since Fatima.

"You *must* meet the visionary. It's so wonderful that we are being blessed with Mary's presence."

I was silent. Martha read my doubts. "I know what you're thinking," she said, "but this is real. Mary herself will prove it. She's been promising for some time that she will work a miracle."

"Where is this apparition occurring?" I asked.

"In Diamond at St. Mary's church. You know, that little chapel that hasn't been used in about a decade."

I knew the place, not far from Clinton. Before it was closed, my great-aunt and -uncle celebrated their fiftieth wedding anniversary there. "Perhaps I'll go sometime," I answered, though it would be more to relive the past than to check out someone I figured would be half-crazy. "And is this restaurant somehow connected to that?"

"Father Skip and I opened the coffeehouse and the bookstore as a service to the pilgrims visiting the area. They're hungry for information, and this gives them a place to congregate. St. Mary's is strictly for worship, as she herself requested."

"Oh," I said, swallowing a bite of omelet.

"The profits go right back into promoting Mary's messages," Martha insisted.

"I don't doubt you."

I finished eating and Martha insisted on signing the check. She walked me out to the van, grabbing an umbrella on the way. The hard rain had given way to a gentle mist.

"What do you need to get started?" she asked.

"I'd like to talk to Tom and Jimmy," I said. "Can you give me Tom's address and tell me where Jimmy is staying?"

"Your best bet to catch Tom would be at the Big Sycamore Gym in Terre Haute. I've heard he practically lives there. It's near the university. As for Jimmy, I don't know where he's staying. He never said, but I'll try to find out." Then she added, "Promise me you won't reveal Papá's depression to anyone."

I opened the van door. "Don't your brothers know?"

She shrugged. "For a long time, even I didn't know."

"Martha, before I get too far into this, I'm going to give you some advice. The best thing you can do, really, is to tell the police everything you know—admit your grandfather's depression and get his psychiatrist to tell the police he was cured. Maybe then they'll take another look at it."

Tears welled in her eyes. I offered her my handkerchief, but she declined. "There are things I can't tell the police," she sputtered. Then she turned away and dashed back into the coffeehouse, her umbrella bobbing after her.

"And are there things you're not telling me?" I asked the perfumed air that remained.

THREE

BARELY OUT OF the parking lot, I was already haunted by second thoughts. I couldn't believe I'd actually agreed to look into Iavello's death. What was I thinking? Did I really believe I could hide this from Joan? Had I given in because of the money, or was that only a part of it? I needed something to do.

Terre Haute and the Big Sycamore Gym were only half an hour away, time enough for the oatmeal and omelet to settle. I hadn't done my workout yet, and I figured I could kill two birds with one stone if I drove over there. I stopped by Dad's house, stuffed my exercise clothes into a gym bag and was just about to leave when I noticed Dad had taped a note to the back of the front door. "Stephanie and I will meet you at Miller's restaurant at 1 o'clock for lunch." I recalculated the travel and workout times, but decided I would still be able to question Martha's brother and do my workout. I raced over to Terre Haute.

A quick look through the yellow pages in a vacant phone booth netted me the address for The Big Sycamore Gym on Wabash Avenue. I pulled into its small parking lot, found no spaces, and ended up circling the block before finding a place to park on the street. I noticed the logo painted on the picture window of the gym—a hugely muscular, war-painted Native-American. Damn, I thought. This was not a "health club," this was a sweat-filled, iron-clanging, muscle-flexing, vein-popping hard-core gym.

The Franklin Iron Works, where I worked out at home, wasn't a hard-core gym. Although we had a few bodybuilding devotees, the clientele was mostly normal. The few serious bodybuilders were attracted to the place by Mark Zoringer, the owner, a former Mr. Indianapolis, Mr. Indiana, and as far as I could tell from all the trophies on display, Mr. Everything Else. I knew Mark well enough to call him a friend. After all, he had saved Joan. In some ways he had also saved me. His weightlifting regime had helped get me through a tough period of self-doubt.

But while I had done a little bodybuilding, there was something intimidating about being in a bodybuilding gym. I stood outside the Big Sycamore Gym for a moment, ran through a focusing mantra Mark had taught me, and went in.

"Since it's your first visit, you can work out for free," a trim, blond receptionist told me. I filled out a card listing my name, address, and phone number, which she didn't bother to look at. "The dressing room's in the back," she said.

The gym smelled like sweat. The biggest part of the workout area contained straight, incline, and decline weight benches in neat rows with weight trees among them holding tons of iron plates. Surrounding the exercise area were racks with paired dumbbells increasing in weight from three pounds to 150 pounds each. I'd seen Mark Zoringer use 150 pound dumbbells, but I wondered how many other people could actually use them.

As I padded across the gym's worn brown carpet toward the locker room, I was relieved to see most of the other patrons were like me—fit, but not obvious bodybuilders. In fact, the only sizable body in the gym belonged to the man I'd come to see, Tom Iavello.

Tom was easy to spot, alone, hanging from a chin-up bar. He wore dirty navy-blue gym shorts and a ragged, purposefully ripped gray T-shirt that hid little of his massive upper body. A leather weight-lifting belt wrapped around his waist was connected to several large barbell plates hanging down around his bent knees. He methodically lifted his chin to the bar, performing wide-grip chins, pumping them out one after the other as though he felt no strain. Finally he slowed on the last repetition, lowering himself so gradually it made my muscles ache in sympathy. When he was down, he let go of the bar and immediately stepped in front of a mirrored wall, flaring and flexing his back muscles. I was impressed by how wide and thick his back was, but I noticed it was also pockmarked with pimples and scars. On an adult, that frequently meant steroid use. I ducked my head and moved quickly to the locker room.

When I emerged in shorts and a red Nike rag top, I threaded my way toward the dumbbell racks. I ran through a series of warm-up exercises with light weights and kept my eye on Tom, thinking I could 'accidentally' encounter him. It didn't look like it would be too hard. Everyone else seemed to be avoiding him.

Tom, however, was concentrating so intensely he didn't notice me, even though I passed him a couple of times during my workout. I didn't have time to fool around, so after I finished, I followed him to the water cooler.

"Come sta?" I asked.

Tom abruptly turned and scowled at me. *"Non c'è male,"* he growled, leaving little doubt his answer was instinctive, not sincere. "What are you doing here?"

"Working out," I said, trying to stay pleasant. "I just came over to tell you how sorry I am about your grandfather." I extended my hand to shake his, but he ignored it. Letting my hand fall back to my side, I stood there stubbornly, trying to figure out how to break the impasse.

"You still know some Italian," he said coolly.

"Some phrases. I never could carry on a conversation in Italian, like I'm sure you could with your grandfather."

He held me in his gaze before he replied. "Papá and I hadn't spoken in a couple of years," he said. He turned and walked away from me. I followed him over to a mirrored wall.

"I'm sorry to hear you and your grandfather didn't get along," I said.

He didn't reply. Instead, he flexed in front of the mirror. Standing next to him, I was struck by the impressive absurdity of his size. His arms looked bigger than my head.

"Unbelievable," I muttered.

For the first time, he smiled. "I am, aren't I?" he said. He flexed one of his biceps right in front of my face. "Twenty-one inches, pumped," he said. "I'm gonna wipe the floor with my competition at state this year."

He hit two more poses, then regarded me. "You're still pathetically thin, aren't you?"

His appraisal flew in the face of how much I'd improved, but this was not the time to defend myself. If he was bent on intimidation, I'd go along with it. Anything to get him talking. "Well, I'm not exactly a bodybuilder."

"That's obvious," he said, crossing his arms over his chest. "Why don't you tell me why you are here, as if I didn't know."

"I came here because I actually do exercise, even if you don't think so. Why do you think I came here?"

He sneered at me. "Because my sister and her band of religious idiots are convinced Papá was killed. I'm high on her list of suspects. You're investigating it for them."

I was amazed at the effectiveness of the Clinton grapevine. "Have it your way," I said.

"Don't be taken in by Martha the Pure," Tom said sharply. "She's not the holy, innocent woman she would have you believe. She's had her eyes on Papá's money since the day my grandmother died. The only reason she wants it to be murder is that his insurance policy won't pay double indemnity on a suicide. A quarter-million dollars if someone proves it's murder. And she'd love for me to take the fall.''

Tom stepped in close. Now I was getting nervous. I took a step back. "If I had wanted to kill him," he said, lifting his hands at me in demonstration, "I would have wrapped my hands around his neck, lifted him off the floor and shaken him until he was dead." He said the last few words through gritted teeth.

Keep him talking, I thought. I backed up another step. "So you didn't do it?"

Tom laughed. "I didn't need to. He was old. I was going to get his money soon enough."

"Do you think he committed suicide?"

"If anybody killed him, it was Martha. Two weeks ago she got him to change his will. Half his estate now goes to that crazy group she founded. She didn't tell you that, did she?"

My face must have registered the surprise. "No," I said.

"'Children of the Second Advent.' Martha is chairman. Papá was so senile I'm not surprised she got him to change the will. I wouldn't know about it yet, except my brother found out from the lawyer. We're gonna challenge the will, if it ever gets read. Martha's managed to put that off until Friday," he said, suddenly mimicking Martha's tearful delivery, "'because it would be too painful to hear it so soon.'"

Tom paused, almost gloating. "Martha can't afford for it to be suicide. That would demonstrate his mental illness, show that he wasn't of sound mind when he made the change. Score one for Jimmy and me. Martha's no saner than Papá was, promoting a woman who says she talks to the mother of God."

Tom's voice became suddenly menacing. "You're not

much of a detective, are you?'' he said. He took steps toward me again. Displaying a little fear to keep him talking hardly required a stretch of my acting muscles. I was worried things were getting out of hand. Backing up, I bumped into a weight bench.

"Did she tell you he tried to commit suicide last year?'' he asked, getting louder. "That he almost succeeded? That she managed to hush it up?''

People started to gather, curious to see what was going on. I maneuvered around the weight bench.

"Do you know who owns Second Advent's restaurant and bookstore? It's not her group, it's her. Check it. You don't know shit, do you? Do you?'' Tom stopped moving when he reached the bench. He was two feet away from me and breathing surprisingly hard. "Get out of here,'' he said.

I wanted to say something but thought better of it. Still, I walked, not ran, back to the locker room, trying to deny him some satisfaction. I showered, dried off and then dressed quickly. When I re-entered the gym, he was busy training a kid who looked like a college football player. Tom noticed an older man performing lateral raises incorrectly. He gently interrupted him, showed him the proper form, and then returned to the football player. The action seemed so kind I was struck by the incongruity of what had just happened to me.

I slipped silently out the front door and let out a breath. Much as I didn't want to admit it, Tom was right. I wasn't much of a detective. I hadn't asked Martha any of the right questions, and I had a lot to check up on.

There was a big dent in the door on the driver's side of the van as though someone strong had hit it with his fist. Damn, I thought, for the second time that day. It had to be Tom—my shower had given him time to do it—but proving that would be time-consuming and troublesome. Thinking of ways to get even, I climbed in and tossed the gym bag on the passenger seat. A crumpled white envelope blew onto the floor. I picked it up and read the typewritten note inside.

"Stay away from Martha Iavello," it read. "Go back to Franklin. This is your only warning."

"Great."

FOUR

THE DENT HAD TO BE from Tom but I couldn't be sure about the note. I'd put the gym bag on the passenger seat when I left Dad's house, but might have missed a note since I hadn't been looking for one. Theoretically it could have been there since the coffeehouse. And I was beginning to think there might be more people than just Tom who would want me to stay away from Martha.

It was interesting that the note hadn't said anything about the *signore*'s death, just to stay away from Martha. I shoved it in my pocket and tried not to think about it as I drove back to Clinton.

Miller's restaurant was on 9th Street. Built back in the early fifties, it still had the old diner motif inside, although the Millers had updated the outside with brick when they had taken it over about five years ago. I hadn't eaten there in a while but Dad had pronounced the Italian food "almost authentic," which was the highest praise he gave any restaurant meal. I figured it would be good, and I was looking forward to lunch.

The rain had stopped. There was a line out front. I spotted Dad and Stephanie midway back. After parking the car on a side street, I joined them. Stephanie waved excitedly when she saw me coming. "Hi, Daddy!" she squealed.

"Hey, little one," I said, picking her up and giving her a kiss on the cheek. I smoothed her light brown hair, the color a cross between my own dark brown and the blonde of her mother. "Did you have fun with *Nonno* this morning?" I asked, looking into her dark espresso eyes. They were perhaps the only physical feature she'd inherited from me. Beyond that, she was clearly her mother's child.

"We went to see Lucy," she said. Lucy was the daughter of my cousin Helena. "We played with Beanie Babies." It was then I noticed Stephanie clutching two bean bag toys, a rabbit and a cat, I hadn't seen before. "Where did you get those?" I asked.

"I gave them to her," Dad said defiantly. "They were two she didn't have."

I sighed. Dad spoiled Stephanie rotten, but mostly I didn't make an issue of it. I supposed it was his grandfatherly prerogative.

"Dad, where are all these people coming from?" I whispered, indicating the line. I gave Stephanie another kiss and set her down.

"A little economic engine called Second Advent," Dad said, his voice low. "It started picking up steam about a month ago."

"You've never mentioned it when we've talked."

"Only because it's nonsense," he replied. But he didn't say it like he thought it was nonsense. And he didn't look at me. He looked around at the crowd.

"Is it nonsense, Dad? I mean, Father Skip must believe it, and I know Martha Iavello does. She's started a coffeehouse and bookstore on Main. What do you know about the apparition?"

"I haven't been out to St. Mary's, so I don't know much. But people claim to have seen statues crying and Mary's Immaculate Heart dripping blood. It's bringing in the crowds."

Stephanie slipped her hand in mine. I gave it a squeeze and winked at her. "I bet old Mayor Bazzani's happy," I told Dad.

"Privately, yes. But he can't take a stand on the apparition. Not everyone is happy."

I looked at the people in line and thought of all the tourists I'd seen on Main Street. "You're kidding."

Dad shook his head. "Some people feel uncomfortable with the whole idea of an apparition. A few fundamentalist groups around here have even denounced it. Loudly."

We finally reached the hostess; she seated us at a window table with a booster chair for Stephanie.

"So what did Father Skip want?" Dad asked.

"As if you didn't know…"

"I don't know," he protested.

"Dad, somebody had to put the notion into Father Skip's head that I would do an investigation for him."

Dad grinned. "Okay, he did come to see me about asking you for help. But it was his idea. And all I know is it involves Martha. Really!"

I looked at Dad's still-youthful face, sparkling eyes pleading his case. I believed him. "He and Martha want me to find any evidence that Signor Iavello was murdered," I said. "They think it was made to look like suicide."

Dad let out a low whistle. "Why not a detective?"

"That's a question I've asked and haven't gotten a straight answer to yet. Father cites the Cindy DePasse case, but there's got to be more behind it than that."

Stephanie held her Beanie Babies over the floor as if she would drop them, glancing my way for a reaction. I smiled at her. "Don't do that," I said in sing-song voice.

"Okay," she said. "Daddy, I wanna eat."

"I know, honey, so do *Nonno* and I. I'm sure it'll be soon."

I turned to Dad. "She wants attention."

Dad nodded but went right back to the Iavello death. "Why don't they think it was a suicide?" he asked.

"The logic runs something like this: Signor Iavello was

a happy, well-adjusted person and he wouldn't have done it.''

My father smirked. ''We must be talking about a different Gregorio Iavello, then.''

I chuckled. ''Not exactly how you remember him?''

''Gregorio was clinically depressed, you know,'' Dad said.

So much for Martha thinking nobody knew. ''There was evidence left at the scene which supports that,'' I replied.

''It's been the big rumor the past year. He never really recovered from his wife's death, you know, and he'd become something of a recluse. Never even went to church, although he did come the Sunday before last. He even stayed around after Mass.''

I thought about that. Why would he have chosen the Sunday before he committed suicide to go to Mass? Was he searching for a reason not to do it? Was suicide in his thoughts at the time?

''Daddy,'' Stephanie said, pointing at her Beanie Babies, now on the floor. I picked them up and handed them to her.

''Be more careful,'' I said.

Just then the waitress appeared. Dad ordered rigatoni al forno. I ordered a child's spaghetti plate for Stephanie and spaghetti with a chicken breast for myself. Low fat and high protein, I thought, congratulating myself on my restraint. But when the waitress returned with a basket of high fat garlic bread, I ate over half of it. The road to love handles is paved with good intentions.

I wanted to stop talking about the investigation and my guilt for taking it on. ''So who is this person Mary's supposedly appearing to?'' I asked.

''Oh, you know her,'' he said. ''Anna Veloche.''

My jaw nearly hit the table. Anna Veloche?

The last time I saw Anna was several years ago in Indianapolis, back when I still worked as a reporter and she worked as a public relations consultant. A scandal involving the governor's office had unfolded, and she was at the heart of it. I covered the story. The governor's press secretary had awarded a chunk of work to the firm Anna represented. Someone with a camera had come up with evidence that Anna had spent long nights in a hotel room influencing the press secretary's selection. To make matters worse, the press secretary was married.

Anna faced the press bravely, but the evidence was substantial. She resigned in disgrace then disappeared. It was one of those rare times I was glad *not* to be the one to break a story. Having known Anna since high school, I found it hard enough just to report on it.

She'd done it to herself, but I felt sorry for her. She had had a tough life. At one time I was even involved in it. But hearing she was back in the limelight, I couldn't help but be suspicious.

"Anna Veloche?" I said, disbelievingly. "I'd like to think she's for real, but my fear is she's just figured out a new way to get attention."

Dad scanned the people in the diner. "I would think that, too," he said, "but some people say she's really changed, that she's taken a hard look at herself."

A woman about Dad's age two tables over waved at him. He winked at her and waved back. "Who's that?" I asked.

"Just a friend."

"A friend?"

"*Nicolo,*" he said, using my Italian name, "I loved your mother very much. I always will. But I have to move on now. I'm dating. I get around to the dances. You understand, don't you?"

I looked at him across the table. Dad had aged well. He'd gained a few pounds since Mom died, but nothing he couldn't carry. His face maintained its oval shape—no jowls, no saggy second chin. His hair was still black. No doubt he would be pursued by widows and divorcees. "Of course I understand," I said, thinking of something Mom had told us before she died, that she didn't want Dad sitting around the house all the time. But still, I looked over Dad's dance partner a little more carefully. Too much makeup, I thought.

The food finally came after we'd demolished a second basket of garlic bread. The spaghetti was good and I ate much too quickly. Stephanie, having filled up on the bread, wasn't much interested in her lunch and tried feeding spaghetti to her bean bag toys. I noticed it too late to save the white cat who now had orange fuzz on his lips. I shook my head and checked Dad. He ate his rigatoni slowly, savoring every bite.

Before long, my thoughts returned to Iavello's death. The one person who always knew what was going on in Clinton was Dana Rardin, editor of *The Daily Clintonian* and my former mentor. It would be helpful to find out what she knew of Iavello's death. I checked my watch. *The Daily Clintonian* was an afternoon paper, but it ought to have hit the stands by now, meaning she'd be available.

I hoped Dana could also shed light on Martha Iavello. She might have some idea if what Tom had said about Martha were true. I wondered now if Martha were as religious as she appeared. In my struggle over whether or not to take the case, I had forgotten to be skeptical of people who claimed to see supernatural things—and I lumped UFOs, ghosts and the Virgin Mary together in that category.

"Does Joan know you've taken on this case?" Dad asked.

"I didn't say I had."

"You didn't have to."

I shoved my hands in my pockets. Was I that easy to

read? I wondered if I would have that kind of knack with Stephanie when she was my age.

My hand fingered the threatening note in my pocket. "I've thought about not telling Joan, just saying that I wanted to spend a few days here with you," I said, "but I don't think that's wise. The way things are, she and I need to be honest with each other. I'll tell her what I'm doing, no matter what that might bring."

"You're finally taking a step forward," he said.

I almost got angry. The last year had been a real struggle trying to balance everything—Stephanie's needs, Joan's emotional distance, my own regrets about what had happened to my family and my seeming inability to make the situation better. I'd tried to keep life stable, especially for Stephanie's sake, but Dad didn't seem to see that. All he could see were changes he felt made me a lesser person. Where I saw Joan as a victim, Dad saw her as a tyrant. But she was my wife, we'd been happy for many years, and I wasn't willing to walk away from my marriage to her. At least, not yet. I kept hoping that, given time, she would get better.

I held my tongue with Dad. "I ought to call her when we get back home. Then I thought I'd go see Dana Rardin."

Dad nodded. The waitress came by with the check and Dad grabbed it.

"You don't have to do that," I told him.

"I want to. We're celebrating your return to being an investigative reporter."

I gritted my teeth and thanked him.

Stephanie wanted to ride with *Nonno* so I walked them over to his car. I gave her a kiss and told her I'd see her back at *Nonno*'s house in a few minutes.

But it turned out to be longer than a few minutes. I knew that when I got within viewing distance of the van. Someone was waiting for me in the passenger seat.

FIVE

"I'VE GOT TO start locking my van," I thought.

My earlier encounter with Tom and the resulting dent in the car had made me cautious that someone might want to put a dent in me. So I carefully approached my visitor from the driver's side, straining to see who it was. Somehow the occupant knew I was approaching and turned to look at me, giving me a smile I recognized instantly, one slightly too wide for her face, with perfect teeth in straight rows. It belonged to Anna Veloche.

My heart beat rapidly at seeing her. Quit being foolish, I told myself. This was a much different Anna than the one I'd known in high school, although seeing her here in Clinton—well, it was easy to forget the more recent scandals and the way she had used people. In high school, Anna had been mixed-up too, but in a sweet, naive way. Though rumored to be "easy", she had had heart, I thought. And there was one other thing I knew about Anna which would always cloud my ability to think rationally about her.

I opened the door. "Hello, Anna," I said.

She smiled again. "It's good to see you, Nick. I apologize for being so presumptuous, but when Martha told me you'd agreed to help, I just had to find you right away. I wouldn't have gotten in your van, but it's cool out, and the door was unlocked."

I climbed in the driver's seat. She certainly sounded like the sweet Anna. And she looked the part, too, with black

hair that had grown long and fashionably frizzled. She wore
blue jeans and a flannel shirt, topped by a navy cardigan
sweatshirt.

"How did you find the van?"

"Martha described it to me. After I didn't find you at
your dad's house, I started looking around. Clinton still
isn't a very big place."

"Where's your car?"

"I bicycled from the bookstore," she said, gesturing toward a cherry red mountain bike lying on its side near the
van's front bumper. "We really need your help."

That brought back Tom Iavello's comment about half the
estate being left to Second Advent, with more money on
the way if I could prove the *signore* had been murdered.
Of course Anna would have a vested interest in encour-
aging me.

"I didn't realize you knew Signor Iavello so well."

She caught the skeptical tone in my voice. "C'mon,
Nick. I say 'we' need your help because Martha is a dear
friend. I knew Gregorio well enough to say he wouldn't
commit suicide."

"Let me ask you the same question I asked Martha: why
would anyone want to kill Signor Iavello?"

"Beyond what Martha's told you, I'm sure I don't
know." Her voice and expression seemed honest and natural.

"Why won't Martha tell the police her grandfather was
cured of depression? They already know he was depressed—I'm sure they checked out the prescribed medication. What's the big secret?"

Anna paused, considering. When she spoke, it was in her
carefully-worded, public relations voice. "The circumstances are something I think Martha feels uncomfortable
with. In time she'll be ready to talk about it."

"If his death was murder, she may not have much time.

His body's already been buried. Another couple of weeks and she won't have a prayer of getting anyone to act."

"That's why Father Skip called you. To help us now, before Gregorio's death has been forgotten."

"I can't help her as much as she can help herself."

"Nick, please. Check into the death. I'll talk to Martha, but I'm not sure I'll have much influence." Anna hesitated. "I have something for you," she said, reaching into her pocket.

She pulled out a necklace of some kind with a medallion. I didn't get a good look at it before Anna undid the clasp, leaned forward and set her arms on my shoulders. I felt her hands behind my neck, re-clasping the necklace. When she didn't move away, I thought she was going to kiss me, and I wondered what I would do if she did.

Instead, she held my eyes with a steady gaze. "We've been sinners before, you and I. God's forgiven us for that, but we shouldn't do it again." She sat back and returned her hands to her side.

Her eyes were a beautiful walnut brown. I continued to stare into them. "You know, you were the first," I said.

Anna grinned, lips pressed together as though holding back a giggle. I reddened. Of course she had known.

"Don't be embarrassed," she said. "You were sweet, really—so concerned about my pleasure, much more than others." Anna gave me the once-over. "If I had known how you were going to turn out…" She shook off whatever thought she had. "That's behind us now."

"What is this?" I asked, holding the pewter medallion away from my chest, trying to see what was on it.

"It's called a Miraculous Medal, though I hate to use that term. In 1830 in Paris, Mary appeared to a nun named Catherine Laboure, revealed an image of herself and asked Catherine to have a medal struck with it. She said those who wore the medal with faith would receive great graces."

"And have they?"

Anna gave me a patient smile. "That's how it's come to be called the Miraculous Medal," she answered. "Catherine's body, for instance, never decayed after death. It remains on display at the shrine dedicated to 'Our Lady of the Miraculous Medal.'

I wondered if Anna had actually seen the uncorrupted body or was just reporting it. The image on the medal looked familiar. It was almost a dead ringer for the statues of Mary I'd seen in Martha's restaurant and at Father Skip's office, except Mary wasn't pregnant in this one.

I had never worn a necklace before and it felt uncomfortable. I pulled at the chain, wincing.

"Please don't take it off," she said. "You might need graces more than you know."

Anna was working some kind of magic on me, and I found it difficult to express my cynicism. Then she disarmed me completely. "I know Martha has told you about me," she said. "Do you believe I'm receiving messages from Mary?"

"You ask the tough questions up front, don't you?" I said. I turned away from her and noticed that the windshield had fogged. "Look at that," I said. "Maybe we should talk somewhere else."

"You could start the engine," she said. "And you're avoiding the question."

I started the car, then cleared my throat. "I don't know yet what to believe. Do you really think you're seeing the Virgin Mary, that it's not some overactive part of your imagination?" Or psychosis or neural disorder, I thought.

Anna looked me in the eyes, unembarrassed by the question. "Oh, yes, I couldn't do this otherwise. After I left Indianapolis, I swore I would never put myself in the spotlight again. When Mary told me about these messages, I begged her not to use me, to use someone else. I didn't want to face the media again."

"What did she say to that?" I asked. It was strange how I adopted Anna's habit of talking about Mary as if she just dropped in to borrow a cup of sugar.

"She pointed out my skills as a speaker. I told her I had no credibility. She said I had God on my side and asked how much more credibility I needed. It was a gentle reprimand."

"I'm not sure credibility is important these days," I said. "Look at all the folks who appear on talk shows."

Anna stared at me. "That's what Mary said."

Great, I thought. Now I'm channeling Mary, too. I changed the subject. "What about the statue I've seen several places? Where did you get those? Is that how Mary really appears?"

"Martha contacted someone who makes statues. He made those to my specifications. And yes, that's how she appears, although when she first came to me, she wasn't pregnant. That's been only in the last six months. Otherwise her appearance hasn't changed. She's very beautiful. She wears the long robes that were common in her time. Often she wears white, but when she's sad or delivers a disturbing message, she sometimes wears gray or a dark color. But never black."

"Does 'Second Advent' mean what I think it means?"

Anna answered matter-of-factly. "If you mean that we're living in the 'Last Times' now, then yes, you're right. But Mary says she doesn't know how long it will be before the Second Coming, and she doesn't encourage speculation. She reminded me that her Son once told His disciples He would return 'soon,' almost 2000 years ago. God's time is not our time. But what she wants to do in *this* time is to unite her children. By bringing us together, Catholic, Orthodox, and Protestant, she is preparing the way for her Son to come again.''

''Do you have any idea how hard this is for me to believe?''

''Yes, I do. For months after she first appeared, I wondered if I were crazy. But there have been signs. And now she's promised me that she will work a miracle soon.''

''What kind of signs?'' I asked. The uncomfortable chain made me itch my neck. Anna grabbed my hand, holding it in hers as she tucked the medal into my shirt with her other hand. Her fingers brushed against my chest.

The touch had felt light but deliberate. Anna's eyes glistened just a little, and I felt drawn to her face. Part of me wanted to kiss her, but I held back.

She turned her face away. ''I'm sorry. I didn't mean to do that. Please forgive me.''

I swallowed hard. ''It's okay,'' I said.

''I need to leave.''

''Yes.''

''*Arrivederci, caro,*'' Anna said. She squeezed my hand.

''*Purtroppo. Arrivederci,* Anna,'' I replied. I was both relieved and sorry when she left the car and rode off on her bicycle, never looking back.

And I knew that although I planned to tell Joan the truth about this case, Anna was one part I'd better leave in the dark.

SIX

AFTER GIVING DAD an edited version of my talk with Anna, I tried the pharmacy number. Joan answered on the second ring.

"Hi," I said, "it's me."

Her voice changed from professionally cool to wavering. "Nick! Is everything all right? Is Stephanie okay?"

"Everything's fine, relax. How are you?"

"Okay," she said, after a moment's pause. Her voice returned to normal. "That prescription hasn't been filled yet," she told someone on the other end. "The doctor wrote it for a dosage the manufacturer discontinued. I haven't been able to get an answer back yet. Just a minute, Nick," she told me. "The Achgills picked up that antibiotic an hour ago. This prescription must be for one of their other children…"

"Joan," I barked, trying to break in. "I know you're busy. I just want you to know I need to stay in Clinton for a few days. I'll call you tonight to explain."

"That's fine," she said. I could tell her mind was on something happening at the other end.

"I suggest you heat up the leftover meatloaf for dinner," I added, testing her. She hated meatloaf.

"What?"

"I'm kidding. About the meatloaf, I mean. I do need to stay longer. I'll call you tonight."

"Okay." I could hear someone talking to her.

"Good-bye, Joan. Love you."

"Loveyoutoo," she rushed.

I hung up first. Stephanie trudged in, eyelids heavy, clutching her new bean bag toys. I picked her up and kissed her on the cheek. "Hey, little girl," I said softly.

"Hi, Daddy." Stephanie yawned and buried her head in my shoulder, rubbing her eyes against my shirt.

"Tired?" I asked.

"Mmmm," she murmured. I glanced at the clock. It was a little early for her nap, but she had undoubtedly played hard with her cousin Lucy all morning.

"Do you need to use the potty first?" I hated potty-training almost as much as Stephanie did, but I had to ask. When she nodded, I sent her into the bathroom before taking her upstairs to put her to sleep.

Dad wouldn't let me leave until I gave him the rundown on Martha's list of suspects. I suspected he was up to something but he protested that he was just curious. After promising to keep him up to date on everything, I left to see Dana Rardin at *The Daily Clintonian.*

Newsprint and coffee were the two smells that defined *The Daily Clintonian* offices, and the familiar mingling of the scents hit me as I entered the building. The receptionist, Mrs. Santrach, whom I had known practically forever, jumped up and gave me a big hug. She paged Dana without an explanation as to why I was there. Dana gave me a hug herself and hauled me upstairs into her office.

"Nick, you are a sight for sore eyes. Sit down," she ordered. I obeyed, taking the chair next to her desk as I had years ago as a reporter. With the exception of new computer hardware and a few more awards on the plain white walls, her office hadn't changed much. I was willing to bet the dusty miniblinds in the window overlooking Elm Street had seen more history than current high schoolers.

Dana sat on the edge of her desk. Although in her sixties,

Dana looked younger. The number of lines in her face hadn't increased, and her eyes held the same spark of inquisitiveness. Always a little overweight, she had put on a few more pounds, but not to the point where it was unattractive. She wore her auburn hair in the same wedge. "How have you been, Dana?" I asked.

"I've been good," she said, punctuating the last word of the sentence. "I can see you're doing fine. How's that sweet little girl of yours?"

"Stephanie is terrific. She's staying with my dad while I'm out running a few errands."

"I see your dad from time to time. He's still as handsome as ever," she proclaimed. "Looks like you're taking after him." She paused. "I don't suppose your being here has anything to do with the death, or might I say murder, of Gregorio Iavello?"

"You still know everything that goes on around here, don't you, Dana?"

"Actually, that was a guess, and you still haven't learned how to play poker," she said, laughing. "Always could see right through you. Well, how about it?"

Making sure it was off the record, I told her about Father Skip's call, his belief that Iavello had been murdered, Martha's asking me to look into Iavello's death and Anna's follow-up visit. I also told her about my strange encounter with Tom at the gym. I stopped short of revealing Iavello's bout with depression, even though Dana was sure to know, feeling bound by my promise not to bring it up. "Level with me," I said, "how did you guess I was looking into it?"

"That's a bit of a story. Martha was distraught when I interviewed her for the *DC*'s article about her grandfather's death, but she said at the time she didn't think it was a suicide. The police only let out details about the self-inflicted gunshot, but Tom Iavello made an offhand comment to a *Terre Haute Tribune-Press* reporter about a pre-scription bottle at the scene. *The Press*'s editor is a friend. When Tom wouldn't confirm what he'd said about the bottle and the police refused comment, he called me to see what I knew, which was nothing. But I filed that fact away.'' Dana paused. ''Tom knows something but won't say. Neither Martha nor the police will answer questions. It's enough to make a crusty old editor very suspicious. Then I heard you were at the funeral, which seemed odd. And Betty Santrach saw you and Martha talking together at Martha's coffeehouse. I put two and two together and figured you're back in the investigative business.''

''What does your intuition think about the death?'' I asked. ''Murder or suicide?''

She stood up, walked behind the desk and plopped in her chair. ''Wouldn't it be interesting if it were murder?'' she said, playing with a pencil on her desk. ''Who could have planned it so well? What was their motive?'' She looked up at me. ''You have a lot to work on.''

''Yeah, I know,'' I replied, ''but I'm rusty. And I got this note warning me to stay away from Martha.'' I pulled the note out of my pocket.

Dana examined it. ''Where?''

''I found it in my car after I saw Tom at the gym. But it might have been in there since I left Martha's coffeehouse this morning.''

''It's typewritten,'' Dana said.

''I may be rusty but I can see it's not handwritten.''

Dana hmphed. ''No, I mean it's not laser printed or jet printed. This was done with an actual typewriter. Impact printing. Trust an editor on this one.''

''Does that mean anything to you?''

''Only that the person who wrote it probably doesn't use a computer. But it might mean more later.'' She handed the note back to me. ''Watch your step.''

"I will. Dana, if Signor Iavello was murdered, Martha has to be a major suspect. Tom's information, if it's right, means Martha now controls over half of the estate." I scooted my chair a little closer to her desk. "What do you know about Children of the Second Advent?"

"It's an organization set up to promote the messages Anna Veloche is supposedly receiving from the Virgin Mary," Dana said. "They have a book out now, not very thick, maybe about 100 pages. Martha sells it at the bookstore. I bought a copy before I did a story on Anna a few weeks ago. It's around here somewhere."

She hunted through her office. From the papers stacked over the lip of her in-box and the mess I saw in her file cabinet, I knew Dana hadn't become any more organized than when I worked for her.

"Here it is," she said, handing me a book with a light blue cover and a stylized drawing of the pregnant Mary. The title read, *Messages From Our Mother of the Second Advent to Anna Veloche*.

I flipped through the book. Father Skip had written the introduction. The last entry was dated two months ago. "Is Anna crazy, on the level, or just a good actress?" I asked, looking up from the book.

"Could be any of those," Dana replied, sitting down again. "I went to her Wednesday night prayer group at St. Mary's when I was writing the article. Everyone was saying the rosary when suddenly Anna knelt in front of the statue of Mary. Anna's face took on this look of ecstasy, as though she were looking at something incredibly beautiful. A couple of people claimed to see a white light near the statue, but I didn't see anything. The apparition lasted about three minutes. When it was over, Anna led the prayer group to finish the rosary. Later she told everyone what Mary had told her."

I folded my arms across my chest. "What was the message?"

"Similar to a lot of others you'll find in that book. Mary thanked the prayer group for their faithfulness, said their prayers were needed for the unity of Christians throughout the world, and urged everyone to continue to fast and pray."

"How many people are in the group?"

"I don't know. There were lots of people in the church, but Anna said not everyone was officially part of the prayer group. The crowds grow from week to week. Martha buys an ad in the paper every Friday. Last week she said they had almost two hundred people."

I must've looked skeptical, because Dana chuckled a bit. "Hey, we've got religious oddities all over the area," she said. "Just a minute." She disappeared into the front office and reappeared with a copy of *The Daily Clintonian.* "This is from last Thursday," she said, finding the page she was looking for and thrusting it in my hands. "Right here," she said, thumping an ad. "Have you heard of the Church of the Mystical Jesus? It's located on the south edge of Clinton. Minister's name is Carl Young, and he's something else. Looks television perfect." Dana smiled dazzlingly in a mock pose. "He's always saying, 'Be healed!' and smacking people on the forehead. Has them wearing these silly crystals with pictures of Jesus embedded in them. But the crowds love him. About a year ago he came out of nowhere and took over a small abandoned church. Now he's filling it up every Sunday and looking for someplace bigger."

I shook my head in amazement. Then I remembered my doubts about the case. "I don't know how to approach this case, Dana. I'm not doing well so far, something Tom Iavello effectively pointed out. I don't know if I've lost my touch or if I just can't think like a detective."

"Of course you can't think like a detective," Dana said, shaking a finger at me, "you've never been one. But you used to be a damn good reporter—of course, you had a terrific teacher." She grinned.

"Modest, too," I added.

"Now when you solved that murder in Franklin, you were thinking like a reporter. You've got to get back into that mode. Build a story. In fact, build *me* a story. If Gregorio's death is a murder, I'll hire you to write the articles."

Something stirred in my brain. A reporter's credentials would get me access to some police information without letting anyone know I was working for Martha, which would be a plus. "Can you hire me right now?" I asked, and told her what I was thinking. "But I can't promise you there'll be a story."

Dana shrugged. "I'll hire you tentatively. But the pay's tentative, too. It's completely contingent on your writing. You understand that, don't you? Even though we're friends."

"You're so frugal, Dana. But I accept."

"I'm cheap and you know it. Oh, and I want an exclusive."

"You got it."

Dana reached into a desk drawer, pulled out a reporter's notebook, and threw it at me. I laughed, feeling a lot better than I had when I came in.

"What are you still doing here?" she said, pushing me out the door. "Get out there and get me some column-inches."

SEVEN

I COULDN'T RESIST the temptation to stop by the police station armed with my new credentials. Dana was right. Detecting was for the police. I just needed to use my reporter skills and concentrate on building a story.

The police station was just off Main at Vine Street, near the depot where the train used to stop when Clinton was a destination. I turned into the uneven parking lot, drove past the front of the beige brick building that housed the mayor and other city officials, and pulled into an angled parking spot near the far door. There was only one other vehicle in front, a forest green Jeep Wrangler bearing the license plate "B HEALED." I remembered Dana's comments about the faith-healing minister in town, but it was hard for me to conceive of a minister who would feel at home driving such a yuppie, get-out-of-town-for-the-weekend vehicle. The jeep looked new. Ministry must be going well, I thought.

I hesitated outside the door, realizing I hadn't prepared a set of questions to ask, but decided to wing it. I pushed on the door and went inside.

The waiting area was as small as a walk-in closet. I stood on a patch of scuffed-up linoleum and stared at the two large, heavily tinted windows in front of me. Behind them lay the dispatch center, but no one slid the windows open to see what I wanted. So I tried the door on my right, which led into the police area. It was locked.

The window slid open. An overweight woman in her late

forties with short, greasy black hair glared at me. She wore a telephone headset and her tiny office was crammed with communication and computer equipment.

"Can I help you?" she asked, sounding like she wanted to be anything but helpful.

"Hi, I'm Nick Bertetto with the *DC*. I was wondering if I could talk to someone about the Iavello suicide." The tiny badge pinned to the dispatcher's powder blue blouse told me her name was Suzy. Suzy looked doubtful about my request.

"The chief would have to be the one to talk to you, and he's tied up right now," she said without checking. I tried to peer around her to see into the police station, but her body blocked me like an offensive lineman's.

"Can I talk to him sometime today?" I asked. "It's for tomorrow's edition."

Suzy looked even more doubtful. "I don't think I've seen you around before," she said, "and the paper already ran the obituary."

"They did," I agreed, "but I just wanted to ask a few questions about the autopsy." I didn't know if they had done an autopsy, but it was the first thing that popped into my head.

Then I got a break. "Suzy, who're you talking to?" asked a voice behind Suzy. A friendly face appeared. We sized each other up. He looked familiar.

"Someone from the *DC*," Suzy told him.

"You look like Nick Bertetto," he said.

My brain worked furiously, trying to place the officer who was now squeezing out a place next to Suzy. "I am," I said, sticking out my hand. "It's been a long time."

He was not fooled, and he smiled, dimples forming in his cheeks. "You don't know who I am, do you?" he said, giving my hand a good, firm shake.

"I'm sorry. I know I should know you..."

"It's okay," he said. "Charlie Cammack. I was a friend of your brother's."

"Sure," I said. Charlie really hadn't changed much from when he hung around with my younger brother John. Charlie's skin was tanned but freckled, and his eyes were gray-blue, set back in his face a bit thanks to pronounced cheekbones. He had short curly reddish-blonde hair, and he looked like could have auditioned for a beach volleyball player in a light beer ad.

"How is John?" he asked.

"Great. He lives in Phoenix now." We exchanged pleasantries until Suzy grunted and sat down.

"I just finished some paperwork," he said. "Why don't you come in?" He scooted around Suzy and opened the door.

The station had been rearranged since I'd been there last. I entered into a large room with four desks in the center and filing cabinets lining the sides. The chief's office was across the room, door closed. The station still smelled like pizza, though. "I can't believe you remembered me from that long ago," I said as he directed me to his desk.

"Are you kidding?" Charlie said. "The *DC* had your story about the murder in Franklin on the front page for almost a week last year. I recognized you from the pictures right off." He grabbed a chair from a vacant desk and set it next to his desk. "I'm impressed with what you did, I mean locating the body, rescuing your wife and all that. It was a gutsy thing for anyone to do, but especially a civilian."

I felt a pit at the bottom of my stomach. Finding the body, helping with the rescue, Joan's condition. I didn't need to be reminded of that. "In retrospect," I said, "I'm not sure I did the right thing. If I hadn't gotten so involved, maybe things would have turned out better."

Charlie shook his head. "You can't second-guess the

past. You're alive, your wife's alive. Concentrate on how right that feels. Now, what can I help you with?''

The chair was hard, and I tried to get comfortable. ''Dana Rardin asked me to check on the Iavello death to see if anything new had come in. I was wondering if there was an autopsy report.''

''Isn't the *DC* a little tame for you?'' he asked.

I tried to look modest. ''I'm just helping out. I'm in town visiting, and since Dana's an old friend, I couldn't turn her down when she asked. And Martha Iavello is a friend of a friend.''

Charlie must've bought it. ''I didn't work on the Iavello case,'' he said, ''but I can't imagine we'd get an autopsy report that fast. There might be a coroner's report, though. Let me see if it came in this morning.'' He got up and thumbed through a set of files, then thumbed through them again. ''It's not there,'' he said, puzzled, and shut the drawer.

The door to the police chief's office creaked open and two men walked out. One of them had a model's face—clear skin without scars, blemishes, or freckles—and he looked fit. He was dressed in a navy blue blazer, light gray slacks, and white pinpoint oxford shirt. A crystal pendant with a picture of Jesus embedded in it hung from his neck. He had a full head of powder white hair, which made him look older than the age I guessed, late thirties. A thick leather appointment calendar was in his hand. The model moved gracefully, and I expected this afternoon he would be out at a country club walloping an opponent in tennis, 6-2, 6-0.

I followed Charlie over. The model's companion, who looked flabby by comparison, had a sun-dried, leathery-looking face. His nose appeared to have been broken more than once and not properly set. With his salt-and-pepper hair cut in a crew, he looked a tough fifty years old. I presumed he was the police chief.

"Chief, did the coroner's report come in this morning on Gregorio Iavello?" Charlie asked him. "I couldn't find it. This is Nick Bertetto from the *DC*. He wanted some information about the death. Seems Martha Iavello is a friend of his."

The captain of the tennis team turned toward me. "I was deeply sorry to hear about the death of your friend's grandfather," he said, studying me with his sky-blue eyes. "My name is Carl Young, but everyone calls me Pastor Carl." His voice flowed sweet and rich, like the drippings of a liqueur-filled candy. Clearly this Hollywood package was the "B HEALED" minister.

I started to stammer out some pleasantry, but the pastor cut me off. "Mr. Iavello was such a good person and a pillar of this community. What will happen to the good town of Clinton with his being called to heaven is anyone's guess."

He stood there somehow managing to smile and look sad at the same time. Annoyed by being talked over, I didn't say anything, which was probably just as well. Despite the sincerity of his voice, his eyes had shown me something else. He looked more concerned about making an impression than my welfare. I wondered if his little speech was something he said after every funeral, changing the name like a fill-in-the-blank form.

The police chief jumped in to answer Charlie's question. "The coroner hasn't issued his report yet. I talked to him this morning. He's been busy, but he promised to get it to me in a day or two." He turned to me. "I'm Captain Slater. Is there some question?"

"Just wanted to make sure that everything was still the same about Iavello's death. The gunshot is still the cause of death, right?"

Slater looked at me suspiciously. "What else would it have been?"

"Oh, I don't know," I answered. "It was a suicide, right?"

Slater looked over at the obnoxious minister. "Would you excuse us, please?" Slater, Charlie and I moved several feet away, but I could tell the pastor was straining to hear what we said.

"Of course it was suicide," Slater said. "Mr. Iavello's prints were the only ones on the gun. Are you getting at something? If so, spit it out. This is Clinton, Mr. Bertetto, not the set of 'Murder, She Wrote.'" The guy was definitely an outsider—he pronounced the first 'n' in Clinton. Natives pronounce it "Clitton."

And I didn't like his attitude. "I just want to make sure I have the facts," I replied. "Tom Iavello said something about seeing a prescription bottle on the floor next to his grandfather. Did you check the prints on it, too?"

Charlie Cammack looked puzzled. "A prescription bottle? I hadn't heard anything about that."

Slater narrowed his eyes at Charlie to silence him, which worked. But what I saw in Charlie's eyes told me plenty about their relationship, and I knew I would do my damnedest to make Charlie my new best friend. Just as soon as the chief left.

"Mr. Bertetto, there is nothing new to report on this case," Slater told me. "When there is, *if* there is, we'll call a press conference."

I followed him back over to the pastor, pretending to write his comment down. "Thank you," I said.

"You're welcome," he said with finality.

Young pulled a business card from his calendar book and handed it to me. "If I can help you in any way with your feelings about Mr. Iavello's death, please call me," he said.

The chief grabbed him by the arm and ushered him away.

Before they left the building, Young took a pen from his book, and I heard him ask Slater to repeat my name.

I turned to Charlie. "Nice guy, the police chief."

Charlie frowned. "Captain Slater's been here about a year. The mayor hired him because he had a reputation as a good drug buster."

"Drugs? In Clinton?"

"Drugs are everywhere, Nick. We haven't had too many problems, but just before Captain Anzo retired, there was an incident at the high school that became news. Led the mayor to hire someone tough on drugs instead of promoting from within."

"Have you had any arrests since he came?"

"A few small time crack dealers. Also nailed a guy dealing steroids. Nothing major. Now, what was that about a prescription bottle?"

"The Terre Haute paper heard about it from Tom Iavello. I just wondered if there were fingerprints on it, and if so, whose they were."

Charlie regarded me. "You don't sound like you think the Iavello death was a suicide."

"I don't know," I said, shrugging. "Can you find out about the fingerprints?"

"Probably should check with the chief, first," he said with a smile, "but he'll be out for an hour or more with Pastor Goldentones."

Charlie's humor was so unexpected I laughed out loud, then lowered my voice. "You don't approve of him," I said.

"Have you heard of his church?" Charlie whispered. "The guy uses crystals, for God's sake, crystals with pictures of Jesus in them. People like him take an idea morons believe in, like 'the healing power of crystals,' relate it to Jesus and use it in church. What's the next thing? The psychic hotline for Jesus?" He began to imitate a fast-talking cable TV announcer. "Call the psychic hotline now, 1-900-555-7929, and talk to Jesus! Mediums standing by right now to take your questions! $2.99 the first minute; kids, make sure you have your parents' permission!"

I couldn't help laughing again. "You know, if this police job doesn't work out, you have a future in cable TV."

"The guy can't remember a name for anything. He carries an appointment book stuffed with things he's supposed to do and people he's supposed to remember. The sad thing is, his church is packed. Captain Slater's one of the elders." He shook his head. "C'mon," he said, leading me back to his desk, "I want to see about this prescription bottle."

Charlie located the Iavello file and read through it. Then he hunted. By the time he finished checking the file cabinet, the secretary's desk and a back room, however, all he had was a look as blank as the page sitting in front of me. "It's gone," he said. "There was a prescription bottle according to the report, but I can't find it anywhere. It's not here, it's not in the evidence room. It's just disappeared. We've got pictures from the scene, fingerprints from the gun, statements from Martha and Tom Iavello, everything. But no bottle or fingerprints from the bottle." He stood motionless with a frown on his face.

"What kind of medicine was it?"

"An antidepressant. Amitriptyline, specifically. That's all off the record, you know."

I nodded. "Can I look at the fingerprints from the gun?" I asked.

"Sure." He handed me the fingerprint record.

I compared the fingerprints from the gun to those taken from Iavello's right and left hands. "These are clear fingerprints," I said. "Looks to me like they're an exact match for the right hand. Of course, I'm no expert."

Charlie looked over my shoulder. "They're a match,"

he said. "But now I want to know if there were any fingerprints on that bottle."

"When you find them, will you give me a call?"

He hesitated.

I gave him my most trustworthy look. "I promise I'll
keep anything you tell me confidential until you say I can
release it."

He hesitated some more, but I think the fact that I was
John's brother helped. He finally said, "Okay."

I rose to leave.

"Don't misjudge the chief," Charlie said. "He's a hard
ass and maybe even a control freak, but he's all right."

"Sure," I said. I gave him my dad's phone number as
a way to reach me. We shook hands and I left.

Things were getting more and more interesting, I thought
as I opened the door to the van. Where was that prescription
bottle, and why had it vanished?

EIGHT

IF IT HADN'T BEEN for a billboard promoting Iavello's Food Market, I would have zipped right through town still thinking about the prescription bottle. As it was, the sign reminded me I said I would make dinner for Dad tonight. I pulled into the parking lot off Sixth Street and rang up about $25 for Italian sausage, peppers, zucchini, tomatoes, a bottle of Chianti, a gallon of milk, and a couple of other items to get us through the next few days.

Dad's house, the same one I'd grown up in, was a split-level stone house with a basement. Located just outside the city limits of Clinton, it was actually closer to a little burg named Blanford than it was to Clinton. I pulled up in the driveway and parked in the empty half of the attached two-car garage. The door opened into the kitchen, and Stephanie must have heard the van pull up because she was standing there when I walked into the house. "Hi, Daddy," she said.

"Where's *Nonno?*" I asked, looking around.

"On the phone."

"Have you had a snack yet?" I set the groceries on the kitchen table.

She nodded. "*Nonno* gave me a snack. A *good* snack," she reported.

"Oh?" I knelt down and looked in her eyes. Sure enough, they had that slightly out-of-focus look—a sugar high. "What did he give you?"

"Cookies, lots of them. And Coke."

My father came in behind her. He looked unapologetic. "She was hungry, and I didn't know when you'd be home."

"Coke? We'll be lucky to get her to sleep tonight."

No response. Dad nosed through the bags.

"It's just the stuff for dinner," I said.

"How much was it?"

"Not much." I whisked away the bag containing the sausage and the vegetables. Dad's kitchen is L-shaped, with the counters, stove and refrigerator on the long side and the kitchen table on the short. I moved the bag to one of the counters. "You bought lunch," I reminded him, nabbing the receipt, crumpling it and tossing it in the trash can.

Dad pulled the Chianti out of the second sack. He retrieved a corkscrew, opened the wine and poured us each a glass. Stephanie followed him to the counter, dragging her two new Beanie Babies.

"Salutè!" Dad said, and we clinked glasses. Stephanie looked left out, so Dad poured some grape juice into a paper cup and touched his container to hers. She giggled and drank with us. First Coke and now juice, I thought. She'd be wired tonight, not to mention primed for a potty disaster.

"I need to start dinner," I told Dad. "It'll take about an hour to cook."

"What are you making?"

"Italian sausage and peppers, just like Mom used to make."

"Mmmmm," Dad said appreciatively, "one of my favorites."

I pulled the ingredients for dinner out of the sack and set them on the counter.

"Ask me what I did while you were gone," Dad said.

I eyed him suspiciously. I'd thought he was up to something before I left to see Dana. "What did you do?"

"I found out that Jimmy Iavello isn't staying in any hotel or bed and breakfast in Clinton, Terre Haute, Brazil, Rockville or anywhere close."

"How did you do that?"

"While Stephanie napped I called every listing in the phone book and asked them to ring the room for Jimmy Iavello. No one had him listed."

"Oh." I poured a tablespoon of olive oil in a large skillet and plopped the Italian sausages on top of the oil. While the sausages browned I started cutting up zucchini, peppers, and onions.

"He could be listed under an alias," I said. Dad looked deflated by my comment, and I felt bad. "Of course, it would be difficult for an Iavello to get away with that around here," I added. "Everyone knows the Iavellos. Word probably would have leaked out if he were using a different name." Dad perked up a bit. What I'd said was true, and Dad, being a retired foreman from the Eli Lilly plant in Clinton as well as being well-connected through the Knights of Columbus, would have heard such gossip.

"More likely he's staying with his brother," I said, though it was hard for me to imagine anyone living with the testosterone monster I'd encountered at the gym. "Tom said Jimmy told him about the will being changed."

"Jimmy was at the lawyer's office first thing this morning, according to someone I know."

"You have been busy."

"I also found out that Martha, not her Second Advent group, owns the coffeehouse and the restaurant. She got the loan from Clinton First Savings Bank, but Gregorio cosigned the loan."

I was impressed. More than impressed. "Dad, how did you find that out?"

He shrugged his shoulders. "I know the right people. What did you find out from Dana Rardin?"

I told him about the prescription bottle found next to the body, and how Dana "hired" me to write the story. Then I went over my visit to the police station and Charlie's discovery that the prescription bottle was missing. By the time I finished, the sausages were browned on both sides. I drained them on paper towels, sautéed the onions and peppers, then added the zucchini. The spicy aroma was wonderful, but it made me recall I'd missed my extra weight-gaining meal at mid-afternoon. It would be okay for one day but I'd have to do better tomorrow.

"Do you think the will was really changed?" Dad asked.

"I'm beginning to think it was. I have a lot of questions to ask Martha now. The problem with the will change is, if the death was in fact murder, then Martha becomes the prime suspect. And she's the one who hired me."

"Maybe to divert attention from herself?"

"There was never attention on her. The police already declared it a suicide. If Martha was guilty, the best thing would be to lie low and let it ride as a suicide." I shook my head. "No, something odd is definitely going on here."

Stephanie climbed on *Nonno*'s lap. "Let's go play Candyland," she said.

"In a minute, sweetheart," Dad told her.

I suddenly realized Stephanie shouldn't be in here listening to us discuss murder.

"Stephanie, how would you like to watch a video?" I asked. Since I don't let her watch TV often, she went for it in a big way. Dad set her up in the living room and then returned to the kitchen.

"Let's review Martha's suspects," Dad said, "in light of what we now know. What about Tom Iavello?"

"The only motive I can see is money, and I don't think that's enough. Tom is huge and he loves to intimidate people, but he denied he killed his grandfather, and oddly enough I believe him."

"Why?"

"I don't think he needs the money that desperately. He never married so he doesn't have a family to support. He drives an old Chevy that's got to be paid off by now. Since he works at the gym he doesn't have to pay fees. And given his size, I bet he's attracted a boatload of personal training business. Unless he's got some unusual debts or costs, like maybe being on steroids, he surely can support himself in bodybuilding." I checked on the sautéing vegetables and splashed some Chianti in with them, then added back the sausages and placed the lid on it to simmer.

"Steroids are illegal," Dad said.

"Yes, but they may not be all that expensive or difficult to obtain. I need to check with my friend Mark Zoringer at the gym on that one."

"What about Jimmy Iavello?"

"Too much unknown. Martha painted a picture of him desperate to get his hands on the Iavello fortune, and Tom backed up that image when he said he and Jimmy were going to sue over the new will. The fact that no one can find him certainly makes me suspicious."

I flipped on a light in the kitchen. Both kitchen windows face north and don't get much light late in the day. "Dad, what do you know about Blazevich and Ronchi, the two farmers Martha suspects? Mining is a volatile issue, and if the *signore*'s plan to sell land hurt their ability to farm…"

Dad shook his head. "I can't picture the Ronchis or the Blazeviches as killers. If Angelo Ronchi was the one to kill him, you know he wouldn't have been clever enough to make it look like a suicide. He probably would have taken credit for it."

In spite of the fact we were talking about murder, I laughed. 'Ronchi *Antico*'—old man Ronchi—we kids used to call him. He was quick to anger, and we were merciless in playing tricks on him. Dad was right. If Ronchi had gotten mad enough to kill Gregorio Iavello, he would have stood over the body until the police got there. Then he would have told the police exactly why Iavello deserved it.

"Bill Blazevich has a cooler head," I said. "If the threat of mining near his farm was great enough…"

Dad shook his head. "The government is paying Bill not to grow crops on nearly a fourth of his land—it has to do with price supports. I think Bill would be able to work around mining for a long time before he'd get desperate enough to kill."

"Isn't the Blazevich home just down the road from the Iavellos?"

"The original farmhouse is," he replied. "Blazevich owns a lot more land now. He has houses on acreage scattered all over, some of it in Illinois. He's doing well. I can't see he'd gain anything from killing Gregorio."

I would still have to do some checking, but I trusted Dad's assessment of the mining situation. "If we exclude Martha, assuming she wouldn't hire someone if she committed the murder, that takes care of Martha's short list."

"What about Anna?" Dad asked. "You said she tried to be manipulative in the car."

"One minute she seems sincere about this apparition, and then the next she does something that doesn't seem right. If she's making up this whole Second Advent thing, then she definitely has the motive. If she knew about Iavello changing the will, she may have been anxious to get her hands on that money."

The rice came to a boil. I covered the pot and turned the heat down. "I'm going to let this simmer for awhile," I told Dad. "Joan ought to be home from work now. I need to call her."

Dad stood in front of me. "I'm glad you're back," he said, giving me a squeeze on my arms. I couldn't tell if he meant back home or back at investigative reporting.

"I'm just doing this one job, and it could be a very quick one. I may just ask around, conclude the police are right about it being a suicide, and go home. But even if there's evidence it's murder, I may not go further. Joan may not be here, but I still have to be sensitive to her feelings."

Dad leaned against the counter and said carefully, "How much longer will it be before Joan gets better and you can get on with your life?"

I chose my words carefully. "Dad, I still love Joan. I will wait for her." Dad remained expressionless.

"It's my life," I stated.

"So it is," he replied.

I cut around him, struggling with the frustration of my love for Joan and the reasonableness of Dad's question. Should there be a limit to my patience? Even when Joan's condition was my fault?

I used the phone upstairs. Anticipating that Joan would have objections, I tried to soften her up by letting her talk to Stephanie first. I put Stephanie on when I heard the first ring.

"Hello," Steph said quietly.

"Is that you, Stephanie?" I heard Joan ask.

Steph nodded her head. "Say yes," I urged her.

"Yes," she repeated.

"Are you being a good girl for Daddy and *Nonno?*"

Steph nodded again. "Say it," I reminded her.

"Yes," she repeated.

Joan asked several more questions and I prodded several more answers. Finally Joan asked Stephanie to put me on.

"It's Mommy," Steph said, as if I didn't know. I sent her back downstairs.

There was a pause after Joan and I said hello. "So why are you staying?" she asked. "What did that priest want?"

I couldn't beat about the bush. "Father Skip thinks

there's something strange about the *signore*'s death. He wants me to make sure it's a suicide.''

"What else might it be?"

"A murder," I said.

"That's what I thought." Silence. "So I guess you're going ahead with this, that I don't get a vote?"

"Joan, don't do this, please. I'd like to stay here another day or two just to help Father Skip get answers about the death. Personally, I think it's a suicide. There won't be any danger."

"What about Stephanie?"

"Dad's taking care of her. They're having a great time."

"This will probably set back her potty training, you know."

"I don't think so. She hasn't had any accidents today and I was gone for quite a while."

"Why don't I get any input in this?"

"Joan, you're safe. You're two hours away from here. This is the kind of work I enjoy, and I'll get paid for it. It's just this one case and then that's it. Besides, Stephanie and I are getting to spend some time with my dad, the kind of time we haven't had since Mom died. It feels great."

There was quiet on the other end of the line. In my mind I could see her trying to decide what to do. Not giving me her blessing to do what she knew I was going to do would drive more distance between us. But my staying meant that I would investigate something that she knew could be a murder, even if I'd told her it wasn't.

In a thin voice, she said, "Promise me you'll come home as soon as it's over."

"You know I will."

"Okay," Joan said. She did not sound happy.

"How's work been?"

"The same. Well, I'd better be going. I have to get myself something for dinner."

"Just one question before you go, Joan, a pharmaceutical question. What do you know about 'amitriptyline'?"

"Amitriptyline? It's an antidepressant. Kind of an ancient one, though. Most psychiatrists prescribe drugs in the latest class of antidepressants."

"Can you check the PDR for me?" Having lived with a pharmacist for so long, I knew about the Physicians' Desk Reference, a thick book that defined drugs, their actions and some indication of effectiveness.

Joan put the phone down with a thunk. "I was right," she said, when she got back on. "It's to relieve the symptoms of depression. The drug is more likely to be effective on depression caused by the body."

"What does that mean?"

"Some depressions are caused organically, like from a chemical imbalance in the brain."

I wondered if Signor Iavello's depression was organic. Another question to ask Martha. "Are there any warnings about its use?"

"All drugs have that. I gather the guy who died took it."

"Some say he did, some say he didn't. He was in his eighties and lived alone."

"That old, huh? There's a special entry on oral dosages for elderly patients. Oh, and the drug can be injected, too."

I looked around for something to write on but couldn't find anything. I hoped I would remember all the information.

"Joan, is there a description of what someone would do if they overdosed on it?"

"A pretty long section. It can cause temporary confusion, disturbed concentration, hallucinations, and a bunch of other things. Deaths by deliberate or accidental overdose have occurred with this class of drugs."

"But not specifically amitriptyline?"

"That's just the way they write it. May well have occurred with amitriptyline."

"If someone who wasn't depressed took it, could it cause hallucinations?" I asked, thinking of Anna and her visions.

"I don't know for certain, but in theory I think that would be possible."

"Thanks," I said. The silence lengthened. "I guess I'll let you go. Take care of yourself. I love you. Good-bye."

She said good-bye and hung up. No "I love you" from her. I told myself it didn't mean she didn't love me; it only meant she didn't love what I was doing. I gave a brief sigh and hung up.

"Nick!" Dad yelled from downstairs. "Stephanie's had an accident." I went running. At least it hadn't happened while I was on the phone for Joan to find out.

I started downstairs when the phone rang again. "Would you get that?" Dad yelled.

I picked up the phone. The voice on the other end sounded like Anna.

"Nick, you have to come to St. Mary's tomorrow night for the prayer group meeting."

"Anna?"

"It's at 7 o'clock. Promise you will."

"I don't know if I can."

"You have to. Martha and I think Mary's going to announce the miracle, and we think it concerns Gregorio's death. And Nick, there's something else." She paused.

"What?"

"Well, Mary gave me a message for you."

A what? "What does it say?"

"I'm not going to read it to you now. I'd rather give it to you in person tomorrow. I'll call you when you're at Martha's house to set up a time. Good-bye."

She hung up the phone quickly and left me with the dial tone buzzing in my ear. I set it down.

Here I was, less than twenty four hours on the job, getting messages from heaven. I couldn't decide if this was a good thing or a bad thing. Was I so inept that Mary felt I needed extra help, or was I so good that she was going to confide in me?

Was Anna making all this up?

I would have to think about it.

NINE

I DIDN'T TELL DAD about the message, but I did tell him about Anna's request for me to be at the prayer service the next day. Even if I wasn't sure what to make of it, Dad was enthusiastic about going. I reminded him we didn't have a baby-sitter for Stephanie, and he called my cousin Helena. She was happy to help out.

Earlier Dad had told me of his plans to go to a dance tonight with Gina, the widow we'd seen at lunch. Though he had offered to cancel, I had persuaded him not to. Now he left, and I let Stephanie play a shape-matching game on the computer while I made a phone call to Mark Zoringer at the Franklin Iron Works.

"Hi, Mark, this is Nick Bertetto," I said when he answered.

"Nick, where are you?" he said in his distinctive, low growl. "You didn't come in today. Trying to get out of a leg workout, aren't you?"

I laughed. "No, I'm in Clinton. I came for a funeral."

He changed his tone. "I'm sorry, I didn't know."

"It's okay, it's no one I'm close to. I'm calling because I ran into someone today I suspect is a buddy of yours."

"Really, who's that?"

"Tom Iavello."

"Tom Iavello," he repeated, "my buddy in the light heavyweights. I suppose he bowled you over with his charm."

"You could say he tried. He's certainly not grieving, even though he's the grandson of the deceased." Mark's phone was close to the bench press area, and in the background I could hear weights clanging and the familiar, "C'mon, one more rep" patter of encouragement. Then it hit me. "Wait a minute, did you say *light* heavyweight?"

"Yeah. He's not in the heavyweights. That's my class."

"He's not a light heavyweight anymore. He's huge," I said.

"Come on. Where did you see him?"

"At a gym in Terre Haute."

"He was probably just pumped from his workout."

"I've seen you pumped, Mark. I'm telling you, he's bigger than you are. When was the last time you saw him?"

"Last summer, the Indiana Bodybuilding Championships. Are you comparing us off-season to off-season? You know I go up thirty pounds in the off-season."

"You're in the off-season now, and I saw you two days ago."

"Hmmm," Mark said. He was quiet for a moment.

"Are you thinking 'steroids'?"

"Yeah," he admitted, "I am."

"I'm asking because Tom's grandfather may not have committed suicide, as the police think. I'm looking for reasons Tom might have needed the money. The family is wealthy."

"Man, to go up that much weight he either must have found some incredible training program or he's pounding the juice. Any signs of acne?"

"Lots, on his shoulders and back. He was wearing a ripped T-shirt and it didn't hide anything."

"What about his attitude? He's never had a sweet personality, but did he show any mood swings?"

"Hard to say. From the moment I started talking to him,

he had this air of superiority that never left. Then he started intimidating me.''

"What about his eyes? How did they look?"

"His eyes? Well, now that you ask, I'd say he looked like he was high.''

"Bingo. That's a giveaway. Another is that builders who use steroids are always pumped. They never lose the look, even before they pick up the first weight of the day.''

"Are steroids expensive?"

"They're illegal, at least for bodybuilding, so you have to pay a price. Tom's probably stacking several of them, so that would be a bundle.''

"Define bundle.''

"Maybe $200, $300 a month.''

"I think he could afford that,'' I said, disappointed at having to dump one of my theories. There was no response on the other end. "Mark?'' I asked.

"I gotta know, Nick. Are you sure you're not exaggerating? He's really that big?''

"I'll take a picture, Mark. Thanks for the information. Good-bye.''

Martha Iavello must've called while I was talking to Mark, because Dad's voice mail had logged a message from her. She told me—not asked—to meet her at her grandfather's house at 9 o'clock the next morning to go over his business records. She also told me to be at St. Mary's for the prayer service tomorrow.

Now I *had* to be there. The boss told me to go. I briefly debated calling Martha back with some questions I had, but then I decided they could wait until tomorrow.

Steph was really good when I persuaded her to take a bath. The upstairs bathroom was tiled in white and blue around the porcelain tub, and Steph drew circles with soap suds against the blue tile. Her own tub at home was a plain white plastic formed tub, so the tub at *Nonno*'s house held

great fascination. When I finally convinced her bath time
was over, I dried her off and brushed her teeth. I diapered
her as a precaution, remembering the earlier accident. As
usual she wanted me to read *Goodnight Moon* for her bed-
time story. After reciting the tale of the great green room
practically from memory, I got her to sleep. She lay there,
hugging one of her new Beanie Babies. I gave her a peck
on the cheek.

I gathered together the few things I'd collected that day
before heading to my bedroom to read. The Second Advent
book was on top. The eyes of the pregnant Mary made me
shiver.

Walking into my old bedroom never felt the same after
I left for college and Mom turned it into a guest room.
She'd removed all my baseball pennants and rewallpapered
with a pattern of tiny pink roses and pencil-thin periwinkle
lines. The look clashed with my furniture and the remaining
baseball paraphernalia, which she'd left. Not wanting to
hurt Mom's feelings, I'd never protested the change. But I
still hadn't grown accustomed to seeing the bedroom this
way, either.

I settled onto the bed to read. Since I hadn't had a chance
to look at *The Daily Clintonian* Mrs. Santrach, the receptionist, had given me before I left the *DC* office, I took
some time to study it. Iavello's funeral was covered briefly
on page three by a reporter whose last name was Italian
and seemed familiar. The story didn't contain any new information about the death.

I reread the notes I'd scribbled after talking to my friend
on the police force, Charlie Cammack, adding some details
I remembered but hadn't had time to write. Joan's information about amitriptyline also went into the notebook.

The note warning me to stay away from Martha fell onto
the floor. Perhaps I should tell Charlie about it, I thought.

That would mean admitting I was working for Martha, though, and I couldn't do that. I put it aside.

The newspaper containing Dana's article about Anna stuck out of the Second Advent book and I took a look at it. There were two pictures with the article, one of Anna in prayer in front of the Immaculate Heart statue, and the other of her talking to a group of followers. The captions didn't offer anything new. I moved on to the article.

Headline: A Message of Unity

Diamond, Ind.—The crowds grow weekly, coming with reverence to the small, white-framed St. Mary's Catholic Church, filling the pews and spilling out onto the lawn. Those outside turn toward a weather-worn statue of Mary and pray.

On the lawn, some sit in chairs and others kneel in the grass or dirt. Most twist rosary beads through their hands with practiced care. A few gaze skyward, hoping for a sign, perhaps a duplication of the miracle of the sun that allegedly occurred in Fatima, Portugal, in 1917, when 60,000 people saw the sun spin, change colors, and hurtle toward the earth only to be drawn back into the sky.

Today's pilgrims, like those in Fatima, have come to hear the words of the Blessed Virgin Mary as revealed by an unlikely source. In Fatima, it was a group of three peasant children. In Diamond, on this Saturday, as it has been for nearly six months, the source is Anna Marie Veloche.

If that name sounds familiar, it is not in a religious context. Veloche was a main player in the Indianapolis scandal three years ago which led to the resignation of the governor's popular press secretary Jeff Henderson and several of his top aides.

"I am a sinner," Veloche says, acknowledging her part in the scandal. "That I have been forgiven by God and brought back to faith in Jesus Christ is one of the great miracles in my life."

But the miracle people expect this morning is even more improbable. It is the regular 9:00 a.m. appearance by the Blessed Virgin Mary, whom Veloche says has been giving messages to her since the first apparition on May 9th of last year.

"At first," Veloche says, "the messages were simple and personal. As time went on, Mary began to give me messages she says are for the world."

Mary's first message did not come to Veloche in Diamond or even in America. It came in Medjugorje, Bosnia-Herzegovina (formerly part of Yugoslavia), where Mary reportedly has been appearing since 1981 to six children, now adults. The site has been the destination of many religious pilgrimages, such as the one which brought Veloche there.

"At the time, I was suffering from a great depression," she says. "My problems in Indianapolis were plastered all over the newspapers and TV, and there wasn't anywhere I thought I could escape. I came back to Clinton, my hometown, but here I was tormented by the memories of my teenage years, which were sinful. Finally, I hit bottom, and that was when God sent Martha Iavello into my life."

Martha Iavello had delayed taking her vows as a nun to return to Clinton and help her father manage the family's financial holdings. Veloche met Iavello through a support group at Holy Family Catholic Church. The two became friends, and Iavello invited Veloche to Medjugorje. It was there Mary first appeared to her, Veloche says, curing her depression and telling her when she arrived home to go to St. Mary's

Church in Diamond to thank God for His mercy.

When she did so, Veloche says, she found St. Mary's Church was unlocked—surprising since services were no longer held there.

"I went in," she said, "knelt at the altar, and said a prayer of thanksgiving. It was then Mary spoke to me from the statue of the Immaculate Heart. She told me her Son had heard my prayers and healed me because of my repentance and sincerity. I was also told to start a prayer group to meet once a week and that Mary would give me messages for the group."

Iavello said she was skeptical at first when Veloche told her she was cured. "Not that I doubted God could do it," Iavello says cautiously, "but the Church urges great discernment in the case of miraculous cures. And there are so many people nowadays who claim to be receiving messages from Mary and Jesus that I couldn't understand why we should have one more."

Iavello said she became convinced when Mary, through Veloche, predicted an event which happened to her the following day. Iavello declines to reveal the circumstances.

No one else can see Mary when she appears to Veloche, which Veloche says now occurs twice a week, once during the Wednesday night prayer session and again on Saturday mornings. The messages are different.

"On Wednesday, Mary usually talks about the importance of prayer and asks us to pray for certain intentions," Veloche says. "Saturday morning messages used to be just for me, but about six months ago she appeared to be pregnant. When I asked her about it, she told me she was revealing herself as Our Mother of the Second Advent. She said she would be giving me messages for the world concerning a new era of trust in her Son's salvation."

On this Saturday, it is 9:10, and Veloche has left St. Mary's Church. She heads for a statue of Mary which sits up on a small hill near the church. Faithful pilgrims crowd around her, asking her for prayers of healing.

Veloche touches all who are close to her. Though she declines to talk about it, it is clear the throng of worshippers today believe, or want to believe, that Veloche has been given the gift of healing.

"If God chooses to work through me, I am honored," she has said. "But it is not my doing."

Veloche kneels before the statue of Mary, making the sign of the cross and saying a quick prayer. Then she stands and gives the message she received inside the church, reading from a notebook.

"My children, thank you for being here in such great numbers today to pray. Since I first announced the imminent Second Coming of my Son, many of you have been asking, 'When?' 'How?' My children, no one knows but the Father, as my Son foretold you long ago.

"However, I have come at the Father's request to help guide you in this. In order for Jesus to be among you again, you must become one with Him and with each other. He has not divided you, you have divided yourselves. Why do you let theological differences stand in the way of unity? I tell you, you will never know complete Truth unless the Father reveals it to you on the Last Day.

"He has placed among you many guides—some, my beloved priests; others, faithful ministers who also trust in my Son. Know, however, that all of you have understanding which is limited by your humanness. Do not rush to condemn others by your inadequate comprehension of the greatness of God's Plan. Rejoice in the knowledge that you have, that believers will be saved. As you become one, the triumph of my Immaculate Heart will be complete.

"The Holy Spirit is already among you, healing divisions and helping you find communion with one another. Pray for this work, and be at peace with one another."

Father 'Skip' Scipiannini of Holy Family Catholic Church in nearby Clinton is an outspoken supporter of Veloche's, the only priest in the area to take an unreserved stance that the apparitions are real. He is also president of 'Children of the Second Advent,' a nonprofit organization formed by Martha Iavello to promote the messages Veloche receives. Iavello serves as chairman of the group.

The Archdiocese of Indianapolis, which is responsible for both Holy Family and St. Mary's, remains noncommittal about the apparitions, although it is aware that the crowds are growing. It has approved the reopening of St. Mary's, closed for many years following a reorganization of nearby parishes, for the Wednesday and Saturday meetings. Father Scipiannini has been appointed administrator for St. Mary's.

The article went further, adding a sidebar with comments from professors at various colleges who had studied such phenomena. I folded the paper and went to the book.

I read Anna's messages until nearly one a.m. As I put the book down, I found myself thinking that a lot of good points had been made in the messages. Of course, Anna still could have made it all up. But I found myself hoping she wasn't a fake. There was something special about her, and I found myself liking Anna again. And I was very curious about this message that had been sent to me.

I yawned and wondered if Dad had come home yet. Then I reminded myself I had no right to know when he got home.

Slipping out of the room, I checked on Stephanie to make sure she hadn't kicked off her blanket. Then I returned to my room, burrowed under my blankets, and tried to sleep. But instead I tossed and turned. When I finally drifted off, it was into something far different from the peaceful slumber I'd hoped for. I dreamt I was caught up in a maze. Though I struggled, there seemed to be no way out except up. And to do that, I would need the help of someone far above me.

TEN

I woke to the smell of bacon, eggs and coffee drifting up the stairs into my room. For a groggy moment I felt I was still in high school, and that if I got up and stumbled downstairs I would find Mom cooking, spatula in hand. I could almost hear her laugh and say her exaggerated, "Good morning," which she said more to herself, finding some amusement in dealing with the morning grumping of her teenage son.

Glancing over at the clock, I saw the wallpaper and remembered I was not in high school anymore and that Mom would not be downstairs. I got up and ran my hands over the pattern of tiny roses she'd applied. It didn't look so bad after all. I put on a robe and went downstairs.

Stephanie sat at the kitchen table with a big glass of grape juice, eating raisins out of a small box. Dad stood over the stove.

"So you do cook sometimes," I said, half-jokingly.

"At breakfast. Did you think I ate toast and cereal every morning?" he asked.

In truth, I had. But I lied. "Of course not. Good morning, Steph," I said, giving her a hug.

I poured a cup of coffee for myself and one for Dad. The coffee was very, very dark. I eyed it, trying to gauge its strength, and then added lots of cream and sugar. Dad made his coffee the old-world way, powerful.

When I sat down at the table, he laid a plate of bacon

and eggs in front of me. They looked shiny and tasted wonderful.

"I make the eggs just like your mother used to, frying them in the bacon grease," Dad said, setting down his own plate. I gave in to the glory of having fat and cholesterol for breakfast, savoring each bite. Any thoughts of eating healthy while I was here were gone.

Dad placed a bowl of sugar-sweetened cereal in front of Stephanie. She began to eat it with her fingers, dry, and I thought she must find Grandpa's house to be heaven. I never let her have that stuff at home.

In response to my questioning, Dad told me he had had fun last night and that the band had been good, although his widow friend seemed to like slow-dancing with him better than dancing the faster numbers. The slut, I thought, then reprimanded myself. It was not her fault my mother was dead.

Dad was much more interested in questioning me about what I'd learned. I told him about my conversation with Mark Zoringer and my conclusion that even if Tom Iavello were on steroids, he wouldn't need the money from his grandfather's estate to get them. I also told him what I'd read about Anna and her visions. "Children of the Second Advent has to be involved somehow, Dad. They had the most to gain from Iavello's death."

Dad pushed his plate aside. "You make it sound like Martha and Anna are your prime suspects."

"They're the best ones, Dad. Much as I hate to admit it, Father Skip is also in that category. He's president of the group."

Dad's brow furrowed. "Now why would they ask you to investigate this if the police thought it was a suicide, and they get the most from it being a suicide."

"I don't know," I admitted. "I just keep thinking of the

advice Deep Throat gave to the reporters investigating Watergate, 'Follow the money.'"

Dad still looked skeptical.

"Speaking of money," I said, "Martha okayed my going through her grandfather's records today." Dad wasn't listening. He was looking at Stephanie, who had a wild, panicky look on her face. I knew that look. "Do you have to go the bathroom?" I asked hurriedly. She nodded. I yanked her chair out from the table and rushed her up the stairs to the bathroom. When she was seated on the potty, I heard Dad yell from downstairs, "Did you make it?" I laughed and yelled, "Yes."

Dad insisted on taking care of Stephanie while I went to Signor Iavello's house. I was relieved, though I told him I could have taken her with me. At 8:45, I headed west, away from Clinton and toward the Iavello farmhouse.

The day was cool but sunny, and I put on sunglasses for the first time in several days. The van acted like it was going to slide when I took the curves a little too fast (among other things, it needed new tires), so I had to slow down. At least it let me view the scenery better as the road zigzagged around the farms, forming artificial boundaries where there were no natural ones. I saw the broken corn stalks from last year's harvest still in the ground, a testament that the no-till erosion prevention policies were taking hold. The coal mines were out there, too, though I couldn't see them. Thinking about the mines reminded me of the Blazeviches and the Ronchis, both of whom remained minor suspects in my playbook for murder. Nothing made sense about this case. If there was a case.

I turned left onto Iavello Road and began hunting for the driveway. About a hundred yards ahead on my right was a thick grove of sugar maples which I guessed marked the entrance to the Iavello homestead. I slowed to make the turn.

The Blazevich farm is on this road, too, I thought, down about a mile and a half. I'd have to check it later, since I was already five minutes late.

Signor Iavello's house sat far back from the road and was concealed by a circle of hickory trees in addition to the maple grove guarding the driveway. There was a detached, single-car garage behind the house. The safety light above the garage door was on, as was the light outside the back door. I knocked. Getting no answer, I went around to the front.

The house looked impressive. It was a large Victorian three-story with a wide porch that went all the way around the sides. The paint on the house was in good shape, but the shade of blue on the house and the winter white on the shutters didn't quite complement each other, and it gave the house a stark look. I could see a light through the window to the right of the door. I wondered if Martha was already there, although there was no sign of her car.

This time I skipped the doorbell and knocked, but as I rapped the door, it nudged open. I pushed it open a little more.

"Hello?" I said tentatively, sticking my head in. "Hello?" I said louder. No response. I opened the door and went in.

"Martha? Father Skip?" I heard nothing but the slight echo of my words. I closed the door behind me.

To the right was a huge family room, which I checked. The air was cold and smelled of burnt ashwood. The flue in the dominating fireplace at the end of the room had been left open. I shut it and the furnace kicked on almost immediately, which made me jump. Calming down, I investigated the house.

The kitchen, dining room, master bedroom and every other room on the first floor looked tidy but dusty, as though no one had lived in them for some time. I checked once more at the front door to see if Martha or Father Skip had arrived. They hadn't.

"I wish someone else were here," I said aloud, just to hear the sound of my own voice. Nothing is as creepy as searching the empty house of the newly dead. I climbed the staircase to the second floor.

The double doors to Iavello's study were open and I walked in, fumbling for a light switch. The drapes were drawn tightly, making the room dark. I noticed a floor lamp next to the desk across the room. I made my way to the lamp and turned it on.

The light wasn't bright but it provided enough for me to realize I'd just walked over the spot where Iavello had died. I shivered a bit. Examining it more closely, I remembered how the body was positioned in the police pictures Charlie Cammack had shown me. There was no trace of anything now.

I studied the room. The highly polished wood floor looked original to the house. Three Oriental rugs were laid in the room, one in front of the desk, another in front of the double doors, and a huge one covered nearly a fourth of the room to the left of the double doors. A loveseat, coffee table, and two Queen Anne chairs formed a sitting area on the large rug.

The walls rose to a high ceiling and were paneled in a rich, dark wood. The stately furniture, including Iavello's large desk, was mahogany. Floor to chair rail-height bookshelves were built-in on the wall next to Iavello's desk, which straddled a corner in the back of the room facing the double doors.

Across the room in the other back corner was a bathroom, which I discovered was connected to the bedroom Signor Iavello must have slept in. The nightstand bore a picture of his wife, Lizbetta, as she looked not long before she died. Over the double bed hung an oil portrait of a much younger Lizbetta holding her son on her lap. I decided to check the bedroom later and looked around the bathroom. In the medicine cabinet, the only prescription medicine was Zantac.

Disappointed, I closed the cabinet and checked the vanity. Nothing unusual there. Likewise, there was nothing under the sink except a wastebasket, and it was empty. I reached for the bathroom light switch to turn it off.

"Well, you could open the drapes," a voice said.

My heart nearly jumped through my rib cage. Light poured in as Martha Iavello opened the drapes.

"I'm sorry. Did I scare you?" she asked. I clutched the doorjamb to the bathroom, a dead giveaway.

"Just a little," I said.

"Where's Father Skip?" Martha glanced around the room, looking puzzled.

"He's not here." I straightened up. "The front door was open. I thought you were already here, so I let myself in."

"The door shouldn't have been open," she said. "I locked it when I left Monday."

"Who else has a key?"

"I'm the only one, I think, although Papá may have given keys to my brothers. Father Skip has a key I gave him yesterday. I thought I'd be late this morning."

"I haven't seen Father."

"He said he'd be here," Martha replied.

I shrugged. Martha walked over to the desk. She wore flat shoes with a soft heel that didn't make a sound against the hard floor. Her clothes, a navy blue wool skirt and pale pink blouse, were a slight variation of what she'd worn the day before. She wore little makeup, only a trace of blue eye shadow and lip gloss that nearly matched the color of her lips.

"You said you wanted to go through Papá's papers," she said. "He did all of his business work at this desk. One of my earliest memories is of him working here while Tom and I played games over by the sofa.''

She sniffed a little, which annoyed me. I had the same feeling I'd had yesterday, that she wanted to appear sorrier than she actually felt.

I tried to be gentle. ''Martha,'' I said softly, ''you and I have to level with each other or I don't have a hope of finding anything new about your grandfather's death.''

''What do you mean?''

''I don't know how to ask this, but were you really that close to him? I mean, at the end? Is it true he tried to commit suicide before? And why didn't you tell me yesterday he left half his estate to Children of the Second Advent?''

Martha stared at the floor for a moment, then began to cry, quietly at first but picking up steam. It was a real cry, I thought. And then she began to sob.

I felt terrible. If it had been Joan, I'd have tried to console her. But this was someone I hardly knew, and I stood helplessly by her, hoping she would pull herself together.

The sobbing finally subsided and she steadied herself using the desk. I handed her the box of tissues on the front corner of the desk. She pulled out several and wiped her eyes. ''I'm sorry,'' she said. ''It has been such a long, long week.'' A tired smile appeared on her face. ''Let's sit down.'' She led me to the sitting area where I took one of the chairs. She sat on the loveseat, leaning her forearm on the armrest and pulling her feet up next to her.

Martha took a deep breath. ''You didn't know Papá very well, did you?''

''Not at all.''

''He was a difficult man, at least where I was concerned. Papá didn't love me, at least not the way he loved the boys. He thought they were everything. To hear Papá talk, Jimmy was the smartest person in the world and Tom the best athlete. That was when we were younger. I was always left out, an afterthought. My job was to help my grandmother, Mama. He loved Mama, but only because she knew her place. At least that's how he saw it. I didn't realize until much later how smart she'd been. She knew more about business than Papá did. She just maneuvered him into making the right business decisions while letting him think it was all his doing.''

Martha exhaled and touched the tips of her fingers to her mouth. She thought a moment. ''I guess my grandmother loved me,'' she said, ''but she was old when my parents died, and it was hard suddenly having to raise a small child. I don't think she ever recovered from losing my father. Sometimes I thought her ability to love died when he did.''

''Why'd you almost become a nun?'' I asked.

''Jesus was the only person I knew who loved me,'' she replied. ''I knew it because I heard it every day at Holy Family grade school and every Sunday at Mass. I got used to that love. It was never conditional, always forgiving. I wanted to give myself to that love.''

I shifted uneasily in my chair. ''Will you go back to the convent?'' I asked.

Martha stared at a spot across the room. I wondered where she was looking for the answer.

''How much do you know about Children of the Second Advent?'' she asked.

''Only what I've read. You're chairman and Father Skip is president, right?''

She nodded. ''There are many ways to work for Jesus, and one of them is this way, through Mary.'' I remained quiet, trying not to give off an aura of skepticism.

''You live in Franklin, don't you?'' she asked suddenly. ''Perhaps you know some of my friends at St. Rose. How about…'' She stopped as I shook my head.

''I don't go there,'' I answered quietly.

"Oh." She smiled as though she had already known that answer. "Have you switched to another religion?"

"No, I just…I just don't go. Although I've thought about going back. Stephanie's old enough to start Sunday School," I added. I didn't want to say more than that, about my slide away from religion during college when church attendance just hadn't seemed important, nor about my courtship and marriage to Joan, who was agnostic.

When Martha finally spoke, it seemed she had decided to try a different tactic. "Do you remember why we venerate Mary?"

Years of grade school catechism suddenly paid off. "Before Jesus died on the cross, He said to Mary, 'Woman, behold your son,' and to John, 'Behold your mother.' Through that, Mary became mother to us all, our Heavenly Mother."

"Very good. I'll have to tell Father. He didn't think you'd remember, especially since you don't attend church anymore."

So she had known. And Father Skip, too. I didn't like the idea that the two of them had been gossiping about my personal life. "When were you talking about me?"

"The night after I found Papá dead. Father persuaded us to let him call you about the murder."

"That brings up a question I've had since yesterday. Why *did* Father Skip call me? I mean, I'm flattered that he thinks so highly of my investigative skills, and I know I can do the job, but I also know you have the money to hire a high-powered private detective who does this for a living."

Martha worded her reply carefully. "He chose you, and he should be the one to tell you why. I'm sure he'll be here any minute and you can ask him."

"I don't see the need to wait, and remember, we need to be honest with each other."

Martha sat still for a moment, running something through her head. I remained silent. Finally she said, "Do you believe Mary is appearing to Anna Veloche?"

"That's not an answer, Martha."

"I'm getting to that. First answer my question."

I cleared my throat. "Anna asked me that herself," I said. "I don't have an answer. All I know is, I've known Anna longer than you have. She has a knack for drawing attention to herself. She thrives on being in the limelight. I'm not saying she's a bad person or that she's deliberately misleading everyone, but the new Anna strikes me in some ways as an extension of the old Anna."

"Believe me, I've thought of that."

"Now what does this have to do with me?" I asked. "You're not going to say Mary told Father Skip I was to investigate this?"

Martha squirmed. "Not exactly," she answered, but she didn't elaborate.

"What exactly did happen, then?"

"Anna, Father, and I were at St. Mary's, discussing what to do about Papá's death. None of us believed he committed suicide. We sought Mary's help. When she appeared, she told Anna to let Father decide what to do, that the Holy Spirit was guiding him. Then he told us he'd been thinking about hiring an investigator, and when Anna pressed him for a name, he gave us yours."

The whole thing was too unbelievable, but my right hand trembled a bit anyway. "That's it?" I asked.

"Not quite. We asked Anna what Mary thought of Father's suggestion, and Mary told her, 'He has chosen wisely.'" Martha leaned back a bit and watched for my reaction.

I felt a chill but shook it off. I stood up. "That's about the most preposterous thing I've heard," I said. "It's time

I left. When Father Skip gets here, tell him we've got to talk. I don't know that I really want to do this.''

"Don't leave,'' she commanded, and rose from the love-seat. She lost her meekness and moved suddenly toward me. Her face changed abruptly, and I saw an echo of Tom Iavello in her manner, although she did not have his threatening presence. Perhaps the Iavellos were simply used to being obeyed. "If this will change your mind,'' she snapped, "I'll pay you $25,000 to prove by Friday my grandfather was murdered.''

ELEVEN

"TWENTY-FIVE thousand dollars?"

"Why not?" she said. "I have the money, and I'll get more from the insurance company if you prove Papá didn't commit suicide. I want his name cleared."

I frowned. My head hurt from trying to figure out what was real and who was on the level. "Be honest, Martha. At $25,000, you can hire an entire team of investigators. Why are you so desperate for me to do this?"

"You may not believe Mary is appearing to Anna, but I do. If Father Skip has chosen you, and Mary has approved it, I'll make you take this case if I have to bribe you to do it."

I closed my eyes and rubbed my temples, trying to get rid of the developing headache. "Okay, let's sit down and start this all over," I said. I returned to my chair. Martha sat on the loveseat with her arms crossed over her chest. "Why Friday?"

"Papá's lawyer, Daniel Tripp, is scheduled to read the will on Friday. When Jimmy and Tom officially know he left half the estate to Second Advent, I'll be in for a fight. They'll claim that since he committed suicide, he was obviously not of sound mind when he changed the will."

"That was a recent change?"

"A week ago Monday."

Jimmy and Tom could make a good case, I thought. I wondered if they could go even farther, denying Martha

her portion of the estate. I wasn't sure she was of soun
mind. At the moment I just hoped her bank account wa
of sound deposits.

"Why did your grandfather make the change?" I asked

Her voice softened again, and she returned to the humbl
creature who had spoken to me of needing love. I wondere
which of her personas was the mask. Maybe both wer
Maybe there was a third Martha Iavello I didn't want t
meet.

"I told you my grandfather was a hard man to please,"
she began. "It didn't get any better when Mama died. H
was so lost. I was away at the convent, and I had no desi
to come home. He asked me—almost begged me—to tak
Mama's place looking after him. I told him no, but Mothe
Superior and the archbishop told me to 'honor my father
It seems Papá was a big contributor to the convent an
some Catholic seminaries. So I came home and was mis
erable for a time. I looked for opportunities to get away
Then I met new friends, like Anna. Went on some trips I'
been wanting to take, like Medjugorje. Things becam
more bearable. Finally I decided to treat working for Pap
like a job. I moved to a house of my own. Came over t
fix him breakfast and lunch. Made sure he had evenin
meals, but didn't stay to eat with him. I even took Wednes
days and Saturdays off."

She looked at me with one eye lowered, as if trying t
elicit some sympathy. I nodded as sympathetically as
could to keep her going.

"A year ago last month I found him nearly dead on
Monday morning. He'd tried to overdose on aspirin, bu
passed out before he could swallow enough tablets. He wa
in bad shape. I have a friend who's a paramedic over i
the next county. She was off duty and came over with tw
helpers. They quietly fixed him up without letting anyon
know. I don't know what made me handle it that way.

guess I thought it would hurt him to find himself alive but have everyone know he'd tried to kill himself.''

''He was suffering from depression then?''

''Yes. Maybe he couldn't live without Mama. Maybe he just hated himself for discovering he couldn't live without her. I don't know, but her death was at the root of it. I persuaded him to see a psychiatrist. He chose one in Greencastle because it was far enough away he could be almost anonymous. Even then, he always went on Wednesdays so I wouldn't see him go.''

''Who's the doctor?'' I asked.

''Her name is Patricia Crowley. I'm sure I can find the address for you.'' Martha stood and walked over to the *signore*'s desk, but I interrupted her before she could start her search.

''Why'd he leave so much money to Children of the Second Advent?'' I asked. ''Was he a believer?''

''Not at first,'' Martha admitted, looking up at me from the desk. ''But in the last month he did. After he was cured.''

My eyes widened. ''By Anna?'' I asked. I must've looked skeptical again because Martha's mouth tightened.

''By God, through Mary, by Anna's hands,'' she said. ''Look, I can't make you believe this, but I expect you to believe that we believe it. Can you do that?''

I paused. It was time to come clean. ''Martha, you said you wanted me to be honest, and I will be. Children of the Second Advent had the most to gain from your grandfather's death. Like it or not, you, Anna, and Father Skip are all suspects. I'd like to believe all of you believe, and if you're all innocent then you probably do, but…'' I raised my hands and shrugged.

Martha's face contorted before she responded, and I guessed she was struggling to maintain her meekness when she wanted to get royally angry at me. ''Very well,'' she said, "but don't spend too much time investigating my friends. We're all innocent, and you only have until Friday to solve the murder."

There were many ways to respond, but since I'd already made my point I passed on them. I stood and walked to Signor Iavello's desk. "Is this where your grandfather kept all his files?"

"Everything that I know of." From the folds of her skirt she produced a set of keys. She unlocked the desk and two four-drawer file cabinets against the wall. "The file cabinets contain old business records. I don't imagine you'll need them, but you can look through them if you want."

"Thanks," I said. Martha located Patricia Crowley's business card for me then stood around peering over my shoulder while I sorted through the desk drawers. Ignoring her as much as I could, I located Iavello's files on all the businesses, a ledger book for each, a file on charities he donated to with notations on when he had given last, and personal financial records. I also located assorted pens, pencils, paper, paper clips, a three-hole punch, and a calculator. There wasn't a computer or a typewriter anywhere, though.

"Did your grandfather use a computer?" I asked.

"No. All his records were kept by hand."

"How did he do his correspondence? I don't see a typewriter."

"Oh, I did all his typing. I have a small office downstairs."

"Do you mind if I take a look at it?" I asked. I hadn't seen it when I looked through the house earlier, but not wanting to admit I'd been snooping, I kept quiet.

I followed Martha down to the main floor. Her office was a small room off the back of the kitchen. It couldn't have been more than eight by ten feet, cramped with a desk, a two-drawer file cabinet and a small typewriter stand. Painted in a drab ivory, the room had a wallpaper border of ducks at chair rail height. The ducks wore country blue bows at the neck and matching hats with frilly little things on them. I couldn't imagine any self-respecting duck looking like that. I wondered if Martha had put the border up. She hadn't struck me as a country fancier.

Martha's computer dominated her small desk. "What kind of records do you keep?" I asked, pointing at the computer.

"I keep correspondence on disk, so we don't have a lot of paper around. The letters we receive I keep in the file cabinet."

"Who kept your grandfather's checkbook?"

"He did. He wrote all his own checks, both for business and personal matters. They're in the file cabinets in the study. I checked on them the other day, so they should still be there."

"May I look through your files?" I asked. She said yes coldly, as if I planned to indict her. Then she said she was going to make coffee and went off to the kitchen. I booted up the computer and looked through a few electronic files that sounded interesting but weren't. Everything seemed ordinary. I also examined Martha's file cabinet, spot-checking some files but not finding anything suspicious. A search of the top and bottom of each drawer also turned up nothing.

When I smelled coffee I went to the kitchen, only to find Martha staring at the knife block. She turned a puzzled face in my direction when she heard me walk in.

"What is it?" I asked.

"There's a knife missing. I must've misplaced it, but I can't think where. I've searched the cabinets and drawers. I wonder if someone took it."

"When did you use it last?"

"The day of the funeral. Jimmy, Tom and I came back here after the service. You know how people bring food to help out. I used the knife to cut meat or something. I'm not even sure I got around to washing it. The three of us argued and I finally left.''

"Do you need it for something? There are lots of other knives in the block.''

"I know. It's just that I used that knife a lot when I prepared meals for Papá, and it should be here.'' She shrugged it off. "The coffee's ready.''

She poured us each a mug. I doctored my coffee with cream and sugar and returned to Iavello's study to look around some more. Martha said she'd be up in a minute.

I studied Iavello's desk calendar. His weekly appointments with Dr. Crowley were on Wednesdays, as Martha had said. Iavello must've connected with the good doctor, because about two months before he died he'd changed 'Dr. Crowley' to 'PC' on the calendar. Maybe I needed to visit Dr. Crowley.

I found the two checkbooks Martha had talked about and went through the check registers. Iavello hadn't dealt with any unusual companies, but he had developed a habit of writing a weekly check to 'Cash' in the amount of $5000. It started seven weeks prior to his death. I crossed-checked the dates and found they were all written on Wednesdays. I pointed out the entries to Martha when she came in.

"Any idea what he used the money for?'' I asked.

"No, I don't,'' she said. "That's really unusual for him. He kept very little cash around.''

"Could he have been blackmailed?''

"I don't think so. Papá was a hard businessman. I don't think he did anything illegal.'' Martha puzzled over that for awhile and I finished making some notes.

"Where did you find your grandfather that last morning?'' I asked. I knew what the answer should be from the police photos, but I wanted to see if she told me the same thing.

"Right here," she said, pointing to the same spot in front of the desk. She contorted her body as though enacting the position of the corpse. Suddenly her eyes started tearing. She grabbed a tissue from the box on the desk and stifled a cry.

"Papá and I didn't get along all that well most of his life, but he was my responsibility, and in the end, after he was cured of depression, I could see how much he respected me. People never got a chance to see the change in him, and I never got a chance to get used to it. I'm really sorry about that." She cried a little.

I knelt to inspect the spot where he was found. "Where was the gun found?" I asked.

"To his right. The glass from the bathroom was next to it, along with the prescription bottle."

"What glass?"

"The glass he supposedly used to take the antidepressants. The police have it."

I'd ask Charlie about the glass. I continued to study the spot. "Your grandfather was right-handed?" I asked.

"No, he was left-handed. So was my father. Tom is, too, but Jimmy and I are right-handed." She stopped. "Why do you ask?"

"Look at this. The drinking glass, gun and prescription bottle were all found on the right. That would be normal for you and me." I popped open an imaginary prescription bottle and, using my right hand, dumped the imaginary tablets into my left hand. I brought the hand to my mouth and followed with an imaginary drink of water with my right hand.

"But your grandfather would have done it the other way." I fumbled around with my hands, trying to do it all with my left hand. "The same with the gun. When he died, everything should have been on the left side," I concluded.

Martha gasped. "That proves it!" she said.

"Not really," I cautioned. "It only raises a doubt. The fingerprints the police have from the gun are definitely from your grandfather's right hand, and a lot of left-handed people do some things with their right hand. But it gives us more to go on. If it was a murder, it must've been someone who was in a hurry or who didn't know your grandfather was left-handed." I wondered why the police didn't notice this. "How long were the police here?"

"Maybe two hours. They acted like it was an obvious suicide. I tried to tell them that Papá wouldn't have taken the antidepressants, but they just sort of humored me."

"Did the police block off the house?"

"Sure, while they were here. Then the funeral home came and took the body away."

"Who cleaned this up?"

"I don't know. Probably one of my friends. I was too stunned to notice anything."

I stood back and tried to imagine the scene as Martha must've seen it. I walked around the room and looked at it from several different angles. Martha was quiet while I did that, and we were both so lost in our thoughts that we jumped when the phone rang.

"Oh!" Martha said. The second ring broke the tension, and we laughed in spite of ourselves. "I'll get it," she said. "It's probably Father Skip."

It was Anna Veloche. The secretary at Holy Family Church had called her looking for Father. No one had seen him that morning. Anna had told the secretary she would call Martha, since she knew he was supposed to meet us at the *signore*'s house.

"We haven't seen him, either," Martha said.

I looked at my watch. It was 11:00 a.m. There was a sensation in my stomach, and I wondered if it was hunger or a reaction to Father Skip's absence. It bothered me a little that he hadn't kept our appointment. As for Anna, I had expected her to call, but about Mary's message to me, not Father Skip.

"Anna wants to talk to you," Martha said, handing over the phone.

"I'm worried about Father Skip," was the first thing she said to me.

"I am, too," I replied, "but there must be half a dozen reasons why an active priest would miss a meeting or skip going to the rectory first thing in the morning. Surely he's done that before?"

"Yes, but not very often." She thought a moment. "You're probably right. I'm sure he's fine. And I know he'll be there for our prayer meeting tonight. He never misses one. Are you coming?"

I had already decided to go, but $25,000 made it all the more appealing. This was the main stage, the place where Second Advent was created and from which the movement sustained itself. I reminded myself it was also the place where Father Skip decided to bring me in on the case. "Yes, I'm coming," I answered. "Is there any way I could look over the church beforehand, maybe this afternoon? I'd like to see it without the crowds. And you can tell me more about this mysterious message you received."

"Why don't we meet at St. Mary's in an hour? I'll bring lunch."

Martha and I wrapped things up after I finished talking to Anna. She let me take a few things, including Iavello's appointment calendar. She said she'd try to find the canceled checks for the weekly $5000 cash, to see if her grandfather had written any notes on them hinting at what the money was for.

I got in my van and drove to the end of the driveway. Remembering the Blazevich farm was west on the same road, I turned to search for it. Discouraged after several miles, I looked for a driveway to turn around when I no-

ticed a green Ford Escort pull out of a driveway ahead of
me. As the car passed, I glanced at the driver. My mouth
opened in surprise—Jimmy Iavello, the one Iavello I hadn't
questioned yet, the one who seemingly didn't want to be
found.

Quickly I sped up to turn around in the driveway he'd
left. When I pulled in, I received my next big surprise. The
name on the mailbox was one of the farmers Martha suspected, W. Blazevich.

TWELVE

I THREW THE CAR into reverse and backed out of the Blazevich driveway. Speeding down the road, I tried to catch sight of the Escort so I could follow at a distance. Too bad Jimmy had a good head start. I didn't know if he was racing, too, but if he had recognized me when we passed, he probably was. The Clinton grapevine seemed to go ahead of me everywhere I went.

I drove east on the county road as fast as my van could safely take the turns, which wasn't swift considering the state of my tires and the van's disturbing need to shudder when I cornered too fast. Reaching the Iavello homestead, I had a sudden flash of intuition that Jimmy may have lurched in there, so I slammed on the brakes in time to make the driveway. When I pulled up in front of the garage, though, Jimmy's car was not there. Martha's car was gone, too, though it had been less than ten minutes since I was there. I checked the garage and found it empty. No Martha, no Jimmy. So much for my intuition.

At the risk of being late for my appointment with Anna, I decided it was time to check in with the Blazeviches and see what kind of story they might tell. I drove back to their farm.

The Blazevich house was closer to the road and less concealed than the Iavello homestead. In contrast to the Victorian mini-mansion I'd just been in, the Blazevich home was a long, rambling ranch. Parts of it appeared newer, as though the family had added to the house throughout the years. The look was unified by a good coat of white paint and a neat white picket fence around the property. I parked my car to the side of the driveway, leaving room for any farm vehicles that might need to get past.

Mrs. Blazevich answered the door. Once I saw her, I remembered her. She was short and round, with a moon-shaped face that matched her body. Her blonde hair was pinned up in a bun behind her head and she wore no makeup. Over her white shirt and denim skirt she had tied a hearts-and-flowers print apron. She smiled as though she recognized something about me, even if she wasn't sure who I was. "Can I help you?" she asked.

"I'm Nick Bertetto, Mrs. Blazevich. I don't know if you remember me, but I used to live in this area. I've been looking into…"

"Nick, of course," she said, interrupting me and clapping my elbow. "Come in, come in. Have a seat. What are you doing back in these parts? I heard you live in the big city, now. What can I do for you?" She rattled everything off at once, leaving me unsure which question to answer first. Better start with the last and tell her what I was here for, I thought.

"I've been looking into the death of Gregorio Iavello. It's for a story I'm doing as a special favor for Dana Rardin, the editor of *The Daily Clintonian*," I said. "One problem I'm having is tracking down Jimmy Iavello, and someone said they thought you might know where he was."

Mrs. Blazevich's eyes narrowed, and she hesitated. When she responded, she tried very hard to do it in the same friendly manner with which she greeted me, but it was strained.

"Well, now, I don't know anything about Jimmy Iavello, and I'm surprised somebody suggested that we would. We haven't been on the best terms with the Iavello family for awhile. But if you want, you can talk to my husband about it. Maybe he might know something about where Jimmy is."

She disappeared into another room for a moment as if looking for him, then shouted, "Bill!" I heard a muffled voice respond from another part of the house. "You'll have to excuse me," she said, returning to me, "I'm fixing lunch for the farmhands. Bill'll be here in a minute. Sit down." She directed me to the couch, then left.

I surveyed the small room. There was a fireplace at the end with an oval throw rug in front of it. Furniture was crammed into the remaining space. The couch I was sitting on was lumpy, stained and old. Someone had thrown a crocheted afghan over the top of the couch, and I peeked to see if it was covering a major stain or burnt spot. It wasn't. There was an antique rocker next to the couch.

Pictures of kids and grandkids were everywhere. The Blazeviches had five children and maybe fifteen grandchildren. Family photos showed smiling, nuclear families in all cases but one. The eldest daughter was pictured with three young children—two boys and one girl—but no husband. I examined it more closely. The oldest boy I guessed to be ten. The two others were probably eight and six. The younger children had the same features as their blond, big-boned mother, but the oldest boy had haunting, stormy eyes, and an athletic build. His smile resembled a sneer. The lack of husband didn't necessarily mean divorce, I reminded myself. Could be she's a widow.

The room filled with the aroma of fried chicken, and my empty stomach suddenly demanded food. When I tried to quiet it, Bill Blazevich lumbered into the room, chewing a piece of chicken and making my stomach feel even emptier. Bill was a beefy guy, four or five inches taller than me and sporting a big belly. His face was wide with a bristly double chin and leathery tan. Whatever he was chewing, he swallowed with a gulp before we exchanged greetings. I stuck out my hand and he shook it, insisting I call him Bill.

"Ginny tells me you think we might know where Jimmy Iavello is," he said.

"Someone suggested I try here. I need to talk to him for a story I'm doing on Signor Iavello for *The Daily Clinton ian.* It would help if you knew. I've been having trouble tracking him down."

"If he's anything like his grandfather," Bill said, finess ing his large body into the rocking chair, "he'd be hard enough to pin down when he's in the same room, let alone track."

"I understand you've had some disagreements with Si gnor Iavello."

Bill crossed his arms. "Now, if you mean we've wran gled over his having the mineral rights to my farmland, then I guess you're right. He's got them, and I'd like to buy them back. Of course, now that he's dead, I hope to get them back from his family."

"You don't exactly sound sorry about Iavello's death."

"What's that supposed to mean? You're the one who came here looking for Jimmy. You think I'm awful just because I didn't like Iavello? Heh. There's a lot of people who'd be in that category."

Now I'd offended Blazevich, not the right approach to take with a guy like him. This would get me nowhere. "I'm sorry, Bill. It was just an observation, one that I've made more than once since starting this story." Bill uncrossed his arms, which I took as a sign we were back on track.

I gave Bill my best look of trustworthiness. "You said you're hoping to get the rights back from the Iavellos. Have you talked with any of them about it? Jimmy, for in stance?"

"Iavello's only been dead a few days," Blazevich re sponded calmly. "I want to give the family a little grieving time before we talk business. Don't you think that's a good idea?''

"Sure," I agreed. I noticed he didn't say that he hadn't talked to the Iavellos, though. "Bill, I know this is none of my business, but how did Signor Iavello come to have the rights? Aren't those usually sold with the property?''

Bill began to rock the chair. "It goes back maybe thirty years ago. I needed cash to buy more land near the Illinois border. The price was good and it was right next to my other farm. I was pretty strapped, and the banks were hesitant to lend. Iavello was shrewd. He knew I wanted the money and he had it to lend. Giving him the rights seemed like a bargain at the time.''

The lumpy couch was uncomfortable and I leaned forward. "Why do you want the rights now? I mean, mining has all but been shut down in this area. And you'd have to sell the land to a coal company for him to exercise the rights, wouldn't you?''

"True enough. The mineral rights don't look like much right now. There's a lot of opposition to mining, what with the damage that's been caused to homes and farms by all that blasting. But the coal companies are still buying land around here. Did you know that?''

"No," I lied, letting him go on.

"Guess who had been negotiating to sell about a thousand acres of farmland to a major coal company, land which happens to be adjacent to one of my farms?''

"Iavello?''

"Land and mineral rights. For a large sum of money. Rumor is that there's a big new vein of coal that's been discovered, one that might be profitable to strip mine. The fact that the coal company wants the land adds fuel to the fire.''

"I thought Midwestern coal had a lot of sulfur in it, that burning it had environmentalists up in arms.''

"Yesterday's news," Bill said, gesturing with his hand as if dismissing my concern. "With all the experimental research being done on clean coal burning, it might become valuable again. A coal company would be smart to buy now and get a good price. Anyway, if Iavello's land gets sold, it'll put pressure on me to sell mine. No one wants to farm near an operating mine. It's disruptive.

"Of course, I can't sell the land at a good price because I don't own the mineral rights, which is the only way the land is valuable to the coal company. I could get stuck if the deal were to go through."

"No agreement's been signed?"

Blazevich shook his head. "May not be, now," he said, very matter-of-factly.

"Oh," I said. "So you're trying to talk Iavello's grandchildren out of selling the land, as well as getting your mineral rights back. That explains why you've been talking to Jimmy Iavello," I added, hoping to trip him up.

"Sorry, but I haven't talked to him." The words came quickly and were firm. Blazevich was lying, but at least he was cool about it. If I hadn't just seen Jimmy pull out of his driveway, I'd have believed him.

I touched my forehead as though I'd made a careless mistake. "Of course, you mentioned that already."

"Don't get me wrong, I'd like to talk to Jimmy about this. I'd sure rather talk to him than his muscle-head brother or lunatic sister. We could talk businessman to businessman. But I heard the will hasn't even been read yet. I'll wait until the right time. Then I'll get hold of him."

"You know where he's staying?" I asked, raising my eyebrows in hope.

"No. I mean, I imagine he's staying at his grandfather's house, but I don't know for sure."

"I just came from the house, and he's not there."

"Perhaps he's just out."

"I went through the house with Martha. There's no sign of him."

Blazevich pursed his lips in annoyance. "Well, I'm sure he'll turn up," he said.

Ginny Blazevich, perfumed with the smell of fried chicken, interrupted us. "I've got the farmhands sitting down to lunch," she told her husband. "You want anymore to eat?" Then she turned to me. "Would you like to stay and have a bite?"

"No, thank you," I said. My stomach growled at me in anger. "That's very kind of you, but I have to be going." I turned to Bill. "Sorry I interrupted your lunch. Thanks for the information. If you do happen to see Jimmy, would you ask him to call me? I'm staying with my dad."

He said he would and walked me to the door. Just as I stepped out, I had a sudden thought. "Your farm butts up against the Iavello homestead," I said.

"Yes, it does, but that's miles from here."

"How far is your land from the Iavello house?"

"Not too far. You can see it from the edge of my property, but it's still a good walk."

I thanked him and left. There wasn't much else I was going to get out of him. He knew something he wasn't telling me, and it concerned Jimmy Iavello. Why else would he deny Jimmy had been there? Blazevich also knew the will hadn't been read. For all his protestations of not having talked to anyone, he was getting information from someone close to the Iavellos.

I had little time to keep my appointment with Anna. Diamond wasn't far away, but I didn't trust my memory enough to use the back roads. Taking the longer route on better-traveled roads would make me late, but it was preferable to getting lost.

After my meeting with Martha, I'd focused on Anna as the likeliest suspect of the beneficiaries. Martha seemed sin-

cere once I got the full story from her, and I couldn't think
of Father Skip as a killer. But Anna, if she were faking the
apparitions, might have decided to get the money from Iavello as soon as he'd changed the will. The only problem
with that theory was that my heart kept saying Anna wasn't
guilty. I wondered if I could trust my heart.

And I wanted to know more about this mysterious message Mary sent through Anna.

I was ten minutes late when I saw the cross atop the
church steeple appear above the surrounding trees. St.
Mary's was built into a hillside in a wooded area just before
the woods gave way to farmland. I pulled into a makeshift
driveway beyond the church and circled around some trees
to bring the van to the back. Anna was nowhere in sight. I
turned off the engine and sat there, studying the building.

The thing that struck me most was how good the church
looked, even after so many years of disuse. The wood siding seemed sturdy and it gleamed white when the sun hit
it. The colored glass of the tall, narrow windows sparkled.
Martha and her group must've refurbished it. I left the van
for a closer look.

The church was long and rectangular, with a compact
entrance that jutted out the front. The bell tower and the
steeple rose above the entrance. As I circled around to the
rear, I remembered the Sunday bean dinners and chili suppers I had attended. I pictured those relatives I'd known,
now gone. Before I got melancholy, a voice rang out, star-
tling me.

"Nick, over here!"

I turned and saw Anna walking along a path in the
woods, coming toward me. She emerged unhurriedly. Today she wore blue jeans with a white turtleneck and carried
a prayer book in her hands.

"I wondered when you would get here," she said.

"I ended up talking to Bill Blazevich after I left Martha. It took a little longer than I expected."

Her eyebrows went up. "Is he one of your suspects?"

"Yes," I said. "Unfortunately, if it's a murder, almost everyone's a suspect."

"I'm sure I must be." Anna looked into my eyes as she said it, searching for confirmation. There was something disarmingly honest about the way her brown eyes explored mine.

"Sorry," I said, "you are."

"Don't be sorry. You have to sort it out for yourself." Anna turned away and walked under one of the two huge maple trees guarding the east side of the church. "I've stored the lunch over here. Let's sit down and eat."

There was a slight breeze which felt cold in the shade of the tree. Anna spread a blanket on the ground. She seemed oblivious to the chill. I zipped my jacket and told myself I wasn't cold.

Kneeling on the blanket, Anna laid out sandwiches. I saw slices of hard Italian salami sticking out the Hoagie buns and they made my mouth water. She handed me a milk carton and opened one for herself. Rummaging through her picnic basket, she pulled out two plastic Saints & Angels Coffeehouse souvenir glasses ("Thirst only for living waters—our refills are free") and a bag of potato chips which she placed between us. Still on her knees, she picked up her prayer book. "Let's say a silent prayer of thanks," she said.

I tried to recall the standard Catholic prayer I'd learned as a boy. She read something out of her book. We both made the sign of the cross. She regarded me with interest as I finished crossing myself.

"I hear you don't attend Mass anymore," she said.

"Word gets around," I replied.

"Tell me, what do you think about Mary?"

"I'm not sure what you mean."

She brushed a strand of hair behind her ear. "I'm just trying to figure out where you are, faith-wise," she said. "Do you still think of Mary as your Heavenly Mother?"

I shifted my legs, tried to think of an answer. Biting into the sandwich, I savored the garlicky taste of the salami, chewing longer than necessary. Religious matters hadn't seemed very important up until a few days ago. I felt uncomfortable discussing that.

Finally I swallowed. "I guess in my own mind I still see Mary as someone very special. 'Heavenly Mother' is a good term. Is it important to you what I think?"

She pondered the question. "Maybe."

"Martha said you cured Gregorio Iavello. Is that true?"

Anna grinned at me. "That I can put to rest. I didn't cure him. God did."

"Semantics," I commented. "Did you put your hands on him to be healed?"

"Yes, but if there is any healing, it's not my doing. It's heaven's. And I put my hands out for everyone who wants to touch me. Very few receive a cure." She delivered that statement with practiced ease and humility.

A breeze kicked up and I had to lurch for the potato chip bag to keep it from blowing over. I bolstered it with the tacky souvenir glass. "Tell me about Signor Iavello. Why do you think he was cured and not others?"

"I don't know. I think he had come to believe very strongly in the messages. He was certainly generous before he died, not that that had anything to do with his cure."

"So you knew about the change in the will?"

She gave me a blank look that took me by surprise. "He left us something in his will?"

THIRTEEN

"YOU MEAN YOU DIDN'T know?" I said.

Anna shook her head. There was no mistaking her surprise. "Me personally?"

"No, he left it to Children of the Second Advent. What did you mean, when you said he'd been generous before he died?"

"The things he'd bought. He donated money to set up the Stations of the Cross over there in the woods. He bought several acres of farmland adjacent to the church property. Donated a new organ to the church. In total it must've cost ten thousand dollars or more."

"He did this before he was cured?"

"Started it before he was cured. He first came to see me about four weeks before he died. He was cured two weeks after that."

"Hmmm." I mentally calculated the sum of the money Iavello had taken out in cash. Even if I inflated Anna's estimate, that still only accounted for half of the missing money. Where was the rest of it? And why hadn't Martha mentioned her grandfather's donations?

Anna was equally lost in thought. "How much did he leave?"

"I don't know the amount, but it's half the estate."

Anna walked out of the shade and into the sunlight, thinking. "That must be why Father Skip and Martha have been arguing lately about the direction of Second Advent, how to spend some money. I didn't realize we had so much."

"They've argued?"

"Vehemently. Believe it or not, it started right after the funeral, back at Gregorio's house."

I followed Anna into the sun. The warmth felt good. "It's hard for me to picture Father Skip in a heated argument."

"I didn't see all of it. We had been meeting in the study, but I left after the argument started."

"Was anyone else there?"

"In the house?" she asked. I nodded. "Sure. Whoever stopped by to express sympathy. Lots of people left food. Both of Martha's brothers were there."

"Could you make a list?"

She thought a minute. "I don't think so, not a complete list. Martha recorded the names of everyone who left food so she could write thank you notes. That would be the best place to start."

"I'll ask her for it," I said.

Anna returned to the blanket where we'd had lunch and gathered the remains into the basket. I prepared to politely turn down the gift of the plastic Saints & Angels Coffeehouse souvenir glass, but she didn't offer it.

"Would you like to go inside?" Anna asked. "Father Skip gave me a key since I live here in Diamond and can take care of the property."

I said yes without hesitation. Not only did I want the chance to check it out before tonight's prayer meeting, I just wanted to see it again, to relive some memories. We went up the steps to the entrance. Anna unlocked the door and swung it open, standing back and letting me enter first.

I felt like I was walking back in time. Very little had changed, although the wood floor in the entryway was now highly polished. The thick rope that rang the church bell dangled on the right. I walked over and held it, recalling the times as a child I'd been given special permission to ring the bell.

"It still rings," Anna said. "You can ring it if you want. There aren't twenty people that live around here, and they won't care if you do."

I pulled hard, expecting to hear the sweet musical ringing that summoned us from my great-uncle's farm so many years ago. Instead it clanged dully. I looked up, although I couldn't see into the bell tower.

"Not what it once was, eh? I've asked Martha if we can spend some money to fix it, but she hasn't gotten around to it. Might be cheaper to buy a new bell. Go on inside."

The majestic angel statue holding holy water in a shell was still there, and I impulsively placed my hand in the water and made the sign of the cross as I passed it. I stood next to Anna at the back, looking toward the altar. Short rows of pews flanked the center aisle, eight on one side, nine on the other. The church couldn't possibly accommodate more than 100 people. It was hard to imagine it as full as Dana Rardin's newspaper article said.

In all the times I'd visited as a child, there had never been more than sixty people at any given service. I could picture myself holding my mother's hand, feeling her tug as she pulled me toward a pew. The memory was so strong I genuflected and shuffled into the back pew, letting the kneeler down with one foot and dropping to my knees. I studied the large statue of Jesus with His right hand raised in blessing and refamiliarized myself with the church.

The elaborate white Gothic style altar, tipped in gold, stood against the front wall. It cradled statues of two Slovakian saints whose names I couldn't remember. The Immaculate Heart of Mary statue, which also had a place in the altar, had been moved to a new pedestal near the communion railing. The picture in *The Daily Clintonian* had shown it dripping blood. The statue was adorned with vases of roses, and someone had placed a crown of daisies on the head. Rosaries of white and gold were strung around the feet.

The church felt filled with an undefined something, but whether it was really spiritual or just my own memories trying to break through, I wasn't sure.

Anna knelt next to me in the pew. I leaned over to her. "Is she here?" I said, *sotto voce*. I hoped it didn't sound irreverent.

"No," she whispered back. "And we can talk out loud. It's okay."

I would have preferred to whisper my doubts just in case, but I agreed. We rose and approached the statue of Mary. I carefully touched it, running my hand over the heart that supposedly bled. It felt solid.

"This is where she appears to you?" I asked.

"Yes. The statue just sort of disappears, and there she is."

"Why isn't the statue of the pregnant Mary in here?"

Anna frowned as though I should know. "Because it isn't a statue yet approved by the church."

"What does it feel like, talking to her?"

"It feels like complete joy, only not the joy you experience when something outside of you makes you happy—it's like being inside the joy itself." Anna's eyes looked up toward the face of the statue. Her smile became wider. She opened her mouth a bit and her breathing became shallower, as if just remembering it were enough to bring her incredible pleasure. "It's pure ecstasy, better than the best…" She started to say the next word but dropped it quietly.

I thought I knew what she was going to say, and I stared at her in surprise. She blushed.

"I'm sorry," she said. "I'm not holy, you know. I make

mistakes and I say the wrong things sometimes." Then she smiled at me and lowered her eyes. "At least I related it to something we both know about."

"I guess we do," I replied, uncomfortable. "Has Mary ever confirmed to you that Signor Iavello was murdered?"

Anna wrinkled her forehead. "No," she said, "not directly. But she always encouraged our thinking that way."

"Did you ever think to ask her who murdered him? Might save us a lot of time," I said without sarcasm.

"I haven't asked her, but she would never answer a question like that, anyway."

"What kind of question would she answer?"

"Matters of faith, that kind of thing."

I listened for a hint of insincerity but detected none. So much of this seemed unbelievable, and yet Anna remained so earnest.

"Is it always the same, or sometimes do you think you might be imagining the visions?"

"I'm not imagining them, no. But some visions are stronger than others. When Mary appears crying or giving me a strongly worded message, the visions can be overpowering. Sometimes when she leaves, I pass out."

That would be theatrical, I thought. Then I found myself sorry I'd thought it. She might be crazy, but I was beginning to trust Anna again.

I examined the statue one more time, noticing that it didn't sit firmly on the pedestal. It wobbled when I pushed on it, but it wasn't so unstable as to fall over without a major shove. I tried to see if there were something small underneath the statue that made it sit unevenly, but I couldn't tell.

"Since I'm here, can I see the rest of the church?" I asked. "I'd like to see the basement. I remember playing down there as a kid during the chili suppers."

We exited by a small door hidden behind the altar. The

door opened into a room, which then led to the basement stairway. We descended the concrete stairs, steadying ourselves with a hand against the cold, damp wall since there wasn't a railing. When Anna reached the bottom and flipped the light switch, only a few lights responded. The basement looked dark and forbidding. "We don't use the basement much," she said. "But we've talked about fixing it up and making it an annex, piping the proceedings down here. The crowds are getting so large, I think we'll need it next winter. I hate to see people standing outside in the cold. It's one of the things Father Skip wants to do with the donations."

"Doesn't Martha approve?"

"Not really. She wants to use the funds for distributing the messages, to let more people know what Mary is doing here."

"Surely there'll be enough money to do both."

"Maybe now. Martha's plan is pretty ambitious, though. She's talking about videos, radio programs, even buying time on cable channels."

I moved around in the large, nearly dark room. Tables seemed to appear out of nowhere and I bumped into them. "I can't imagine the Catholic Church allowing that to happen."

"No church funds would be used. It would all be Second Advent moneys. Martha says if TV evangelists can do it, we can, too. She's particularly irritated that the Mystical Jesus church has a call-in radio show on a Terre Haute station and just launched a half hour TV show on Wabash Valley Cable."

I turned back to Anna. "You're kidding? Pastor Carl, that guy with the white hair and smooth voice? He's got that kind of backing?"

"He must. I've never been to his church, of course, but

I hear he packs 'em in for the faith-healing stuff. Probably gets a lot of his money there.''

I made a mental note to find out when the show was on and watch it. What for, I wasn't sure. But all these "miraculous" things happening in the same place at the same time intrigued me. I also wondered if the shows Martha was proposing might not be similar. "In some ways, you're in competition with him," I said.

Anna waved away the suggestion. "Not even close. He must heal ten, twenty people a week, of all kinds of physical ailments. Mary concentrates on spiritual healings.''

"But you claim to have been healed in Medjugorje, and you told me Mary healed Gregorio Iavello.''

"Yes, Mary healed my mind," Anna said. Her voice softened. "She did the same for Gregorio. Some whom I've touched have claimed to be healed physically. They may have. I believe Mary can obtain physical miracles from Jesus, just as she did in Cana when He changed water into wine. But I think, when she works through me, she heals minds and spirits. She says spiritual healings are needed more than physical ones in America today.''

I looked around again, but the basement wasn't at all the way I remembered it and it didn't hold the same appeal. As we started to leave, though, I felt the chain of the Miraculous Medal tingling at my neck. I turned around, but there was nothing behind me but the furnace, and behind it the old coal bin. I itched where the chain touched my neck. Anna noticed.

"I'm glad to see you're still wearing the Miraculous Medal," she said. "That's good." She turned off the basement light and we walked upstairs.

"Are you going to tell me what message Mary left for me? You brought me to hear it, but you haven't mentioned it yet.''

She pulled a small, folded note out of her pocket.

"You're part of the plan, Nick. I'm sure of it. Don't discount us or yourself."

"I won't," I said, sounding non-committal nonetheless. I opened the note and read the message, written in Anna's handwriting on light blue stationery.

"Luke 8:16-17, Isaiah 6:10. Go forward and do not fear, for my Immaculate Heart protects you." I looked up at Anna. "Do you know these Bible passages?"

Her eyes looked deeply into mine, and she said gravely, "Yes, but you need to read them for yourself. Mary cautioned me not to speculate."

I pocketed the note. Dad had a family Bible and I would check the passages when I got home. Whether this was a message from heaven or Anna's imagination gone wild remained to be seen. "Do you know what Mary plans to announce tonight?" I asked.

"She hinted that God would allow her to predict a miracle, but when the miracle would occur or what it would be, she didn't say.

"Since you're coming to the Prayer Service tonight, you need to bring a rosary," she continued. "We start at 7 o'clock, but with the crowds that come, you need to get here earlier."

"I'm not sure I have a rosary..." I said.

"I'll bring an extra one. And don't worry if you don't remember how to say it. I'm sure it will come back to you."

I wasn't sure it would, but I didn't argue. I thanked her again for lunch and climbed in the van. Circling to leave, I glanced back at the church just before pulling out onto the road. The afternoon sun shone hard against the white siding, causing it to take on an ethereal glow. Anna had her back against the church, and the white radiance blazed around her. She had her hands out to her sides, and I gasped at the image created. If she had been wearing a robe instead of jeans, it would have matched the image on the Miraculous Medal.

"Jesus," I said.

FOURTEEN

EITHER IT WAS an incredible coincidence that the car behind me took all the same county roads I did on the way back to Dad's house, or I was being tailed. I didn't want to believe I was becoming paranoid, but working on this case was making me cautious. My road companion had picked me up when I passed through Clinton. Now, approaching Dad's house, I was trying to decide what to do. Did I want to wait until I got there and then confront him? Would it put Dad and Stephanie in jeopardy if I did? I'd been down a similar road with Joan and didn't want to take the chance.

I slowed down, and the car pulled up behind me. Red and blue police lights suddenly flashed in the grill. I eased over to the side, my heart racing.

Every violation I might have committed sped through my brain. I watched the car in the side mirror. When I saw Charlie Cammack step out, I breathed a little easier. He sauntered over to my window, dressed in a very un-police-like gray sweat suit.

"Are you trying to give me heart failure?" I said, rolling the window down.

"Thought that was you. The '41' license plate was a giveaway. I've got some information. Want me to follow you home?"

"You could have let me know it was you. I've been going crazy trying to figure out who was tailing me." I looked at his clothes. "Are you off-duty or undercover?"

"Me undercover and you being tailed? You read too many detective stories, you know that? I'm off duty because I've got to cover the evening shift tonight. What I need is your help. A trade. I'll explain when we get to your house."

Dad was at the window when I pulled into the driveway, and he opened the door before I had a chance to knock. He nodded to Charlie and looked at me with raised eyebrows.

"Dad, this is Charlie Cammack with the Clinton Police. He's a friend of John's from high school." They shook hands. "If it's okay, we'll use the living room. Where's Stephanie?"

"She seemed really tired so I put her down for a nap," Dad said. "She protested all the way but fell asleep quickly."

I offered Charlie coffee, which he accepted. Dad makes a big pot in the morning and drinks it throughout the day. I zapped two mugs in the microwave and added lots of cream and sugar to mine. I recommended Charlie do the same. "Trust me," I said.

"So what do you want to trade?" I asked when I'd settled into a blue upholstered chair in the one room in the house I could count on to be uncluttered. With the piano, good furniture and mauve and teal wallpaper, the living room was more formal than the rest of the house. As kids, John and I would only be found in there 30 minutes a day when we had to practice piano. Other than that, we lived in the family room with the TV.

Charlie sat on the sofa next to my chair. "It's easy on your end. I'm doing a little side investigation of the good pastor Carl Young, and I want you to release the information when I've got something on him. Since the Chief is smitten with this guy, it would be, ah, career limiting, for me to bring him down. I need *The Daily Clintonian* to do it."

"What do you have on him?"

"Nothing confirmed. But I did a background check on some of the folks he's 'healed' recently on TV. Seems they're all from Oregon." He sipped his coffee. "Wow, this is strong coffee."

"Told you."

"Anyway, why would people travel all the way out to Clinton to be healed?" he continued. "The guy just started his cable show, and it's local. Unlikely they would have heard of him in Oregon."

The reporter in me was nearly giddy at the prospect the pastor might be a phony. "Charlie, I think it's the kind of story Dana Rardin would kill for. But I can't make any agreements for the *DC*. I'm not the editor."

"I know you can't speak for Dana. But I don't want to go to her office and risk the chief making a connection. I want you to be the go-between."

We agreed on that; Charlie, for his part, agreed to feed me information on Signor Iavello's death.

"But there's something I have to tell you first. We know you're working for Martha Iavello."

I reddened. Everyone seemed to know what I was doing. "How did you find out?"

"Martha told us. We called to get her permission to exhume Gregorio's body."

My eyes opened wide. "Exhume? Why?"

"This is completely off the record," Charlie said. "The preliminary autopsy report came in. While the blood test indicated an overdose of amitriptyline, the postmortem didn't show any undissolved tablets in the stomach."

"Why is that odd?"

"Well, it's a case of timing. Martha Iavello said she left her grandfather about 10:00. The coroner placed the time of death about midnight. That's two hours. In an overdose, you sometimes find partially dissolved tablets when the person dies before all the medicine is absorbed. If Gregorio took the tablets right after Martha left, then in two hours they *might* be fully dissolved. But if he took them any later, and I mean even ten minutes later, we should have seen some."

"So he must've taken them at 10:00," I said. "The drug had to get there somehow."

"It may have gotten there another way."

I remembered Joan's information. "Amitriptyline comes in an injectable form."

Charlie's look told me he was impressed. "Very good. It might have been given by syringe. Maybe Iavello did it to himself. Or maybe he took the tablets. We don't know what happened."

"Wouldn't an injection leave a mark?"

"I talked to the old guy's doctor. Iavello had just had a blood test. A skilled person could have used the same small area and not attracted attention. The coroner didn't look too hard. At the time it didn't seem important."

Charlie put the mug aside and rested his arms on his thighs, leaning forward. "But suddenly it's important, and the chief wants the body exhumed."

"He thinks it's murder?"

"He wants to know more. The body's going over to Vigo General in Terre Haute for more tests."

"How long before they know something?"

"Could be two weeks, but I think it'll be less. The chief's pushing for a quick resolution."

I pursed my lips. "I don't think Iavello could have injected himself with the drug, not that skillfully."

Charlie shook his head. "Probably not. I talked to the psychiatrist, Dr. Crowley. She never prescribed it in injectable form."

"Hmm." I remembered the 'PC' entries in Iavello's date book and my suspicion that Patricia Crowley and the *si-*

gnore might have been more than doctor and patient. I didn't mention it to Charlie, though. Not now. I mean, it was still conjecture. "When can I do a story on this?"

"The chief won't go public until the pathologist is done."

I ran my finger across my jawline. The police finally thought it was murder. That was good, but also bad. The police would be working to solve the murder now. If they solved it before I did, I could forget about the $25,000. On the other hand, with Charlie's help, I might solve it first.

"Now that you know I'm playing investigator as well as reporter, does that change our relationship?"

"Hardly. I just trusted you with knowledge about Reverend Goldentones that alone could sink me. Look, I reread the articles about you to get the name of the sheriff you worked with. Lt. Polsky told me I could trust you with anything. But he also told me you needed to be warned off doing police work."

I smiled. Polsky would say that. It wasn't his wife who'd been kidnapped. But I had no intention of placing anyone in danger this time.

"I'm going to work on this case, but I won't do anything dangerous."

"I have to ask what you know so far."

I told him most of what I knew—what I had learned of the will and how Jimmy and Tom were planning to fight it, how farmers Bill Blazevich and Angelo Ronchi had motive if Iavello's land got sold to a coal company, and how Martha, Anna, and Father Skip would benefit from the will as it now stood. I also told him that I didn't think they did it.

"Then who did?"

"I'd like to question Jimmy Iavello, but he's hard to locate. There seems to be a connection between him and Bill Blazevich, too, but I don't know what it is."

"There *used* to be a connection, you mean," Charlie said. "Used to be?"

Charlie drained his coffee. "Maybe it was just rumor, but Jimmy supposedly was in love with Blazevich's eldest daughter Margaret when they were in high school. There was a lot of opposition, though. No love lost between the families, you might say. I didn't know it was over mineral rights.

"Anyway, when the two went to college, Jimmy chose the University of Chicago and she chose St. Joseph's in Rensselaer. There was only an hour's driving time between the two campuses. If it was a hot love affair, it apparently cooled off because Margaret married someone else. She had three kids with him before he divorced her."

I shook my head. "How come you knew about it and I didn't? I was only two years behind them. You were a lot younger."

"That's because Pauline Blazevich was in my class. She viewed the whole thing as a Romeo-and-Juliet romance. She blabbed."

"Oh." If there was really some hatred between Jimmy and Bill Blazevich over a lost love, that added a new dimension to the relationship. I wasn't sure yet where it might go, but I wanted to think about it.

"Will the police question Jimmy Iavello?" I asked.

"Yes. He said he was at his home in New York when Iavello died. We have no reason to doubt him, but of course we have to check it out now. And we have other questions, too."

Stephanie appeared at the door, holding the arm of a rabbit Beanie Baby with one hand and rubbing the sleep out of her eyes with the other. "Hi Daddy!" she said.

"Hi, sweetheart. Mr. Cammack and I were just finishing up." She glanced shyly at Charlie and looked adorable. I

had a sudden thought. Martha had said Jimmy was childless. Was that by choice? What did Jimmy care about, besides money?

"I have to go," Charlie said, glancing at his watch. He
stood up to leave. Stephanie came over to me and slipped
her hand in mine. I collected the two coffee mugs with my
free hand and tagged behind Charlie on the way out.

"I hope you can find Jimmy Iavello," I said.

"Oh, we can find him. I just hope it's this afternoon so
I don't have to head up a search party tonight."

I wondered if Charlie was hiding something about the
missing evidence or had just forgotten to mention it. "What
about the prescription bottle? Have you found it yet?"

"No. The chief and I did a brief search of the evidence
room but couldn't find it. The chief seems unconcerned. He
says it'll turn up." Charlie crossed his arms. "We have a
deal, right? You'll talk to Dana Rardin?"

"Right."

"You'll tell me anything you learn about Iavello's
death."

"Promise." Only maybe not right away, I thought.

"Just for my information, what are you going to do next?
And it better not be dangerous."

I laughed. "Hardly. I'm going out to Diamond tonight
to the prayer group meeting. I want to be there when Mary
appears to Anna, to see what I think about it. Second Advent will soon be flush with money. Whatever Gregorio
died for, I have to believe money is at the bottom of it."

Charlie nodded. "Be careful," he said, and let himself
out.

FIFTEEN

I CALLED MY EDITOR, Dana Rardin, at the paper. She okayed the arrangement with Charlie but reminded me that Pastor Carl Young was an advertiser. "Tell Charlie we have to have an iron-clad expose," she said. When I told her I planned to go to Anna Veloche's prayer meeting that evening, she agreed it was a good idea. "Write up a story for tomorrow's paper if there's anything to report."

While Dad fed Stephanie a snack, I located the family Bible, cracked it open and read the two passages. I hated sneaking around but I didn't want to tell Dad about the message from Mary. The idea that I had received some special communication from heaven made me uneasy and not a little embarrassed, and that assumed I believed Anna was on the level, something I wasn't ready to admit.

The passage from Isaiah read: "You are to make the heart of this people sluggish, to dull their ears and close their eyes; else their eyes will see, their ears hear, their heart understand, and they will turn and be healed."

Luke 8:16-17 read: "No one lights a lamp and puts it under a bushel basket or under a bed; he puts it on a lamp-stand so that whoever comes in can see it. There is nothing hidden that will not be exposed, nothing concealed that will not be known and brought to light."

If this was supposed to be a clue, I felt more like the first passage, my ears were dull and my eyes were closed. Still, I wrote the passages word-for-word on the back of

Anna's note and pocketed it again, hoping that something would happen to make it understandable. If this were really a heavenly message. If Anna were really a visionary. If I were as good at this as I hoped.

My cousin picked up Stephanie at 6:15 p.m., and Dad and I left shortly after that. Not knowing what to wear to a prayer meeting, I had decided not to be underdressed. Since I hadn't come to Clinton expecting to stay, I selected from my limited choices the navy slacks from the suit I'd worn to Gregorio Iavello's funeral and paired it with a blue and white striped Oxford cloth shirt. Dad wore gray slacks with a patterned shirt in burgundy. We both took windbreakers to protect against the cool weather and umbrellas in case of a spring shower.

In the van, Dad pulled out the rosaries he'd found and reviewed the instructions on what prayers to say on what bead. Anna had been right, the whole thing came back to me quickly, although I had forgotten that saying a full rosary could take as much as forty-five minutes. With all the other hoopla going on, I did not expect this to be a short service.

Dad had advised me not to try the short cut from Clinton to Diamond because of bad roads, so I had stuck to the main thoroughfares. We turned on a road that led directly to the church and were only about a half mile from it when we were flagged down by a group of two men and one woman. They were waving pamphlets at us and standing in our way, so I slowed down. The men were well dressed and appeared harmless. The woman, also well-dressed, had a smear of red lipstick across her mouth that stood out next to her skin, paled by the glaring van headlights. The three held their ground, and I had no choice but to brake. Dad rolled down the window. The men stuck in their hands, shoving literature at us while the woman shouted behind them.

"Anna Veloche is in league with the devil," she screamed.

My hands gripped the steering wheel. Dad hurriedly rolled the window up, forcing the men to withdraw their hands. He turned to me.

"Where did they come from?" he asked.

Shaking, I applied pressure to the gas pedal and the van pushed forward, forcing them out of my way. "What does it say on the pamphlets?" I asked.

Dad studied them in the reading light. "You'll like this," he answered. "They're from the Church of the Mystical Jesus."

In the rearview mirror I saw the reception committee slide into the background. I relaxed and even chuckled a bit. "I didn't notice their crystal pendants with Jesus in them."

"Probably inside their jackets," Dad said.

We arrived at the church a minute later. St. Mary's parking lot was overflowing with cars. A youth who couldn't have been more than sixteen directed us with his flashlight to a space in an adjacent field.

I checked my watch. We had arrived before the service but not early enough. From the number of people wandering around on the church grounds trying to peer in the windows, I guessed the church was packed. A sheriff's deputy patrolled the entrance. Dad and I went to talk to him.

"Is it always like this?" I asked the deputy.

He was roughly my age and a good four inches taller. He looked down with a taut smile. "Has been the last couple of weeks. That's all I can speak for. I got assigned here when the crowds attracted a group of protesters." He nudged his head in the direction of the group up the road. "There's been some threats."

"Really," my dad interjected. "What kind of threats?"

"I'm not at liberty to say."

I made a mental note to check with Charlie Cammack later. "Tell me, is there a way I can get in the church?" I asked.

The sheriff snorted. "At this point? Not unless you know somebody."

"Nick! Nick! Over here!" a woman shouted. I recognized Martha Iavello's voice.

"Maybe I do know somebody."

Martha waved an unopened umbrella at the far side of the church. "We didn't know if you were going to make it," she said after Dad and I had hustled over. "Anna has asked me twice to check on you."

"Anna's asked about me?"

"Yes, for whatever reason. Oh, hi, Mr. Bertetto," Martha said, noticing my dad and extending her hand.

Dad smiled. "Please call me Victor."

"Is Father Skip here?" I asked.

"No," Martha answered, her voice registering a slight quiver, "and we still haven't heard from him." She produced a key from the pocket of her tan trenchcoat and opened a back door. "Let's get inside." We entered onto the middle landing of the staircase that led from the basement to the church level. We followed Martha up, our shoes clicking on the concrete steps. When we entered the sanctuary from the hidden door behind the altar, my jaw dropped.

Every pew was jammed, every extra folding chair was taken. People stood at least two abreast on the side aisles of the church. A mob gathered at the back. Only the center aisle was clear, that being gently enforced by three strapping young men.

"Where's Anna?" I whispered to Martha, as she led us toward two reserved seats near the statue of Mary.

"In the back near the entrance," she whispered.

One of the ushers saw us coming and let us in. There

was a bit of embarrassment as the three of us looked at the two seats. Obviously they hadn't expected my dad. I insisted on standing, though I felt conspicuous standing so near the front.

The church bell rang seven o'clock with the same dull sound it had made that afternoon. A small buzz of excitement rose from the crowd, and everyone's eyes shifted to the back where Anna made her entrance. Dressed in a simple, floor-length flower print dress, she appeared to float as she moved effortlessly toward the center aisle. Reaching the back pew, she genuflected, bowing her head deeply as her knee touched the floor.

When she stood, pandemonium broke out. Everyone crushed in toward the center aisle, holding up items for her to touch. Anna closed her eyes, I presumed in prayer, and turned to one side. People crowded in around her. The ushers fought in vain to keep control. Anna seemed frightened by the jostling, but valiantly kept her eyes closed and tried to touch every object she could. I was amazed by her concentration and calmness.

The noise level in the church began rising. I tried to watch the scene in front of me as objectively as I could. Most of the items thrust toward Anna were either crucifixes, rosaries or pictures. Some people were pushing pieces of paper into her hands. I nudged Martha and asked her what Anna was being given. Martha said they were probably petitions for God's blessing on the sick.

Anna tried valiantly to shuffle forward. I saw perspiration on her forehead. The mob-generated heat felt sticky.

Eventually those whose items were touched returned to their pews. The ushers formed a small wedge and guided Anna through the remaining crowd. She couldn't possibly know everything she put her hands on, I thought. Some joker could have put up a crystal Mystical Jesus pendant, and it would have gotten blessed.

Anna reached the altar and turned to face the congregation, waiting for the buzz to die down.

"I pray that the Lord will bless each of you," she said quietly. "Thank you for coming to our prayer service in honor of the Blessed Mother. Let's begin by praying the rosary."

Everyone but Anna knelt instantly, even those in the back and on the side aisles who had no kneelers and had to use the hard floor. Anna took out her rosary, an ornate one with white beads, and crossed herself using the crucifix at the end. Then she kissed the figure of Jesus on the crucifix and began to pray aloud.

Dad and I followed Anna's lead. Portable kneelers had been provided to us, so we were able to kneel with some comfort. I recited the prayers with everyone else, all the while scanning the crowd. Then someone moved in the back of the church, which caught my attention. The person was under the choir loft, an area in near-darkness. I watched a few heads turn and used the shifting bodies to pinpoint the location. I strained to see who it was.

Not long after, there was another disturbance in the same place. Whoever it was made his way to the back door and left. I caught a brief flash of light on the person's head, revealing thick white hair. I did a double take. Pastor Carl Young of the Church of the Mystical Jesus? It was too dark to get a good look, but that white hair made me think of him. What would he be doing at a service his church was denouncing?

Back at the altar, Anna stood and faced the statue of Mary. Her eyes anxiously searched the statue.

Anna's recitation of the prayers abruptly stopped and she fell to her knees. The crowd, sensing that the apparition had begun, became quiet. Anna's eyes locked on the space immediately above the statue, and she smiled with excitement. I glanced from her to the statue and back again. I didn't see anything, but as intently as Anna stared, she could have.

Her face began to radiate the ecstasy I'd heard about, and I noticed something odd. Anna wasn't blinking—at all.

There were no falling tears, no pooling in the eyes. The upper eyelids didn't strain to stay open. Anna's eyes were simply fixed on something. I wished I could shine a light in her pupils to see if I could get her to blink, but in all honesty, I didn't think she would.

The crowd gasped. I looked toward the statue where people were pointing. The Immaculate Heart on the statue of Mary had begun to drip blood down the statue's robes and onto the pedestal. My hands started to shake, and I stared at the heart in shock until it occurred to me how regularly the drops were falling. Could such a thing be staged? My intuition said yes, but I couldn't let go of the awe I felt watching the statue bleed.

Anna took her eyes off the apparition once to look to Martha, who handed her a pad of paper and a pen. Anna laid the pad on the railing and began to write. She glanced up at the vacant space every so often, then wrote again. After about ten minutes, she started to put the pen down, then snapped it back up, looking again at the empty space. She paused, turned and pointed in my direction.

Suddenly I felt everyone's eyes scrutinizing me. My ears turned red. I knelt on the floor. Mercifully, Anna turned her attention back to her vision and began to write again. All eyes followed Anna, and I gulped in relief. I rubbed the back of my neck and brushed the chain holding the Miraculous Medal. I followed the chain down to the medallion and rubbed it.

At the front, Anna finished writing, tore away one sheet and gave it to Martha. She put her pen down and bowed her head in prayer. As she was praying, the bleeding of the Immaculate Heart came to a slow stop. Anna remained in prayer for a couple of minutes, after which she stood and turned to face the congregation, holding the pad of paper in front of her.

"Here is the message given to me by Our Mother of the Second Advent," she said.

"'Thank you, dear children, for your devotion and prayers. God is touched by your willingness to be humble and your desire to do His Will. He only wishes all His children were so obedient and would take the messages of His Mother to heart. Still, even among you there are those without faith, who view these messages as a curiosity, not the desire of Heaven. To convince you, by the power and grace of God I shall work a miracle this Saturday. Someone thought to be dead will be raised to life, and someone thought to be alive will be brought to justice. Thank you, my children. I love you. Continue to pray for unity in the name of my Son.'"

And then Anna's legs buckled under her and she spilled onto the floor in a dead faint.

I stood up, concerned, but apparently most everyone else had seen this before because those around me swung into action. Two people rushed to Anna's aid. A heavyset woman in the first pew stood up with her rosary, and, backed by the vocal power of the front half of the church, picked up saying the rosary where Anna had left off at the time of her vision. Everyone quieted down.

A little later the service was over. Anna was still unconscious but coming around. Martha thanked everyone for coming, reminding them to return for Saturday's service and message. She didn't say anything about the predicted miracle for Saturday, but I guessed she needed time to assess what to do about it.

The crowd began to leave. Chairs banged together and clothes rustled noisily. Excited by the prospect of a miracle, people spoke in loud, animated voices. An older lady with styled blue hair walked briskly over to us. I remembered her as the church secretary at Holy Family Church.

"Isn't it amazing?" she told my dad. "Saturday, Mary will bring Gregorio Iavello back from the dead!"

"That's not what she said, Rose," my dad responded. "She just said someone *thought* to be dead would be brought to life. Could mean just about anything."

Rose started to argue with Dad. My attention was caught by a young man wearing a priest's collar who stood at Mary's statue. He held a small test tube in one hand and was trying to scoop the blood into it with a small spatula he held in the other. I left Dad discussing the prophecy with Rose.

The priest was fresh-faced with just enough lines to convince me he was about thirty years old. His brown hair swept across his forehead covering a receding hairline. His clothes were casual, khaki-colored corduroys with a brown Fair Isle sweater over a shirt, the white collar visible in front. He was absorbed by his work on the blood and didn't notice me as I approached.

"What are you doing?" I asked.

He looked up, a little startled. "I'm getting a sample to run an analysis." The voice was flat and matter-of-fact.

I touched a bit of the blood on the statue and brought it to my nose. It had an iron smell, not unlike my own blood.

"Touching what could be blood in this age of AIDS is not a very smart idea," the priest said.

I jerked my hand away from my face and looked for something to wipe my finger on. Not seeing anything obvious, I settled for my pants.

The priest chuckled, an odd, rumbling sound that came from deep in his throat. "It's too late now, but don't worry, we haven't found the HIV virus in any other sample. It's unlikely we'll find it here."

"Who are you?" I asked.

"Father Vincent Kennedy. You can call me Vince, or Father Vince if first names make you uncomfortable," he said, resuming his work at the pedestal. He finished scooping what he could and put a cork in the top of the test tube.

Vince was clearly not going to volunteer information. "Are you from around here?" I asked.

He reached down to a leather briefcase by his feet, pulled out a pouch and secured the test tube inside the pouch. "I teach at St. Mary-of-the-Woods College in Terre Haute. I'm also a Mariologist. The archdiocese of Indianapolis has asked me to investigate this alleged apparition." He placed the pouch in the briefcase and snapped it shut. "Who are you?"

I put out my hand. "Nick Bertetto. Martha Iavello has asked me to look into the death of her grandfather. I'm curious about Children of the Second Advent, whether or not it might be involved somehow."

That got Vince's attention. He shook my outstretched hand and nodded gravely, looking into my eyes for the first time. "Then we're fellow seekers of truth," he said.

"What are you hoping to find out from that sample?" I asked.

"We want to make sure it's blood and that it's the same blood type as the other samples. This is the fourth."

I ran my hand over the statue again, making sure it seemed solid, but carefully avoiding the blood this time. "Is this real?"

"If you mean, is the statue really dripping blood, the answer is yes. If you mean, is this a supernatural event or did someone rig it up, the answer is, we don't know yet. I'm waiting for the archdiocese to give me permission to run an X ray on the statue. Right now, they don't want me to pull the statue out of the church."

"Why not?"

"Could be as simple as indecision. If it's real, they probably want to avoid offending a divine apparition. On the other hand, many people are finding a renewal of their faith in this event. There's also been a number of converts to Catholicism. The archdiocese may not want to know if it's a fake.'' Vince did his throaty chuckle again. ''The pressure to give some kind of approval to this apparition will build as the crowds get bigger. Eventually they'll have to let me borrow the statue. I just don't know when.''

''You seem to know a lot about investigating apparitions.''

Vince looked around to see if anyone was watching us. There were people close to us, but I wasn't sure anyone was listening.

He pulled a business card out of his briefcase and handed it to me. ''I'll discuss this with you, but privately. Can you come to my office tomorrow at 9 o'clock?''

''Sure,'' I said. Then Vince turned and left abruptly. I stuffed the card in my pocket.

Dad, meanwhile, had managed to free himself from Rose with the blue hair. He met me at the statue. ''Who was that?'' he asked.

''A priest who's investigating the apparition.''

Martha approached. ''Anna says to tell you Mary was glad you were here and had read the message.'' She looked into my eyes intently, then squeezed my forearm. She returned to Anna's side.

''What was that all about?'' asked Dad.

Before I could answer there was a disturbance of some kind at the church entrance. Four sturdy men, two in blue uniforms and two in brown uniforms pushed through. Charlie Cammack was one of the officers in blue. The tall sheriff's deputy I'd talked to outside was one of those in brown. Charlie advanced to Martha and pulled her aside. As they talked, Martha began to cry. The officer with Charlie put his arm around her and escorted her out.

Hoping Charlie would tell me what was going on, I walked toward him. He saw me coming and waited.

"What is it?" I asked.

"Tom Iavello is dead," he answered.

"No!" I exclaimed. "How?"

"Poison, in steroids. That's off the record, by the way."

"Poor Martha," I said.

"Yeah," he responded, evenly. "Nick, you need to come with me. We have some questions for you to answer."

"Me?"

Charlie nodded. "We went over the log book at the Big Sycamore Gym. We were surprised to find your name listed as a visitor and hear you and Tom had an argument. Apparently you were one of the last people to see him alive."

Panic rose in my throat. "I didn't have anything to do with his death!"

"Calm down. We don't suspect anyone yet. But we need to talk."

I gave the van keys to my dad and told him I'd be home as soon as I could. He watched as Charlie led me out to the waiting police car. I gave a brief wave of reassurance before I left the church.

But I was far from reassured myself. Tom Iavello was dead. Father Skip was still missing. Anna had promised everyone a miracle. I had a personal message from Mary. And Martha and I were in the custody of the Clinton Police.

SIXTEEN

CHARLIE WAS TIGHT-LIPPED as we got in the car to return to Clinton. He called into police headquarters to let them know we were on the way but said nothing to me for a long time. I waited, on edge, hoping he would say something to indicate he didn't view me differently now. Finally he pulled a crumpled sheet of paper from his pocket and handed it to me. "We found this in Tom's apartment." he said. "What does it mean to you?"

I smoothed it out. It was a version of the note I'd found in my car when I left the Big Sycamore Gym. There were typing mistakes all over it.

"That Tom wasn't much of a typist?" I joked.

"You've seen it before."

"I found a copy in my car after I left Tom at the gym. At the time I wasn't sure he'd written it. The way it was positioned on the seat, I could have overlooked it all morning. The only thing I was certain he'd left was a nice dent in my door."

"Why didn't you tell me about it?"

"I couldn't at first, because then I'd have had to tell you I was working for Martha. Mostly I've been trying to forget about it."

Charlie got quiet again.

"I didn't know it was Tom, honestly. And even if I did, I sure wouldn't kill him for it."

No response.

"I talked to Dana Rardin," I said. "She'll agree to expose the Church of the Mystical Jesus, as long as the proof against Pastor Carl is ironclad. If we still have a deal."

Charlie checked his rearview mirror, but didn't answer.

"Do we still have a deal?"

Charlie's smile was wooden. "Stop worrying about being a suspect, okay?" he said. "We'd be hard-pressed to make a case that you killed him. We just have to ask you some questions."

"Then why don't you act like you trust me anymore?"

Charlie shook his head absently. "I still trust you. Unofficially, anyway. Just too many things have come up. The gym, the note. And we know you took a bunch of evidence from Gregorio's study."

"What evidence?"

"Martha says you have the date book and some financial records."

I cocked my head toward him, annoyed. "The police had written off the death as a suicide when I took those records. It wasn't illegal. And I'll give them to you if you ask."

"It would help."

"They're yours," I said. There wasn't anything in them anyway, except those "PC" entries that hinted Iavello may have had more than a doctor/patient relationship with Dr. Crowley. And that was pure conjecture on my part. "Is there any evidence Tom's death was related to the *signore*'s?"

"We haven't found any yet, but we're looking."

"A friend of mine thought Tom was on steroids," I offered. "I guess he was right."

Charlie grunted. "In spades. Tom was stacking three or four different steroids from the variety of bottles we found. It's a wonder his liver hadn't given out.

"What was going on back there at the church?" Charlie

asked suddenly. "Anna Veloche looked like she had passed out."

The change in subject sounded deliberate. I wanted to pursue Tom's death further, but it was easier to let Charlie lead for now. "She did pass out. Apparently that's not unusual. Five people got up to take care of Anna and finish the service. It looked almost practiced."

"Did you see anything unusual?"

"Oh, no. It was just your typical, run-of-the-mill prayer service where someone sees the Virgin Mary."

"You know what I mean."

"I don't know what's usual or unusual, but Anna's going to have to pull something major out of her hat for Saturday. She told everyone Mary would perform a miracle then." I tried to recall the exact words. "Something about bringing someone to life who was thought to be dead." I didn't bring up my own message.

Charlie whistled. "That is major," he said.

"Another thing. A protest was set up down the road by the Church of the Mystical Jesus. They were passing out pamphlets accusing Anna of being the devil. The deputy I talked to said there had been some threats made against St. Mary's. Know anything about it?"

Charlie smiled. "The Church of the Mystical Jesus is such a fun group," he said. "We heard about it. Pastor Carl refers to the protesters as a small part of his congregation and denies he has encouraged them. Naturally, the chief believes every word. Privately, I'm sure the pastor's behind it. Not that it matters much, since the protest isn't in our jurisdiction."

Charlie had taken the back roads from Diamond to Clinton. They didn't seem as bad as Dad had made them out to be. The moonlight, passing through the trees as we whisked by, cast shadows over Charlie's face and whitened his hair. It jogged my memory. "You can add this to your file," I said. "A guy with white hair left the church midway through the service. He was far enough away that I couldn't swear it was Carl Young, but I had this feeling it was. I kept watching for him to come back and disrupt the service, but he didn't."

"Any reason you can think of that he'd be there?" Charlie asked.

"You can bet it wasn't to say the rosary. I don't know, maybe he was investigating the service. Maybe he sees it as a rival religious event and worries about it."

Charlie shrugged.

Time to get back on the subject of Tom Iavello. "You know, there had to be a lot of people who saw Tom after I did. When I left the gym, he was training a client. It was close to three-thirty. Peak time at most gyms is after work and in the early evening."

Static broke in on the police radio. Charlie paused and listened to the message, then ignored it. "Tom didn't have any later clients," he said. "Seems people had been dropping Tom as a trainer because he had become abrasive. But Tom was supposed to come back after supper. When he didn't answer his phone or come in today, the manager sent someone over. The knock on the door sounded dull, like something heavy was leaning against it. Turned out to be Tom's body."

Charlie wouldn't divulge any more details. He insisted we needed to talk at the police station so our conversation would be on the record. That sounded ominous. I wondered if I should keep quiet and request a lawyer; well, I'd see how things went.

Since Charlie wasn't talking, I leaned to the right and looked up at the sky.

Night had overtaken the dark blue of twilight and stars shone against the black sky. We were still out in the country enough that the stars seemed to blaze, little points of light defying the infinite darkness that threatened to swallow them up.

Was heaven up there, I thought. Was Mary? If she was, would she really bother to communicate with me? The message Anna had given me stirred about in my brain. I closed my eyes. It had been a long day.

I must've dozed briefly because Charlie nudged me into consciousness at the police station. It was just past nine. I struggled to wake up.

The lineup at the station was incredible. I sat on a hard bench for an hour and a half while the police talked to nine people ahead of me. Captain Slater, the police chief, hurried into the station at one point, dressed in his civvies and looking preoccupied. He blew by me, avoiding my gaze. I couldn't tell if it was deliberate or if he just didn't see me. He deposited a small knapsack in his office and came out carrying a notepad. Then he disappeared into the questioning room.

Just when I thought I would be next, a police escort arrived with Martha. Everyone huddled with her for about fifteen minutes. When she came out of the little room, her eyes were swollen red and smudges of dabbed mascara were all over her face. Martha plopped herself next to me, much to the dismay of the tired policewoman accompanying her. "I want to rest a minute," Martha told her. The policewoman went over to the water fountain several feet away.

"It's Tom," Martha whispered to me, her voice dry and gravelly. "He's dead."

This isn't worth $25,000, I thought. "I know," I said. "I'm sorry."

"Do you think it's related to Papá's death?"

"I don't know. Did the police tell you anything?"

She drummed her fingers on the bench. "They're looking for evidence. Who would want to kill Tom, though?"

A lot of people, I wanted to say. Instead, I gently squeezed her hand. "I'm sure the police will find whoever did this," I said as reassuringly as I could. "They'll find your grandfather's killer, too."

Martha opened her eyes wide. "You're not going to stop helping me, are you?" she exclaimed too forcefully for her weakened voice. She went into a raspy coughing fit as she stood up.

The policewoman looked over at us. Before she could react I whispered to Martha, "No, I'll stick around and see this through. But in light of what's happened, I'm questioning how effective I'll be."

"You have to keep looking," she said wildly. "Mary wants you involved. I want you involved. I'm paying you to stay involved."

She began to wheeze from the agitation. The policewoman rushed to her side and held on, giving her physical, and maybe moral, support. Glaring at me, the policewoman said, "Stop upsetting her."

I heard a male voice behind me. "You, come with me. It's your turn." The policewoman hustled Martha out of the way, and I turned to see that the voice belonged to Captain Slater, the police chief. I followed him, relieved to put an angry Martha Iavello behind me.

The relief was short-lived. Slater closed the door and told me to take a seat, the one on the opposite side of the green metal table. Slater, Charlie Cammack, and a detective who looked familiar sat on the other side. The room had no windows. The walls looked soundproof. A tape recorder lay on the table. Slater started it.

"I'm Detective Sergeant Morini," said the tall, stocky detective.

"Joe Morini?" I asked.

"Yeah," he replied, smiling faintly. "I thought you were probably the Nick Bertetto I remembered."

Too bad he was the same Joe Morini I remembered. Morini had been the class bully, and given that I didn't get my growth spurt until late, I had been bullied a lot. He looked much the same as he had then, big and brutish, with the addition of a thick black mustache that curled onto his upper lip and gave his yellow teeth a pompadour.

"We're recording this interview only to save us from taking notes," Morini said. "However, if you want the tape off, we can turn it off. You are not under arrest or under suspicion. We are only seeking information." Morini sounded like a recording himself.

I let them keep the tape on. I told them about the note. We went over the events that occurred at the gym. I swallowed my pride and admitted Tom had intimidated me, backing me against a bench. I figured if they'd interviewed anyone from the gym, it had already come up. They asked if Tom had given me any information about Gregorio's death, and I said no. I didn't mention the will change Tom knew about. I had already told Charlie. No one asked about it.

Charlie sat quietly during the whole ordeal, too quietly for me. Despite the assurance that I was not a suspect, they questioned me at length on my whereabouts the evening Tom Iavello died. I told them I was at my dad's home taking care of my daughter. Since Dad hadn't been there for a good part of the evening, I didn't have a verifiable alibi.

"Now, wait a minute," I said. "Are you implying that I would just blithely leave my daughter alone while I went off to Terre Haute to commit a murder? Or worse yet, that I would take her with me to murder someone?" I started to get hot.

"Calm down," said Morini. "We don't disbelieve that you were at your father's home. It would just be better if you'd been with someone who could back you up. Now, we know Martha Iavello has asked you to check into her grandfather's death. Cooperate with us and stay out of it. Leave police work to the professionals.''

I bit the inside of my cheek to remain mute. Morini rubbed me the wrong way.

We finished shortly after that. Charlie offered to take me home, and I accepted.

We rode in his police car. This time I was the one who was tight-lipped. After a couple of false starts at conversation, he said, ''You did okay back there.''

I shot him an angry glance. ''You could have spoken up anytime in support of me,'' I said.

''No, I couldn't,'' he replied. ''Because if I did, they'd have guessed we're working together. I haven't told them much at all about what you know.''

My attitude changed. ''You haven't? What haven't you told them?''

''The connection between Jimmy Iavello and Blazevich, for one. Also about half the estate going to Children of the Second Advent.''

I regarded him with new respect. ''Why not?''

''Well, Morini is one of those fervent believers in the Church of the Mystical Jesus, although he may have converted in the hopes of getting promoted. Which worked, I guess. Anyway, if they know about where the money's going, I think that will color their investigation. Let's just say I want to solve this case before he does.''

''Charlie, did you get passed over for promotion?''

He smiled crookedly. ''Yes. I'm not saying Morini won't be a good detective, but I had better credentials.''

It was close to midnight when we arrived at Dad's house. I was exhausted, but Charlie stopped me from getting out of the car. ''I need you to get some information for me,'' he said. ''Pastor Carl says he graduated from Oregon Bible College in Salem. Can you check out his claim? I can't be the one to do it." Charlie rubbed the palms of his hands on the steering wheel.

"Is everything all right, Charlie? You seem nervous about this."

"It's nothing I can't handle," he said, refusing to elaborate.

"Do you suspect Reverend Goldentones didn't graduate, or do you know?"

"Suspect. I saw the diploma on his wall. It's not the original. If you look at it closely, you can see the name of the college is not sharp like it would be on a diploma. It's a copy."

I yawned and rubbed my eyes. "There could be lots of reasons for that. Maybe he lost the original."

Charlie's yawn overlapped mine. "Now you've made me yawn," he said, "and I still have half the night to go on my shift. No, there's something funny about that diploma. Trust me. I want you to find out what it is."

I agreed to make some calls and got out of the car. Climbing the front steps, I searched my jacket for my keys, but Dad pulled the front door open when I got there. "What happened?" he asked, ushering me in the house.

I slipped off my jacket. "Can I have some coffee?" I asked.

Dad warmed up the last of his industrial-strength coffee while I checked on Stephanie. Then, sitting at the kitchen table, I filled him in on the little bit I'd learned about Tom Iavello's death.

Dad wanted to speculate on Saturday's predicted miracle, but I persuaded him to go to bed. Talk of the miracle brought out the reporter in me, and I knew Dana Rardin would want something for the next day's edition. Dog-tired, I went to Dad's study and punched out a short article on his computer. I filled it in with some color from my memory and a bit of history about the apparitions. I figured a quote from Anna or Martha, which I could get in the morning, would wrap it up. I logged off the computer and trudged upstairs to bed, looking in on Stephanie one more time.

When I finally fell into bed, it was two o'clock. My head spun. Tom Iavello had written the note warning me to stay away from Martha, and now he was dead. What did that mean? Was I being protected, or was I next on the hit list? Or did it affect me at all? And why had he tried to warn me off? To keep me from investigating the first murder?

Well, now I had two.

SEVENTEEN

IT WAS A SHORT night. Stephanie pushed and prodded me awake at 6:00 a.m. Groggily I pulled her into bed with me, hoping she would calm down and return to sleep. When it became apparent she was more interested in bouncing on the bed, I sent her to check on *Nonno*.

One dream from my abbreviated sleep continued to whirl around in my head, and I didn't know what to make of it. I was back in the maze again, the one with steep sides, and as I turned one corner I came upon a large funeral service with three caskets, one each for Gregorio Iavello, Tom Iavello and me. I wasn't dead, but I was in the casket anyway. We were all at the altar of St. Mary's. The only thing I could hear was a heart beating. I kept assuming it was mine until the pallbearers wheeled me past the Immaculate Heart of Mary statue. It was hers, a huge, red, three-dimensional heart pulsating loudly. I shivered just thinking about it and pushed the dream aside.

Today would be much too complicated. I had a nine o'clock appointment with Father Vince at St. Mary-of-the-Woods College, trying to get a handle on Anna's claims. I had the ''miracle'' story to finish for Dana, calls to place to Oregon Bible College for Charlie, and more legwork to investigate the murder of Gregorio Iavello. What I needed was a good, old-fashioned break in the case.

Two Iavellos were dead now, and I didn't even have a good suspect for the first murder. I was also bothered by the continuing absence of Father Skip, for whom I feared the worst. And what about me, or Stephanie, or my dad? Were we in danger, too?

Stephanie came back to report that *Nonno* wasn't up yet. Not surprised, I thanked her for checking, gave her a big hug and struggled to my feet, reaching for my robe. Stephanie followed me down to the kitchen where I handed her a box of Froot Loops, poured her a glass of milk and told her not to spill anything. I went to the study and printed out the article I'd written for Dana. When I returned she was playing with the loops, picking out her favorite colors. She was being good, so I reread the story.

Amazingly, it was coherent. I rearranged some information and made a few changes, but it held together. All I needed was a quote. I looked at the time. It was closing in on 7 o'clock, too early to call Martha or Anna.

But not too early for me to get called. The phone rang and I snatched it up, hoping to let Dad sleep a little while longer. I recognized the voice on the other end. Joan.

"What's going on over there?" she demanded.

"What do you mean?"

"The front page of *The Indianapolis Star* is covered with news from Clinton. They say Tom Iavello was murdered, his grandfather might not have committed suicide, and there's some crackpot who claims to see visions of Mary, predicting a miracle for Saturday. That's the case you're working on, isn't it?"

"Uh, yeah."

"It had your name written all over it. I knew this would happen. You can't stay away from murder. I want you to come home now."

"Joan, I can't. I have to finish this. The police are looking into it now, which they weren't before, and I'm sure it won't be long…"

"No!" I could hear the hysteria rising in her voice. "You have to come home. Now!"

"Take a deep breath, Joan. This is not like the Cindy DePasse case. You are not in danger."

"I'm not so sure of that. And I won't have Stephanie there. I want her home with me. You can do whatever you want to yourself, but I will not let my child be put in this kind of situation."

Damn. I could argue for hours about my own safety, but Stephanie was another story.

"Look, I'm not saying she's in any danger, but I can understand your point. Do you want to come pick her up?"

"Not on your life. I wouldn't come near Clinton right now. I have to go to work in less than an hour anyway. I want you to bring her home. Today."

One more thing to add to the list. I thought briefly about sending Dad to Franklin with Stephanie, but Dad and Joan didn't mix very well right now. "All right, Joan. I'll have her home by the time you get off work. Then I'm coming back to Clinton."

We tried to talk for a minute more, but there wasn't much to say in the charged atmosphere we'd created. I hung up and tried to refigure the day. Going back to Franklin might not be such a bad idea if I could swing by Greencastle and question Iavello's psychiatrist, Dr. Crowley. But there was so much to do. I needed help.

I wondered if Dana Rardin still had breakfast every morning at 7:30 in the Main Street Kitchen, a small restaurant in downtown Clinton. It was hard to imagine she wouldn't. In all the time I'd known her, she'd never wavered from that tradition, using the time to go over the plan for that day's paper.

I was pretty sure that Stephanie and I could get there if we hurried. Promising to buy her pancakes for breakfast if she dressed quickly, I sent her to her room while I showered

and shaved. I threw on a pair of jeans and a Franklin College sweatshirt; Stephanie wore her favorite, well-worn
pink sweat suit. We didn't look great but certainly presentable for a diner breakfast. I grabbed my story and notebook and left a message for Dad on the kitchen table.

The day was a repeat of yesterday, sunny but cool. We
drove past The Saints & Angels Coffeehouse (Today's marquee: "Try our desserts, they're divine!"), which was very
crowded, and pulled up to the Main Street Kitchen, which
was only moderately crowded. We parked the van on the
street in front of the restaurant just as Dana arrived. She
stepped out of her late model Oldsmobile and gingerly
leaped across the small puddle at the curb, checking her
pants and black flats when she landed. When she glanced
up and noticed us, her face lightened in surprise. Then she
did a double take.

"You look like hell," she said. "Not getting enough
sleep?"

"I didn't get to bed until two."

"Neither did I. You know about Tom Iavello, of
course."

"More than you might think. Let's talk."

After we were seated at the table—Stephanie was in a
high chair next to me—and had breakfast plates in front of
us, I showed Dana my story and we compared notes on
Tom Iavello's death. I shared my concern about Father
Skip's disappearance and brought up Charlie's news about
Carl Young's copied diploma. Talking to Dana was easy,
and I bared my soul about my conversation with Joan and
how I'd promised to make a round trip this afternoon despite all the work that needed to be done. I also told her
that I planned to make a brief stop in Greencastle to see
Dr. Crowley. Dana listened quietly.

"The article's good," she said when I finished. "You
haven't lost your touch. Drop it off when you've got a

quote or two." She picked up her layout for the paper and made a note on it about the story. "If you write down a few details about Carl Young, I can have my secretary place the calls. But about everything else, you're on your own. I especially don't give advice when it comes to spouses." She stirred some sugar into her third cup of coffee and took a sip.

Stephanie tugged at my sleeve, her fingers a gooey mess. She had been dipping her silver-dollar pancakes in syrup, and droplets of the sticky stuff ran down the front of her sweatshirt. "More syrup, Daddy?" she asked.

"Stephanie behaves well in restaurants," I told Dana, "but she does make a mess." I used my water glass to wet a napkin and began to wipe the syrup off Stephanie's clothes. Since she still had more pancakes, I poured her a little more syrup.

Dana's eyes sparkled as she grinned at Stephanie. "She's a doll."

Something caught Dana's eyes and she looked behind me toward the door. "Speaking of dolls, here comes that good-looking father of yours." I turned around to look as Dana waved at him. Dad, always dressed above what was necessary, wore a white turtleneck under a brick red sweater and dark dress slacks. He saw us and came over, slipping off his leather jacket.

"Mind if I join you?" he asked.

"Not at all," Dana said, moving her work to the floor and clearing a spot for him. "How are you, Victor?" she asked, extending her hand.

They flirted while I finished what little of my low-fat, high-protein breakfast hadn't been eaten. I found myself weary of oatmeal and coveting Dana's uneaten toast, practically swimming in butter.

Dana laughed at a little joke my father had made. "Victor, it's been delightful to see you again," she said. She turned her attention from Dad to me. "Well, Nick, I'm sorry to see you running back to Franklin just as things are getting hot, even if you are coming back tonight. But I understand the position you're in. Do what you think is best. And get as much as you can out of the psychiatrist."

With that, she was gone, picking up her part of the bill and paying it on the way out.

Dad glowered at me. "You're running out on this?"

"No, I'm not. But Joan called this morning and insisted I bring Stephanie back to Franklin for her own protection. I think it's best. Tom's murder has me worried."

The waitress interrupted to take Dad's order. Dad scanned the menu and ordered sullenly. Before the waitress had a chance to clear away Dana's plates, I snatched up the leftover toast and slathered it with strawberry jam.

Dad looked at me with displeasure, and I knew it wasn't over the toast. "You won't come back," he said. "The minute you get home she'll start working on you. Pretty soon, you'll give in to her again, and this chance you've got to get back into investigative reporting will be shot." He shook his head in disgust. "You're a quitter. When you couldn't deal with Joan after the kidnapping, you let her go to work while you stayed home. This is not the behavior of a man."

My face and ears felt hot with blood rushing into them. Words tangled in my mouth, so I began counting to ten. I gave up at five when my tongue came untwisted. "You think it's easy holding my family together when I'm the only adult trying?" I said. "You think I don't miss a regular paycheck or the sight of my byline regularly in the paper? You think..." I caught sight of Stephanie, her little head back against the high chair like she was trying to push herself away from us. Her mouth was open. She was getting ready to cry.

I turned away from Dad and tended to Stephanie. Neither

Dad nor I spoke for awhile. The waitress brought Dad's food. I tried to take a bite of toast, but my hand shook. I put the toast down.

"I'm sorry," Dad said.

"Do you really feel that way about me?"

Dad breathed shakily like Stephanie after a crying fit. "No, and I'm sorry I said it."

"I know my giving up my job eats at you, Dad. You still think of me as a grade card for your being a parent. But I did what I thought was best for my family. As for Joan's decision to go back to work, that was hers. And she would have gone back whether or not I continued to work. I just believed it would be better for Stephanie if I stayed home. And it has been."

I tried the toast again. My hand wavered only slightly, smearing a little jam on the corner of my mouth.

"I'm an interfering old man, aren't I?" Dad finally looked up at me. "I should mind my own business."

His hand was across from mine. I reached over and covered it. "It's taken you more than a year to tell me this. I don't think that makes you meddlesome."

The rest of breakfast was subdued.

Afterward, when Dad tried to pick Stephanie up, she clung to me.

"What's wrong, Stephanie? Won't you come with *Nonno?*" he asked.

Stephanie held fast to my leg. "I want my daddy," she said.

I shrugged. "It's probably the argument we had. She's never seen us fight."

Dad looked sheepish, and he got down on one knee. "I'm sorry your daddy and I talked mean to each other. But it's all right now. Won't you come back to *Nonno*'s house and play?"

Stephanie shook her head and buried her face in my

pants leg. "It's okay, Dad," I told him. "She can come with me. It won't be a problem."

Dad left with a dejected look on his face.

I checked my watch. I had figured we were getting close to the critical departure time and I was right—if we didn't start for Terre Haute now, we'd never make the 9:00 with Father Vince. After Steph was securely buckled into her car seat, I sped off.

EIGHTEEN

I HAD FORGOTTEN how much the campus of St. Mary-of-the-Woods looked like a picture postcard, even in early spring when the only colors were the deep evergreen of the pines and the peeled light gray bark of an occasional sycamore. The black naked branches, studded with buds, framed the stately college buildings like a brochure photo from somewhere north, perhaps New England.

A thick canopy of entwined tree limbs shaded the street. I parked illegally along the main drive and pulled Stephanie out of the van. We walked to yellow-bricked Le Fer Hall where Father Vince's office was. The building was so huge it dominated that area of the campus, and I wondered if Stephanie felt any smaller than I did as we ascended the stairs.

Inside, a receptionist directed me downstairs to the faculty offices. I followed a long hallway until I found Father Vince's name on a wooden door. The office had windows facing the hall, but the curtains were drawn. Stephanie looked anxious. I squeezed her hand before I knocked.

Father Vince opened the door. Although I was only five minutes late—close enough in my mind to be considered on-time—he ushered me in like he'd been expecting me for hours, greeting me with a quick handshake and the same humorless expression he'd worn the night before. Today he looked more priest-like, with a black shirt, white collar and black pants. His office looked like I expected it would, a quirky mix of the scholarly and the worldly. His bookshelf contained an impressive set of reference books, both religious and secular, which were thick and bound in encyclopedic coverings. His desk, however, was a mess of reports, loose papers, candy wrappers and the lab equipment with which he'd collected the blood samples at St. Mary's. Next to the desk was a table that held so many little statues of saints at first glance I thought it was a recently completed chess game.

When Father Vince saw Stephanie, he asked if he could give her a piece of candy. I okayed it, and he produced several bite-sized Tootsie Rolls from the pocket of his shirt. Bending down, he handed it to her. "I like these a lot myself," he told her.

Stephanie instantly became his friend for life. She sat down to eat it, chewing thoughtfully as though eating Tootsie Rolls required immense concentration.

"Now, then," he said, "Martha Iavello has asked you to look into the death of her grandfather?"

I told him what I knew so far. I also said that while I really didn't suspect Martha or Anna, I did believe Children of the Second Advent was somehow connected to Gregorio's death since so much money had been left to the organization in the will. "Money is a powerful motive," I said. "That's why I need to know what you think of Anna and her visions."

Father Vince hemmed and hawed like a college professor trying to decide where to begin with a novice student. He paced a bit and then went over to the bookshelf, selecting a volume. "What do you know about the Blessed Mother's appearances throughout time?" he asked.

"Not much," I said. "Is it long and involved?"

"It is, but I'll try to be brief. We have stories, traditions really, that go back over a thousand years, of Mary appearing to people. But we discount most of those as being unreliable. The first of Mary's modern appearances occurred in Mexico at Guadalupe in 1531. She appeared to a young boy, Juan Diego, and told him of her desire to have a chapel built on a certain spot. She said she wanted to show compassion to Juan's people and all who would come. No one believed the boy, of course. Mary sent him with fresh roses to prove to the local bishop she was real. It was winter at that time, and roses weren't in bloom. Juan had been given so many roses he had to put them in his cape.'' Father Vince gathered up his arms like the boy might have.

"When Juan dropped the roses onto the floor at the bishop's house, there on his cloak was the imprinted impression of Mary's image as she appeared to him.'' Father Vince dropped his arms and pointed to his imaginary cloak. "The coat still exists and can be seen in the chapel which was built as Mary directed. Her appearance led to the Catholic conversion of Mexico.''

I'd heard of Guadalupe. It was one of those things I'd been taught about as a child and simply accepted. As an adult, the story seemed almost like a fairy tale. "And as an investigator, you believe this?'' I asked.

He nodded. "I've been there and seen it. The detail on the cloak is quite remarkable. If you enlarge the image of Mary's eye, you can see Juan Diego's reflection in it.''

Father Vince's eyes held no sign of doubt. I felt a chill at the back of my neck, which was becoming commonplace every time somebody mentioned miracles. Before I could ask another question, though, I saw chocolate fingers reaching for the statues on Father Vince's side table. I nabbed Stephanie's hand in time.

"Here Stephanie, let me clean you up,'' I said. I took my handkerchief and wiped away the chocolate as best I could. "Can she touch the statues?'' I asked Father Vince.

"Yes, let her play with them," he said. "They're not expensive or anything."

"Play nice," I cautioned her.

When I stood up I felt the medallion against my neck. "Anna gave me this," I said. "She called it the 'Miraculous Medal.'" I held it out for him to see. "She said it had to do with Mary's appearance to a nun."

Father Vince flipped a few more pages in his book, then turned the book around and showed me a full-page illustration of the medal. "Catherine Laboure, 1830," he said, nodding. He turned the book back around and flipped a while longer. "More sensational, though, was Mary's appearance to Bernadette Soubirous at Lourdes in 1858. Perhaps you've seen the movie, 'The Song of Bernadette?'" he asked.

I shook my head. "You should," he said. "It's an account of the apparition, very good. Won several Academy Awards." He glanced back down at the book and examined a few pages without comment.

Suddenly, he thrust the book in my face. "Ah, here we are, Fatima, Portugal, 1917. This is the most famous of the recent ones. Mary appeared to three shepherd children. Are you familiar with it?"

"Well, I read an article about Anna that contained some references to it," I said, pushing the book back at him. "Mary performed a miracle that had to do with the sun, I think."

"Yes. Virtually all of her appearances have been marked by some kind of miracle. Both Bernadette and Catherine Laboure, for instance, have bodies that never decayed. The bodies are on display for all to see. Fatima was unique because she predicted the miracle in advance and some sixty thousand people witnessed it."

"Anna's apparition is hardly the first since Fatima," he

continued. He turned to the back of the book and handed it to me.

My eyes widened in surprise. Mary had more worldwide sightings than Elvis. In print, there were three pages, single-spaced, of reported apparitions since 1917. Beyond that were Father Vince's handwritten notes in the margin, adding dozens more. One full page was devoted to apparitions since 1980 alone.

I handed it back to him. "All these are real?"

"I didn't say they were all real," he replied, cautioning me with a raise of his finger. "I said they were all reported. Some are more promising than others. Of the current ones, Medjugorje, in former Yugoslavia, and San Nicholas, in Argentina, have the ring of authenticity. I've been involved in the investigation of several in the United States."

I folded my arms. This was very interesting but I had so much to do today, and the round trip to take Stephanie back to Franklin weighed on my mind. Father Vince picked up on my impatience. "But then, you're just wanting to know, is this one real?"

"Precisely," I said.

He cleared his throat. "On the negative side is Anna herself. To be uncharitable, she's flaky. Though she's the visionary, she only occasionally seems able to discipline herself to any kind of holy action. She remains free-spirited and kind of flirtatious. We've never seen that in any other visionary. All the others seem determined to earn heaven. Even Father Skip has commented on it, but he firmly believes in her."

Stephanie, who had apparently lost interest in the statues, had moved around to Father Vince's desk and climbed on his chair. She had hold of a pen and was preparing to make additions to the reports on his desk when I noticed her.

"Stephanie," I warned.

"Would she like to color?" Father Vince asked. "I keep

some markers around here to make drawings of my investigations.''

Stephanie thought that would be fun. Father Vince hunted around and came up with a religious coloring book in addition to the markers. Stephanie sat on the floor and began to work.

''Couldn't a lot of these appearances be brought on by wishful thinking?'' I asked when Stephanie was playing with her new treasures. ''I mean, today, television is everywhere, and if people are getting attention by claiming to see the Blessed Mother, wouldn't that encourage less stable individuals to believe they see her also?''

''Some of it could be. Pilgrimages to Medjugorje have brought money and attention to the area. Unscrupulous people could be trying for the same effect elsewhere. Still...'' He let his voice drop.

''Still what?''

''Even if we discount ninety percent of them, there's a lot left that have no other explanation.'' He recast his eyes at me. ''Does that mean something supernatural is going on? No one wants to be gullible, but some of the seers are very believable and pass all kinds of tests.''

''Have you run any tests on Anna?''

''No,'' he replied, ''although we had one scheduled. Iavello's death put it off.''

I considered that. ''You implied earlier there were some reasons to believe Anna was on the up-and-up. Can you tell me what they are?''

He leaned back against the bookshelf. ''Mary's words have taken on increasing urgency since Fatima. They encourage all peoples to return to God. Through God comes peace, she says, and she says this everywhere. Anna's messages, though, are the first ones to say we are in the Second Advent now, that Mary's desire to reunite all Christian faiths is in preparation for her Son's imminent Second Coming.''

I stared at Father Vince, so calm and clear in calling this a positive. ''You believe this?'' I asked.

He attempted a smile. ''The Church is conservative. None of the recent apparitions has been fully endorsed, nor will be until long after the apparitions have stopped.''

''What do you believe?''

Father took a few steps away from me as if he needed to contemplate his answer. He exhaled deliberately. ''As an investigator, I see both sides. I know there are flakes and fakes among the visionaries. But what about those apparitions we can't poke holes in? How to explain them?'' He shrugged his shoulders lightly. ''Since Jesus ascended into heaven, His followers have looked in the skies for His return. If we truly believe in Him, we should be ready at any time. Even if these worldwide apparitions are the result of some kind of telecommunicated mass hysteria, Mary serves as a reminder that all of us ought to behave as our God expects. That's worth a lot.''

I rubbed my temples. A theologically induced headache was starting. ''What about the blood?'' I asked.

''O positive,'' he responded, folding his arms over his chest. ''Each time. That's the most common blood type there is, so we can't do much with that. Neither Martha nor Anna nor Father Skip is O positive, by the way.''

Mine was, not that it was relevant. ''But how is the statue dripping blood? Can that be explained?''

''Easily, with some kind of pumping system placed in the statue. That's why I want to examine it with X ray. But the dripping could be done in other ways.'' Father Vince unfolded his arms. ''Want to watch me make a statue cry?''

He said it eagerly, like a child anxious to work a magic trick. I nodded, and he motioned for me to come with him. I coaxed Stephanie away from her coloring, picking her up to follow Father Vince. He led us down a side hall to a place where several life-size statues stood in a row. They looked to be made of plaster. The paint on them was either well-preserved or had been kept fresh, because there was no flaking. By the robes I guessed the statues were ancient saints.

"Now look at the eyes on St. James," he said, pointing to the one on my left. St. James had blue eyes in a leathery-looking face with a curly brown beard that protruded about six inches from his chin. Father Vince touched the blue eyes, then reached for my elbow and prodded me to do the same. The eyes felt cold and dry.

"Now look at the eyes on St. Andrew," he said, pointing to the statue on my right. "Notice how his eyes are more pallid, but still have the same dry feel."

I reached up to touch them when Father Vince said, "Oh, look, James is crying." I jerked my head around and sure enough, the eyes of the St. James statue were wet, tears streaming down the face and beard.

"How'd you do that?" I demanded.

Slyly he pulled a water pistol out of his pants pocket and dropped it into my hand. "The old bait and switch tactic," he said, smirking. "I love to do that one."

"But neither Martha nor Anna…"

"Could pull that one off," he finished for me. "True. Too many people are watching. If it's a trick, it has to be a different one. But I just wanted to show you how simple the tricks can be sometimes."

I returned the water pistol to him. The ruse had been clever and insightful, but it wasn't much help.

Coming in, I hadn't decided whether to reveal my special message from Mary or not. But Father Vince seemed so knowledgeable that I thought I'd try it out on him.

"This is so cool," he said, after I'd explained what had happened and handed him the note. "I've been at this a ong time and I've never gotten a message from heaven. You're very fortunate.''

He embarrassed me, not the least because he took the message more seriously than I had. He returned the note after he'd read the passages on the back. ''The quote from Isaiah is a well-known one,'' he said. ''Jesus himself quoted it in Luke, I think, in the very same chapter as this other quote. Did you know that?''

I admitted that I didn't.

''You might want to read it. Could shed some light on how to interpret the message.''

Father Vince and I talked a bit longer. Clearly he wanted to believe in Anna's apparition, but wouldn't let himself until there was proof. He did put one question to me, a surprise, and it came as he walked me out to the street.

''Are you going to be at St. Mary's for the miracle on Saturday?'' he asked, leaning against the hood of the van. I started the motor and prepared to leave.

''I feel committed,'' I replied. ''Are you?''

Father Vince flashed an impish grin. ''I think it will prove something one way or the other. If I were you,'' he said, ''I wouldn't miss it.''

NINETEEN

I HEADED BACK to Clinton with an unsettled feeling in my stomach that had nothing to do with missing another mid-morning meal. I'd learned a lot about apparitions, but it didn't get me any closer to solving Signor Iavello's murder. Anna might or might not be real. Mary might or might not be communicating with her (and me!). Jesus might or might not be coming soon. The only thing I knew for certain was that I was going soon, back to Franklin. And with so much unknown, it was a bad time to leave.

I buzzed by The Saints & Angels Coffeehouse hoping to find Martha and let her know I would be gone most of the day, but she wasn't there. The manager suggested I call her, but since her house was a few blocks away, I drove over. I wanted to talk to her in person, if for no other reason than to make sure she was okay. Too many Iavellos had died recently.

Martha's house was a modest two-story Cape Cod with blue-gray trim, the back yard fully enclosed by a high privacy fence. The front yard had several large maple trees which shaded the porch. When I got out of the van I could hear dogs barking all over the neighborhood. Stephanie's eyes opened like a time-lapse video of a flower blooming. "Don't let the doggies get me," she wailed.

I had forgotten how afraid she was of dogs. "Don't worry, Stephanie, they're all inside their fences," I said, holding her tight. "They won't get out."

She wouldn't let me set her down, so I lugged her to the porch and rang the doorbell twice. When I didn't get a response, I moved around to a window and peered in. No sign of anyone. Still holding Stephanie, I left the porch and climbed awkwardly through the bushes to check the front windows. At first I thought I saw movement in the front room, but it turned out to be a flickering votive light in front of a little shrine for a pregnant Mary statue.

I tried to go around back but was blocked by the privacy fence. I jiggled the gate latch. It was locked. I half-expected some large dog to attack the gate and bark itself silly, but none came. The barking was from the rest of the neighborhood.

I returned to the front door. This time I noticed a small package tied to the black mailbox on the house. My name was on it.

I juggled Stephanie to my left side and opened the package. Inside I found two sets of keys, a note from Martha, and a list of everyone Martha thanked for stopping by her grandfather's house with food after the funeral. The note said Anna had told her I needed the list. I was glad Anna had remembered.

Martha said she thought I might need the keys. One set was hers and included a key to her grandfather's house. The second set belonged to Father Skip, which she had 'borrowed' from his desk in the rectory. She said she had called the psychiatrist to clear the way for me and promised to contact me later.

I shoved the keys in my jacket and returned to the car. I glanced over the list of names and threw it in the back where I'd stashed other materials I'd collected for the case.

The barking of the dogs continued, but there was something very odd about the tone, almost as if they knew something was wrong but didn't know what. I went next door to talk to whoever was home.

A well-dressed, middle aged woman responded to my knocks. "I'm Nick Bertetto, ma'am. I was wondering if you've seen your next-door neighbor today." I pointed in the direction of Martha's house. "I'm trying to find her."

The woman said she hadn't and tried to close the door. I had to be blunt. "Do you notice all the dogs barking? Their barks sound odd to me. Is that normal?"

The woman cocked her ear and said she would be back in a minute. I heard her yell at her dog, but it continued its strange growl and bark. The woman returned to the front door.

"I don't know what it is," she said. "He's back by the garden with his nose under the fence, digging at something. I don't know if it's anything to worry about, but I'll check it out." She closed the door and locked it.

I returned to the van and put Stephanie in her car seat. The neighbor watched me through her front window. I waved and she backed up behind white-lined draperies, but I knew she was still there. Much as I hated being watched by a suspicious neighbor, especially since the Nick Bertetto Fan Club at the Clinton Police Station had only one member, I couldn't shake the bad feeling I had about what the dog might be digging at.

"Stephanie, Daddy is going to climb that fence just to see what is on the other side. I'm going to leave you here in the van where the doggies can't get you. Okay?"

She nodded, eyes still wide, and I closed the van door. Sprinting to the right side of the house where the neighbor couldn't see me, I leaped at the eight-foot high fence and grabbed the top with my hands. Then I did a pull-up to get my head where I could see.

Except there was nothing to see. I needed a view of the left side of the fence where the dog was digging, and the house blocked it. I levered my leg on the top of the fence and jumped over.

Eight feet is a long way down, but I rolled on my side like a parachute jumper as I landed and that helped. I made my way cautiously along the side of the house. Peering into the back yard, I saw something that sent me running toward it.

A body, clad in black, lay face up behind thorny rose bushes that had been cut back for the winter. The face was turned toward the fence, the body contorted as though it had been dropped there. I got close to it and the smell of decay stopped me short. Backing up a few steps, I took a huge gulp of air and then went to see who it was.

It was, as I feared, Father Skip. Other than the purplish hue of his skin, death had not affected his face yet. Dark, matted blood had pooled on his black shirt, and I could see a knife protruding from his side. I turned my head and threw up. Then the smell invaded my nostrils and I threw up again. Kneeling on the cold, hard ground, I closed my eyes and tried to gather my wits.

It was hard to think. The dogs in the area continued to howl, and my mind kept playing video clips of Father Skip leaning across his desk, staring into my eyes just two days ago. I cleared my mind and forced myself to at least try to look at the body dispassionately.

The blood stains were heavier on three parts of the chest and on the side, which led me to believe there were multiple stab wounds. Without touching the knife I examined the handle and recognized it—it was from the set Martha had shown me at her grandfather's house yesterday, when she had noticed one of the knives was missing. I stood up and nudged the body with my foot, finding it was stiff with rigor mortis. I was only a layman about stages of death, but I guessed he'd been dead at least a day.

The dog on the other side of the fence continued to scratch at the ground. Every once in a while I could see its paw. I felt wetness on my cheeks and I looked up at the sky to see if were raining, only to discover I was crying. In shock, I just stood there.

When I was certain I couldn't look at Father Skip's body anymore, I suddenly thought of Stephanie in the van. How long had I been standing there? I ran to the gate and opened it, rushing to the vehicle to make sure she was all right. The poor kid was crying for me, but she was fine. I lifted her out of her carseat and sat with her in the van, holding her in my arms. I kept telling her things were all right, though I wasn't sure if I was saying it for her benefit or for mine. Pulling a tissue from a travel-size box next to me, I wiped the tears from my face. I had no idea what to do next.

On the one hand, the Clinton Police needed to be called. On the other hand, the last thing I wanted to give them was another reason to suspect me. Calling them would mean enduring lots of questions about why I was here and how I found the body, and that would tie me up for a long time. But since I had introduced myself to the nosy neighbor earlier, sooner or later someone else would find Father Skip and the police would want to talk to me. It would be better to do it under my own initiative as the person who stumbled across the body, rather than under police questioning as the suspect who ran from the scene of the crime.

First, though, I wanted to get Stephanie to Dad. Too bad I didn't have a car phone. I had the keys to Martha's house—I could go in and call from there, but with Father Skip dead in the back yard, I wasn't sure I wanted to take Stephanie in the house without checking it first.

I returned to the neighbor's house carrying Stephanie. At first she didn't come to the door, but I rang the doorbell until she did. I was on a mission. "Could I please make a couple of phone calls from your house, ma'am?" I asked her when she opened the door. "I'm afraid there's been a crime committed at your neighbor's house."

TWENTY

FORTUNATELY DAD HAD been home and said he would rush over. I delayed calling the police by five minutes to give Dad a head start. I hadn't had to check with the neighbor about that because when she returned from seeing the body, she had to lie down. Dad arrived a minute before the police, time enough to get Stephanie safely into his arms before I had to deal with Detective Morini. While I led the police next door, Dad took her back to his house.

Watching the police catalog everything was both interesting and gruesome. Through the sliding glass door in Martha's dining room where the police questioned me, I could see them working. They had broken into the house when no one answered the door, wanting to make sure there were no other dead bodies on the property, which there weren't. I could have let them in with the key, but I had some doubts about the wisdom of letting them know I had one.

I told the same story three times to different officers, including Captain Slater. With nothing to hide, I felt I came off as the completely innocent discoverer of the body. Morini clearly would have liked to charge me with something but when it became obvious there was nothing to charge me with, they let me go. As before, I was told not to leave Clinton.

Fat chance I was going to obey that one. Stephanie was going home to Franklin, and I was taking her there.

By the time I left Martha's house it had been two hours since I'd discovered Father Skip's body. I returned to Dad's with precious little time before I needed to leave. I was aware that fitting in a stop at Greencastle for an interview with Signor Iavello's psychiatrist would cramp my time even more.

Dad greeted me when I walked in the door. "How did it go?"

"Okay, I guess. I'm not charged with anything."

"Are you all right?"

"I'll be fine. Did anything happen while I was gone?"

"Dana called about that unfinished article you wrote that needed a quote. I told her where you were and why, and she said she would run the article as is. She wanted you to call when you got back."

I decided to interpret "when I got back" as "when I got back *this evening*," knowing full well Dana would not be happy about it. But since unhappiness was running rampant through Clinton right then, I decided that—like it or not—she could have some, too.

Dad had lunch ready for us, toasted cheese sandwiches. Stephanie had already eaten but wanted to be with me, so I fixed her a small plate of snacks. I poured cups of milk for all of us and took them to the breakfast nook. Dad followed with sandwiches and chips.

We had no sooner sat down when the phone rang. Both of us got up to answer it, but I waved Dad off.

"Hello?" I said.

"Is this Nick?" a voice whispered. It sounded like Martha.

"Yes," I said, straining to hear the voice.

"This is Martha. I need your help." Her voice sounded faint and far away. I scrunched one ear to the phone and plugged the other with my hand to help me concentrate.

"You've got to find the person who killed Papá. It's not me," she pleaded.

"Where are you, Martha? Do you know about Father Skip?" I asked.

"I can't tell you. Anna and I are hiding. Use Mary's message and help us," she said. I heard a click and then the dial tone.

"Martha? Martha?" I said loudly into the receiver.

Dad stood. "It's Martha?"

I shoved the phone back on the cradle. "Was Martha. She hung up."

"What did she say?"

"That she didn't kill her grandfather."

"Did you say she did?"

"No." I thought a minute. "I wonder if Jimmy Iavello did, though. The police were looking for him last night. Maybe he knew something." I ate a bite of my sandwich, but wasn't very hungry. Finding a dead body can have a negative affect on one's appetite. I pushed the plate aside.

"So what do we do now?" Dad asked.

I checked my watch. "We wait to see what happens. I've got to leave now if I want to get Stephanie home before Joan gets there. If the police show up with more questions, just tell them I've run an errand and will be back soon. Maybe that'll keep them at bay for awhile."

"What should I do while you're gone?"

"Wait for me to get back."

That wasn't the answer Dad was looking for. "No, really. There must be something I can do," he said.

I stared at him. Tom and Gregorio Iavello and Father Skip had all been murdered, Martha and Anna were in hiding, and my father was anxious to get out and beat the bushes. "I think you should stay at home, Dad."

"Well," he said thoughtfully, "I guess I'll just have to figure out what you would do if *you* were staying here…"

Great, just great. Now I had to come up with some kind of safe action to keep him busy but out of harm's way. "You could try to track down Jimmy Iavello's phone number and see what he knows. If the police won't provide the information, try the funeral homes in town to see what arrangements have been made to bury Tom's body. My bet is, Martha's hiding means Jimmy is making the decisions, and the funeral home will have some way to contact him."

Dad nodded in agreement. "What else?" he asked.

He wasn't going to give up easily. "I'd call Angelo Ronchi and find out if Jimmy Iavello has been to see him. The mineral rights angle is still a long shot, but if Jimmy's pursuing it, maybe there's something there."

Apparently satisfied, Dad took his plate to the kitchen. Stephanie waited for him to return and asked for a cookie, which *Nonno* was happy to provide. He also prepared a take-home sack of cookies for her and placed it on the table.

While Stephanie scampered off to play one last time with the toys *Nonno* kept at his house, I packed her clothes and loaded them in the car. Deciding it wasn't best to leave all the information I'd collected where Dad could easily access it and think of other ways to get involved, I put it in a box and placed it in the back of the van.

Dad seemed unusually quiet. I had the impression there was something he wanted to say to me but couldn't find the right words. Just before I left, he found them.

"Encora, perdona. La colpa è mia," he said, apologizing again.

"Lo capisco, Papá." I hugged him. "And I *will* be back tonight."

Stephanie cried at leaving my dad, but he kissed her and told her he would see her soon. It didn't stop the crying, but it seemed to make her feel better. I handed her several of her bean bag toys, including the two new ones from

Nonno. By the time we could no longer see his house, Stephanie had stopped waving and the tears had dried up.

The drive to Greencastle was picturesque in an Indiana sort of way, with miles of farms dotted with neat, well-kept farmhouses and barns. We had to make one emergency potty stop in Rockville, but I was glad Stephanie had thought to say something. Potty-training hadn't been foremost in my mind the past two days. We were lucky to be in a town when she needed to go.

There were three things on my agenda with Dr. Crowley. I wanted to know if the *signore* had spoken to her of anyone who might want to kill him. If he had, I hoped it was a short list. People who are depressed can sometimes get quite paranoid. Next, I needed to know how she thought a murderer could have obtained not only a bottle of amitriptyline tablets but also injectable doses. I had no idea how to do that other than by prescription. Third, I wanted her opinion on whether one could be cured of depression simply by believing one was cured. Not that I was absolutely discounting a miracle—I still had faith that such things could occur—but the odds were highly against it. I certainly didn't expect to be privy to one. But if Signor Iavello absolutely believed in the miracle, could he manufacture one? I wondered what she would say.

If I managed to get more than five minutes of her time, I would try to pry out of her what her relationship had been with Iavello. I still had hope the "PC" entries in Iavello's calendar were a clue.

I had no idea where I was going when I entered Greencastle, but it wasn't difficult to find Dr. Patricia Crowley's one-story, red brick office building two blocks from the town square.

I introduced myself to the doctor's receptionist and told her why I was there. She said Martha had called to ask Dr. Crowley to talk to me, but the police had called, too.

"I'm not sure how much Dr. Crowley will say without some kind of court order," the receptionist said, "but she's agreed to at least hear you out. She's with a patient right now, but can see you for ten minutes between appointments." She whisked Stephanie and me into a small interview room and told us it would be a short wait.

Floral wallpaper gave the room a cozy feeling. Three chairs and a couch formed a neat little family-counseling pentagon. I sat on the couch. Stephanie crawled onto my lap. I spread out her coloring books and crayon box, but she would have nothing to do with them. I could tell she was tired.

I scratched the spot where the Miraculous Medal hung at my chest and found myself surprised to still be wearing it, although it hadn't bothered me this afternoon. I didn't really think it would bring me the graces promised by Anna and was contemplating taking it off when Dr. Crowley came into the room.

Awkwardly I stood up, holding Stephanie at the waist with my left hand and clasping the doctor's hand with my right. "I'm Nick Bertetto, Doctor, thank you for seeing me."

Doctor Crowley was in her late fifties, younger than I expected because of the relationship I presumed she had had with Iavello. Her body looked fit and her face was wrinkled from too much sun and wind. An outdoors type in her free time, I thought. Her eyes were bright blue.

"You might want to hold out thanking me until after we've talked," she said. "I don't intend to give out confidential information, not when the police are investigating a murder and coming to see me tomorrow for the same kind of data." She twisted her mouth into a half-smile, a firm one.

Her attitude made me pause. "Fine," I said. "Let's not talk about Signor Iavello, then." I gave her one of my best you-can-trust-me looks, but she didn't soften. "Let me ask you some questions about the murder. Your expertise as a psychiatrist might help me to understand it better."

She continued her stony glare, but I could see my change in strategy surprised her. "Well, you can ask," she said. She sat in a chair opposite me.

I placed Stephanie purposefully on the floor. Steph glanced up, but I motioned to her coloring books. She didn't look happy.

"I have a play area in my other family counseling room," Dr. Crowley offered. "I could have my assistant get a few toys from there if that would help."

"Thank you, but I know we don't have more than a few minutes of your time, and I'm sure she'll be fine." I handed the crayons to Stephanie and she understood. She opened a coloring book.

"Signor Iavello was killed by a gunshot wound, probably not self-administered," I said. "He also received an injected overdose of amitriptyline. You prescribed it in tablet form. How could someone get it in injectable form?"

"By prescription," she answered, speaking slowly as though trying to figure out my game plan. "Any other way would be illegal."

"Why would someone prescribe it in injectable form?"

"I'm not going to tell you why I prescribed the drug to Mr. Iavello," she said, getting short.

"I'm not asking that." I spoke calmly and leaned forward. "But you did prescribe the medicine, at least in tablet form. Did you ever prescribe it in injectable?"

"Not to him."

"Under what conditions would you or any doctor prescribe it in injectable form?"

"You could get that information out of the PDR," she said, countering my forward lean with a backward lean of her own. "It's given when a patient is unwilling or unable

to take the tablets. You replace it with tablets as soon as
you can, if you can.''

"What happens to a person when they get an overdose?'
I played the leaning game again, this time leaning back just
a little as though giving her space. I hoped she would
loosen up.

Dr. Crowley spoke in a professional manner, sounding
almost prerecorded. "Amitriptyline has sedative effects
like many antidepressants. An overdose eventually could
cause stupor or coma. There could be symptoms prior to
that, though. Temporarily, the patient may have hallucinations.''

I mulled that over. "In Iavello's case, then, it's possible
that he may have had some kind of hallucination that
caused him to kill himself?''

"It's possible he had hallucinations, but I'm not sure he
could have killed himself.'' She turned her head slightly to
the side, guarded. "An elderly patient would have been
weak after an overdose, and disoriented. Could he have
found a gun and shot himself? I can't rule it out, but the
odds wouldn't be in favor of it.''

Stephanie tore a page out of her coloring book and
handed it to me. I traced the sweep line of her bangs on
her forehead and murmured, "Thank you, honey. This is
very nice.'' I turned back to the doctor. "In your opinion,
was he the kind who would be prone to hallucinations?''

It must have been her turn to lean forward, because she
did. "I told you I wouldn't discuss those details with you.''
She smiled as though she were pleased with herself for
thwarting me.

"So you did,'' I said as agreeably as I could even though
I was annoyed. "Let's go back to something more general.
Signor Iavello was eighty-six. That seems kind of old to
succumb to depression. Is it?''

"Oh, no,'' she said, returning to a professional tone.

"Depression in the elderly is quite common. As many as fifteen percent of those over sixty-five suffer from depression."

I jotted that down, for no other reason than to keep her talking until I could think of some other way to relate it Iavello's case. "What kind of symptoms do you look for in elderly patients?"

"They lose interest in activities they've enjoyed for a long time, become indecisive, feel sad for long periods of time, are hostile toward others, have loss of memory. There are others," she said. Her voice became guarded. "Those symptoms I mentioned may or may not have been exhibited by Mr. Iavello."

"I see." I wrote out her list. This wasn't getting me anywhere. I looked up and gave her a trusting, albeit impatient, smile. "Dr. Crowley, what would it take to get you to cooperate with me? I didn't ask Signor Iavello's family if they wanted help. They came to me. I'm not even a detective. I agreed to help this family even though it has put me out quite a bit. As much as I can tell, you're not trying to help anyone. You may be trying to protect yourself. From what, I don't know."

I felt tired and cranky. Like Stephanie, I wanted a nap. I began to gather up Stephanie's things because I couldn't decide what else to do and I figured our interview was over. "I've come a long way out of my way to see you," I said. "What is it going to take to get your help?"

I must've pushed the right buttons with her because she looked contemplatively at me while I shoved crayons back in the box. The muscles in her cheeks flexed and relaxed.

Our ballet of indecisiveness came to a halt when the receptionist knocked at the door and entered. "Your next patient will be fifteen minutes late, Dr. Crowley. She just called."

"Thank you," the doctor responded. She rose and closed

the door as the receptionist exited. Turning back to me, she smiled. "You apparently have my next patient on your side," she said kindly. "All right, you've won me over— to some extent. I'll give you a brief history of Mr. Iavello's case, but what I say must be kept absolutely confidential." She settled back into her chair. I stopped packing and grabbed my notebook.

"It was the granddaughter who persuaded him to seek help. He came to me because he thought Greencastle was far enough away no one would find out he was seeing a psychiatrist. That kind of anxiety is typical of the elderly. They often attach a stigma to mental illness."

Stephanie pushed her way onto my lap. I moved my notebook to the right to accommodate her.

"How long was that after his first suicide attempt?"

"Oh, you know about that. Mr. Iavello was quite secretive about it. It was about a month before he began to see me."

"You knew right away he was depressed?"

"Self-destructive thoughts are not uncommon with depression. He had other symptoms as well. In particular, his granddaughter noticed his indecisiveness. He'd been quite a businessman, yet he reached a point where he couldn't make decisions of any kind about money. Apparently he had left some investments in money-losing situations longer than he should have."

I noted the loss in investment money, something I intended to ask Martha about later. The loss would have made both Martha and Jimmy nervous.

"How was his relationship with the grandchildren?" I asked.

Dr. Crowley fidgeted. "I don't want to go too much out on a limb here," she replied. "He dealt with each of them in their own way. He seemed to trust Martha. The younger son, Tom, worked with him as a part of his therapy. I had prescribed exercise, something I often do with depressed patients, and since Tom is a licensed physical therapist, Mr. Iavello suggested him.''

"Tom was a physical therapist?" I asked, taking notes furiously. Martha hadn't told me that, nor that Tom had helped the *signore*.

"Yes. He worked part time at Vigo County General in Terre Haute.''

Stephanie sleepily turned around and buried in her face in my chest. I patted her shoulder, then returned my attention to the doctor.

"Did they work together until his death?" I asked.

"For a while. They had a falling out. I honestly don't know what it was about.''

I sighed. Trusting Martha to tell me the truth about Tom hadn't been smart.

"What about Jimmy Iavello?" I asked, bracing for more revelations.

Dr. Crowley shrugged. "He lived in New York and they didn't talk much. But he did come to Clinton unexpectedly after the suicide attempt. Mr. Iavello wouldn't tell me what they discussed. He called them family matters. I couldn't get him to elaborate. As far as I know, that was the last time they spoke.''

Once again Martha hadn't given me the full story. I made a note to ask her about the meeting and what family matters were discussed. If she knew. If she would tell me. If I could find her.

"It sounds like Signor Iavello wasn't very cooperative,'' I said. I eased Stephanie a little to the left to get her knee out of my stomach.

Dr. Crowley shook her head. "Not really. Why do you say that?''

"Well, you said he didn't give you much information about Tom or Jimmy.''

"That's to be expected." Dr. Crowley took on her professorial tone again. "Very often it takes a long time to gain the confidence of a patient so they'll confide everything to you. Actually, Mr. Iavello was better than most at talking about himself. He was troubled, but he was very pleasant and easy to talk with. He wanted to be cured."

She led right to my next question. "Was he so eager that he would have looked for a miracle?"

Dr. Crowley laughed. "All of my patients come hoping for miracles. We do what we can. The mind, which we try to heal, is not yet completely understood by medical science. Depression is often related to a biochemical imbalance in the brain. We try to repair the imbalance and treat the depression with drugs and therapy. Occasionally, a patient doesn't get better fast enough, and we lose him to suicide. But that doesn't happen very often."

"Was Signor Iavello getting better?" I couldn't get used to calling him "Mister" Iavello. My mind was too fixed by my past.

Dr. Crowley glanced at her watch. "Yes, but we still had much to do." She sat up, signifying that our meeting was ending.

"He just stopped coming to you without telling you why?"

She nodded.

Stephanie's head slipped limply onto my left arm. I heard her easy breathing and knew she had fallen asleep. "Let me ask you a question that may seem odd. If Signor Iavello believed in a miracle, that he was cured, could he have cured himself?"

She gave me a puzzled half-smile, turning up her nose in curiosity. "Miracles again, huh? In my opinion, Mr. Iavello still had problems coping with his age and his wife's death. But he was much better. I guess, and this is very simplistic, if he truly and completely believed he was cured, he might have been able to cure himself. But the chances of that happening are remote. Not from what I'd seen of him.''

There was a knock on the door. The receptionist stuck her head in.

''Your next patient is ready, Dr. Crowley.''

''Thank you,'' she replied. Mrs. Thompson shut the door. Dr. Crowley stood up and offered me her hand. I struggled to get up while cradling the sleeping Stephanie.

Dr. Crowley smiled at Stephanie. ''You handle her well. She seems like a sweet child.'' Then the doctor looked at me. ''I hope I have been of help.''

''Very much,'' I said, ''and thank you for trusting me. One last thing, Dr. Crowley. How would you characterize your relationship with Signor Iavello?''

She turned back to me with a frown. ''It was completely professional. I would not prolong therapy. I was not after his money.''

Her eyes flashed with anger. I began stammering through an apology when she cut me off. ''I assume you had to ask that question. Now good-bye.'' She turned to leave.

''If I have any further questions, can I call you?'' I asked hurriedly, trying to catch her.

She spun back around. ''We'll see. I want to talk to the police first.''

On my way out, the receptionist stopped me. ''I hope you don't mind my asking you to do this,'' she said sheepishly, ''but the bill from Mr. Iavello's last visit hasn't been paid yet. We've sent the invoice twice. Since you're working for the granddaughter, would you give her another copy?''

I wanted to politely decline, but thought it best to keep on the doctor's good side in case I really did call in with additional questions. ''Of course,'' I said. I took the sealed envelope and walked out.

TWENTY-ONE

STEPHANIE SLEPT the hour drive back to Franklin. I had picked up I-70 south of Greencastle and took it all the way into Indianapolis, catching another interstate south to Franklin. It was a boring drive, but quick. Indianapolis was at rush hour when I went through; fortunately I hadn't encountered any traffic jams. When I reached Franklin, I thought for sure I'd beaten Joan home from work.

But I hadn't. Her car was already in the garage. I parked the van next to it and went into the house carrying Stephanie, who was in that half-awake, after-nap state. "Joan!" I called. The only response I heard was a mournful cry from the living room. I ran in. "What is it?" I asked. Her face was buried in her hands, damp blonde hair falling through her fingers. She turned watery blue eyes and flushed cheeks toward me. "It's happening all over again," she sobbed.

"What's happening again?" I placed Stephanie on the floor and knelt next to Joan.

She pointed to the answering machine on the end table. Its red light blinked insistently. I leaned over and pressed the replay button. My dad's voice, choked with emotion, came on after the beep. "Nick, this is Dad. The knife in Father Skip's body had Martha's fingerprints all over it, and Anna's house in Diamond has been broken into. When the police investigated the break-in, they found the missing prescription bottle and a used syringe tinged with amitriptyline. They think it was the one used to overdose Gregorio.

Both the syringe and the prescription bottle had Anna's fingerprints on them. There's an arrest warrant out for both women.

"But like you, I don't think they did it," he continued, lowering his voice to a conspiratorial whisper. "In fact, I've found something suspicious that may help. There's a tire print that was left beside the rectory driveway. The secretary says she noticed it yesterday morning but didn't think anything about it. I found a similar print on Bill Blazevich's land just off the Iavello property…"

I heard a doorbell ring in the background noise of the tape. Joan sprawled on the couch with her head in the throw pillows. I cocked my ear to listen to the faint murmurings in the background of the tape. There seemed to be a discussion of some kind between my father and another person, a man possibly, but I couldn't be sure. The words were almost inaudible. Then everything got quiet, and I heard the click of a door shutting.

I turned up the volume. "There's nothing else," Joan whispered, tilting out of the pillows. "Eventually the phone disconnects. I've tried calling, but the line's always busy. What have you gotten us into this time?"

I snatched the phone off the hook and dialed Dad's number. The busy signal buzzed in my ears. I called the operator and told her what had happened, asking if she could find out if there was any conversation on the line. She put me on hold. When she came back, she said there was no one there. I thanked her and hung up. I felt the color drain from my face.

"What happened in Clinton?" Joan demanded, her voice bolder.

"Just a minute," I said. I called the operator back and asked for the number for Mr. Pesavento, Dad's neighbor. When I got in touch with him I explained what was happening and asked him to check the house. Mr. Pesavento said he'd call me back. After 5 minutes that seemed like 20, he phoned to report that Dad's door was unlocked and there was no one at home, but there was no sign of a struggle, either. He said Dad's car was not in the garage. I told him I was coming back to Clinton and asked if he would call a few of Dad's friends and try to locate him. He agreed.

Joan was still demanding reassurance.

"First of all," I told her, "this has nothing to do with you. You aren't in any danger here in Franklin. The only person who might be in danger is my dad. I have to go back." Joan's eyes widened. "You'll be perfectly safe here," I reiterated. I glanced at Stephanie, who had awakened and was leaning against me. "You need to be strong for Stephanie," I said, trying to give her a mission.

Joan nodded, not convincingly, but it was a start. I handed her a tissue and she wiped her eyes. "What happened?" she asked, her voice more conciliatory now.

I told her as much as I dared, leaving out a great deal about Father Skip. I also tried to downplay my own dread that something had happened to Dad. "We don't know that's he's in danger," I said. "We only know that he's not at the house. Let's not jump to conclusions." I hoped I could follow my own advice.

Joan began pulling herself together and made a sandwich for me to take. I pulled my suitcase out of the van and replaced the dirty clothes with clean ones. The suit I'd worn to Signor Iavello's funeral got left in the van since it looked like I would be attending additional funerals. Finding the unopened bill from Iavello's psychiatrist, I stuffed it in the box with the other information I'd collected. As I finished packing, Mr. Pesavento called to say no one knew where Dad was.

"I have to go," I told Joan again.

"I know," she said. She turned away.

I wasn't surprised that Joan only said good-bye through

the glass of the front window. She and Stephanie waved as I pulled out of the driveway. I knew Joan's eyes were tearing, as mine were, but perhaps for a different reason.

Just before leaving the Franklin town limits, I felt the chain itching around my neck again. I scratched at it but had no intentions now of taking the medal off. I still wasn't certain about Anna's apparitions, but I was certain that I needed my faith and I needed it now. I said a prayer and asked Mary for her intervention. Then I hurried toward Clinton as fast as I could, pushing the speed limit and hoping to shave 15 minutes or more off the two-hour drive.

The setting sun shone in my eyes most of the way. The sky had turned deep blue and stars were out when I reached Dad's house. I leapt up the steps to the front porch. The door was locked. I pounded on the door, but no one came.

Shivering from the cool night air, I pulled my jacket around me. I fiddled with my key-ring, finally found the right key, and let myself in. A note to Dad from Mr. Pesavento was on the table. He apologized for intruding, but cited my call and concern. I searched the house. No Dad.

Wearily I sank into an overstuffed chair in the living room. My head fell back while I stared at the ceiling. What have I done? I asked. No answers came.

I closed my eyes and thought the situation through again. If Dad wasn't in danger, then he was just out doing something. But what? Why walk out in the middle of a phone call? And why leave the door open if he hadn't been forced to leave?

Locking the house, I returned to the van. Dad had said he'd found tire prints both at the Holy Family rectory and in the Blazevich field near Signor Iavello's house. He seemed to think they were significant. I decided to start there.

The Blazevich field butted up against the Iavello property near the back of the Iavello home. I turned onto the county road faster than I should have and had a heart-stopping moment when I thought the van might tip. When I recognized the fence separating the Iavello and Blazevich properties, I pulled over. I parked on a large concrete pad on the Blazevich side and stared in the direction of the Iavello house. The stars only provided enough light to see the gabled roof over the tree tops. I studied the field illuminated by the van headlights. The tire tracks were there, just as Dad had discovered. I pulled a flashlight from the glove compartment and got out to examine them.

The tracks were blurred and nondescript. Some grooves stuck up, cracked and dried, distorted to the point they wouldn't be of much help. Whoever drove the vehicle into the field did it during or just after a rain. Unfortunately, that narrowed the time period only a little. It had rained for more than a week, finally ending on Tuesday night. The tracks were consistent with the time frame for Iavello's death, but there was no evidence linking the two.

I waved my flashlight farther out into the field. The tracks went on along the fence as far as I could see. I flicked the flashlight off. I hadn't found Dad, but I hadn't found any dead bodies either. That was good. They seemed to be plentiful around Clinton.

The Holy Family rectory was next. I located the single tire print, but again, not my father. The single print made me think the vehicle had just missed the driveway but pulled back on. Like the print in the field, it had been distorted by rain and muddy conditions.

The lightless rectory looked somber. No help there. I closed my eyes in frustration and asked for any kind of help.

The chilly weather forced me back into the van. Sitting in the driver's seat, I thought back over my last conversation with Dad. He had asked my advice on what to do. What had I told him?

The words came back. Find a way to contact Jimmy Iavello and check out Angelo Ronchi, the other farmer who didn't want the coal mine. Jimmy was still a mystery, so I backed out and headed for Ronchi's farm.

Angelo Ronchi's place was on a little-traveled gravel road north of the Blazevich home. I slowly approached the farmhouse. My headlights shone on Dad's car, a hundred feet from Ronchi's driveway, half off the road. It was dark and quiet. My heart almost stopped.

I parked behind Dad's car and threw my door open. I grabbed my flashlight and rushed to the driver's side, peering in. Dad lay still, slumped over in the front bench seat.

My hand shook. I grasped at the door handle, trying to open it, but it was locked. I beat on the car. "Dad, Dad!" I yelled. My heart thumped furiously.

Dad jerked up in the seat. *"Che? Che?"* he exclaimed, eyes full of fear. He didn't recognize me in the blackness.

I sank to my knees in relief. I dropped my flashlight and my hands slid against the window. *"Dios mio, Papá!"* I sputtered. "Don't ever do that to me again!"

Dad opened the door slowly, giving me time to move away. "Nick! What are you doing here?"

I stood up and faced him. "Don't give me that, Dad." I was angry now that I knew he was okay. "You left half a message on my answering machine, teased me with some discoveries you've made, then went away before you finished. You left the phone off the hook. All I knew is that you left with somebody, maybe willingly, maybe not. Three people are dead. I'm just supposed to pretend you're all right and not come charging back here looking for you?" I pounded my hand on his car. "And what are you doing here anyway? Spying on Ronchi?"

Dad glanced toward the Ronchi house. He did a double-take and pointed. A light had popped on in the front window. "Let's get out of here," he said.

"Oh, shit," I said. I raced for the van. Dad jumped in his car and started it just as the porch light went on. The door opened and "Ronchi Antico" stepped out in his nightshirt.

Dad sped off. I started the engine and jolted the van into drive, leaving Ronchi to yell at a spray of dirt. In the rearview mirror I saw him, light reflecting off his bald head, pumping his fist up and down in the air. He spit Italian obscenities at our tracks. I laughed in spite of myself. It felt like an escape after an old high school prank. I sobered up and followed Dad back to Clinton.

I finally relaxed as we pulled into the Dairy Nook parking lot. Dad got out of his car. "I'm starving. We've got to stop, okay?" he asked.

My stomach rumbled. The only thing I had eaten was the sandwich Joan had fixed. It was past eleven o'clock now. "Yes, but I have to call Joan first," I said.

At a phone booth inside, I called Joan with the news that my father was safe and to try and get some sleep. I could hear in her voice that she hadn't been to bed yet. I told her I would call again in the morning.

The Dairy Nook crew, just about ready to close, didn't look happy to see us. Still, they let us order. I looked the menu over for a low-fat selection but threw caution to the wind and ordered a cheeseburger, French fries, and milk shake. Dad followed my lead but ordered a Coke with his. He paid for both orders.

"You were spying on Ronchi," I said as we waited for our meals.

"You were the one who told me to do it," Dad answered.

"I did not. I suggested you call him."

"I tried that. When I asked Angelo if he knew where Jimmy Iavello was, I got a stream of profanities. I figured Jimmy must have been there sometime. I camped out after dusk. After a couple of hours of nothing, I guess I fell asleep.''

''What happened during your phone call to the answering machine? Why did you break it off? Why didn't you call back?''

A restaurant employee broke in to hand us our orders. Dad thanked him then lowered his voice. ''Charlie Cammack came to the door while I was on the phone. He was looking for you. You didn't tell him you were leaving. He was upset.''

I chewed on my lower lip. I should have told Charlie. ''What did he want?''

''To see how you were holding up. He knew you'd found Father Skip's body. He told me they still hadn't found Jimmy Iavello. But he also said—'' Dad glanced around furtively—''he said that Anna's house in Diamond had been broken into. The police found more syringes there, but they might have been planted.''

I sipped the milk shake. ''Do they have any leads on who broke into the house?''

''No, whoever did it was careful.''

''Did you go somewhere with Charlie afterwards?'' I asked. I tried to figure out what Dad did in the time between his phone call and his vigil at the Ronchi's. A suspicious thought had formed in my head.

''Charlie just wanted to know how to reach you. I told him I was sure you'd be back, but I gave him your home phone number.''

''But you weren't sure I'd be back, were you? You left the phone off the hook on purpose. You knew if I thought you were in danger I'd come back. That's it, isn't it?''

Dad's face reddened. ''That's not true,'' he said to the hamburger on his tray. ''I really forgot.'' Then he mumbled, ''For awhile, anyway.''

''And by that time, the recorder had stopped and the call

had been disconnected," I finished. "But rather than call back, you left the phone off the hook to see what would happen, didn't you?"

Dad dipped two French fries into catsup and shoved them in his mouth. "The thought had occurred to me."

I started to say something but Dad interrupted. "Look. The police have an arrest warrant out for Martha and Anna on evidence that might have been planted. The police chief wants someone convicted. You've investigated these kinds of things before. I know you can figure this out. The police won't bother once they have Anna and Martha."

Even as angry as I was, it was hard not to forgive him, considering the kind of faith he had in me. "Dad, I can't work miracles," I said with a half-smile.

He grinned broadly. "I know that. But now that you're back, what can we do to find the real murderer?"

"First, Dad, we don't know that Martha and Anna aren't the real murderers. They had the most to gain and their fingerprints are on the murder weapons. But Charlie's right, the evidence could be a frame. Martha noticed the knife missing from her grandfather's house, and she said it was a knife she used the day before."

I took a bite of the hamburger. It was tasteless, another frozen patty defrosted to order. I smothered it in catsup. The French fries, though, were fresh, warm, salty, and oozing with fat calories. I ate the whole bag.

Dad said he had been tracking Martha and Anna's last known whereabouts and found out no one had seen Martha since yesterday morning. He also said that Jimmy Iavello had arranged for Tom's funeral, just as I'd guessed. The Ruatto Funeral Home wouldn't have given out the information except Dad knew the Ruattos so well. Jimmy had listed his grandfather's address and phone number as the way to get hold of him, but calling there had come to nothing. Ruatto also told Dad the coroner hadn't established the time of Father Skip's death yet. I'd check that one with Charlie. If he weren't mad at me.

I finished my milk shake with a noisy sucking sound from the empty straw, a sound my mother used to call "the drugstore blues." The employees hung around waiting for us to leave. "Let's go home, Dad," I said.

By the time we pulled our two vehicles into Dad's driveway it was 11:45, but I was jittery again. Something nagged me about Signor Iavello's house. On impulse, I motioned for Dad to climb into the van. I told him I wanted to drive by the Iavello house.

Intuition finally worked for me. As we slowly approached the house, I could see a light on in the third story bedroom window. Then it went off. I felt goosebumps on my arms. "I never made it to the third story when I was here two days ago."

Dad tapped his fingers on the armrest. "I'd like to know who's in there. Too bad we don't have a way to get in."

I patted the pocket of my jacket for the envelope that had been taped to Martha's house. "We do," I said, holding the keys aloft. "Martha left these."

We contemplated the next move. "It's not exactly breaking and entering," Dad said. "Martha did give you the keys."

"But what if it's someone with a gun? Someone who doesn't want us there?"

Dad glanced back at the house. "No one wants us there."

Headlights off, we crept up the driveway to see whose car was parked in back. The shadows of the leafless trees made the long drive seem longer. I found myself holding my breath.

When we rounded the house, I could see the shape of a car parked near the garage. I didn't need the headlights to know what it was, or whose—it was the same Ford Escort I'd seen Jimmy Iavello driving the day before.

TWENTY-TWO

I PUT THE VAN in park. "It's Jimmy's car," I whispered to Dad. "He's been evading me and the police all week." Dad didn't say anything, and in the dark I couldn't tell if he'd heard. "I wonder what he's doing sneaking around his grandfather's house in the middle of the night," I whispered a little louder.

Dad remained quiet. I sensed his courage had left him— I knew mine was gone.

"Perhaps one of us could hide behind the garage, and the other could drive the van down the road," Dad suggested. "Someone needs to see if he brings anything out. Then when he leaves, we could go in and search. He might be after something."

It wasn't a half-bad plan, assuming Jimmy wasn't settling in for the night. We could avoid a showdown that way and possibly still get information. Maybe when we knew more we could confront him. Assuming we could find him again. Of course, there was always the funeral home tomorrow.

"I'll hide," I said, braver than I felt, but I couldn't let Dad to do the dangerous part. He'd already scared me once that night. "You take the van."

"No, let me hide," he argued.

All at once, the plan didn't matter anymore. The outside light switched on, and Jimmy stepped out the back door leading a blonde-haired woman I recognized immediately as Margaret, the eldest Blazevich daughter. Jimmy stopped short when he saw our van.

"The jig is up," I told Dad.

Dropping Margaret's hand, Jimmy advanced on us, his face contorted in anger.

The engine was still running. I reached for the gearshift and contemplated a quick exit but he'd already seen us. Confrontation seemed inevitable. I rolled down the window.

"Hi," I said.

"What are you doing here?" he demanded, his breath forming little clouds in the cold night air.

I nodded in the direction of Margaret Blazevich, who pulled an unbuttoned cardigan sweater tightly around her. "A more interesting question is, what's she doing here? Does her father know she's with you?"

Margaret shrank back toward the house. Jimmy gave a forced laugh. "She's well past the age of consent. And that's none of your business, anyway."

"None of this would be my business, except your sister hired me to find out who killed your grandfather. It looks as if you've been avoiding both the police and me, which makes me suspicious. You can't do that forever. The police especially want to talk to you now that your brother is dead." He stared hard at me. His eyes were a deep, bitter brown, so dark they melted into the black pupils. The effect was menacing, but I was determined to win our battle of the stares.

His mouth twitched and the corners twisted into a sneer. Where had I seen those eyes and that mouth before? Somewhere, and recently. Margaret Blazevich stepped toward us and the answer hit me. Her eldest son, in the picture I'd seen at her father's house. Jimmy and the boy didn't look exactly alike, but enough to make me think twice about who his father was.

"Margaret, go back inside," Jimmy said. "I'll handle this."

She came up to him anyway and slipped her hand in his. "We can't keep ducking this."

Jimmy stared at the concrete driveway. "For a while, we still can," he said. His voice was tight.

"If you're not guilty, we might be able help you," I said.

He looked up. "And just how are you going to help me?"

"Your grandfather is dead, your brother is dead. The police think your sister murdered them. Now, I don't believe she did it, and I'm going to figure out who did. But if your sister didn't do it, and you didn't do it, then you could be in danger."

He thought about that for a moment. I pressed him. "You don't have anything to lose if you're not guilty. And if you are, well, consider our questioning good practice for the police tomorrow."

Jimmy exhaled forcibly, fighting with something inside himself. "I'll talk to you," he said with resignation. "But it's just you and me."

"No," Margaret said firmly. "We'll do it together."

Jimmy shook his head. "Margaret, I need to do this alone." He squeezed her hand.

Dad looked worried. "I'll be okay," I mouthed silently to him. He didn't look convinced, but he didn't try to overrule me.

Jimmy pulled Margaret close and kissed her, lingering at her ear to whisper something. Then he put keys in her hand. "Go ahead," he said. "I'll call you."

Dad spoke up. "I could drive her home," he offered.

Jimmy scowled. "*You* will stay here."

Margaret silently climbed into the Escort and started it

up. I moved the van out of her way. When she was past, I shut off the motor.

Dad and I followed Jimmy into the house through the back door, past the small office that Martha used, into the kitchen. He turned to Dad. "You sit here," he ordered. He seemed used to telling other people what to do.

Obediently Dad took a seat. His eyes looked grim and tired.

Jimmy and I went upstairs to Signor Iavello's study. He settled into the burgundy leather chair behind his grandfather's desk. Dressed in that casual look rich people affect, with a white, long-sleeve polo shirt and chinos that cost as much as a suit, he looked very much like he belonged there. How long would it be before it was his? I wondered.

"I didn't kill my grandfather or my brother," he stated belligerently. He crossed his arms over his chest.

"I didn't say you did," I responded. "But you've got to admit, you've got motive."

"That I was after Papá's money?" He snorted. "Check with anyone, you'll find I'm a very successful stock broker in New York. I'm worth more than he ever was."

While he could have been bluffing, his voice had a righteous ring to it. I'd leave it to Charlie Cammack to check his claim, but I was annoyed at how wrong it seemed to have been to trust Martha's version. Although, even the rich want more.

"Money is always a motive," I countered.

Jimmy shook his head.

"You knew your grandfather had changed his will," I went on, not about to let him off the hook, "leaving a lot of money to Children of the Second Advent. Tom told me the two of you planned to challenge the will in court."

"Oh, that much is true." All of a sudden he seemed strangely calm. Perhaps he had figured out I didn't know as much as I pretended. "Can't see letting Crazy Martha get her hands on all that money, now that he's gone. But that doesn't mean I would kill to get it."

"Martha says you argued with your grandfather, that you wanted control of the family's money," I said. "She says he shut you down."

"He did, but that's because he didn't feel comfortable with the stock exchange. He knew farming, owning a business, investing in land, things he could see, put his hands on. Mineral rights was about as exotic as he got. He didn't approve of the things I would have invested in. They were too complicated for him."

Jimmy had zeroed in mineral rights. It was the one thing I knew had been a sore spot with the other suspects. "But you're working with Bill Blazevich and Angelo Ronchi on the mineral rights your grandfather owned."

"So what? I'm just trying to wrap up loose ends so we can settle the estate. Martha can't handle it, and Tom trusted me to do the right thing."

Throughout our conversation, the bitterness had never left his eyes. Did that imply he was lying? What was he feeling? Irrational hatred? I examined my fingernails. Something had to be important about the mineral rights. Jimmy was too interested in them. I saw the wedding band on my ring finger, thought of Margaret Blazevich, and hit on an idea. Martha had said he was childless.

"Does this have anything to do with your son?"

"My son?" he said quickly. Too quickly.

"Your son by Margaret. Her oldest child."

"I don't have a son." The bitterness from his eyes edged his voice.

"Sure you do," I pressed. "He has your eyes, your mouth. There's so much of you in him I bet it'd be obvious if you were seen together." I was exaggerating, but not by much.

His dark eyes burned. "You're guessing."

"Not anymore." I leaned forward, defying his glare. "You were in love with Margaret, but her family was against a marriage. So you went to a college just far enough away from hers that it looked okay. But the two of you still saw each other. She became pregnant…" I trailed off, having reached the limit of my guess. "Do you want me to tell you the rest, or do you want to tell it?"

"You don't know the rest," he said, unafraid. My poker face failed again.

"I know enough to make the police interested, maybe forget about your sister."

He knew that wasn't a bluff. He gritted his teeth. "I loved Margaret so much," he said. "But Bill wouldn't let her marry me until we had something resolved on those damned mineral rights." Jimmy gripped the arms of his chair. "To me, it was ridiculous. 'Sell the damned things back to him,' I told Papá. But Papá was stubborn. Bill saw it as something my family wanted to lord over him. It escalated. I hated both of them for what they did to Margaret and me."

If he were telling the truth, and he sounded like it, I could hardly blame him for his anger. I tried to imagine what it was like to have your father care more about money than your happiness. Mentally I thanked my dad sitting in the kitchen.

Jimmy released the grip on the chair and stretched his white fingers. "I tried to talk Margaret into eloping, but she wouldn't get married without her father's blessing. When she got pregnant, she got scared. She latched onto someone she knew her father would approve of, made him think the child was his, and married him. They moved away."

Jimmy's eyes started to water. His voice sounded thick. "My degree was in finance. I went to New York, determined to start over. I got a great job, found someone I learned to love, and got married. Life was going along great. Then we found out she couldn't have a baby. We became obsessed by it. Went to all the best doctors. Nothing worked." Jimmy's voice faltered.

I prompted him, almost feeling guilty doing it, but three people had been murdered and I had to keep pushing for the truth. "Surely you thought of adoption?"

After a pause, Jimmy found his voice. Remorse rung in it. "Adoption was a possibility, but that could take a long time and I already had a son, a flesh-and-blood male heir. I searched for Margaret and the boy. By then, she'd had two other children. The only good news, if you can call it that, was that Margaret's husband had divorced her, then died later. I thought there'd be only minor problems."

Jimmy wiped his eyes with his hands. "I was going for partial custody. I guess by this time Margaret had told her father the truth. They were determined to deny everything, fight me in court, turn my son against me. Unless I married Margaret."

"A major reversal for the Blazeviches," I said. "First they wouldn't let you marry Margaret, then they pressure you to do so."

Jimmy leaned on his arms. "They wanted the kids to have a father, I guess. But I didn't want to divorce my wife, and I only wanted my boy, not the others. I hoped Papá would help me. I knew he wanted the family name to continue.

"He developed a scheme to sell his land to a coal company to put pressure on Bill. Papá thought Bill would come around to our way of thinking." Jimmy reached for a tissue.

"And Bill Blazevich killed him?" I asked.

"No. I know he didn't do it. He and Ginny were with Margaret and the kids the night Papá died. I don't know what happened."

"And you were in New York," I added, fishing.

Jimmy clenched his teeth. "I was in New York. And I wouldn't have killed Papá. You know now, I didn't have a reason to want him dead."

If I could believe him. I didn't know who to believe anymore.

"If you're so innocent, why have you been avoiding me, not to mention the police?"

"Things have become more complicated. I need time to work them out before I face the police."

I raised my eyebrows. "Like your discovery that you still love Margaret?"

He flinched. I was right. "No one will find out from me," I said in my most trustworthy voice.

He looked down at his hands. "I sent my wife back to New York after the funeral. I've been staying with Margaret. She has a separate house on her father's property. It's far enough away he doesn't know I've been there. And I do love her. I don't know what to do," he mumbled.

"You could divorce your wife and marry Margaret."

"But you don't understand," he said, his voice muted. "I love them both."

We sat in silence. His story was convincing. But someone gave Signor Iavello an overdose of antidepressants and killed him. Someone killed Tom and Father Skip. Someone was a murderer.

"Did you know about your grandfather's depression?" I asked, breaking the silence.

"I could see he was depressed, even if he didn't talk about it."

I rubbed my forehead, trying to massage away my sleepiness. "Do you know Martha claims your grandfather was miraculously cured of his depression?"

Amusement flitted in his eyes. "Anna Veloche cured

him?'' he asked sarcastically. He rolled back his head as if loosening his neck. ''That's a good one.''

''So you don't believe it?''

''Do you?'' he asked. He snapped his head back to eye level and looked at me curiously.

''No, of course not,'' I replied. Then I stopped. I had reacted to his disbelief, not wanting to seem crazy. But what I said wasn't quite the truth. ''Actually,'' I stated quietly, ''I'm not sure anymore.''

He snorted. ''You may well be as crazy as Martha is. That's probably why she hired you.''

''Do you think Martha's guilty?''

He leaned back in the chair. ''No, not really. She's changed since she got hooked up with Anna Veloche, but I don't think she'd resort to violence when she still knows how to manipulate to get what she wants. I mean, she's brought Clinton back to life with this Second Advent stuff. Martha's a marketing genius. If she needed money, there's not a bank in Clinton who wouldn't loan it to her.''

''Yeah. I can't imagine anyone who'd want to pull the plug on this miracle. Can you think of anyone who wanted your grandfather dead?''

''I've racked my brain. It may not even have to do with the will.''

''No,'' I said. ''The money has to be involved. Nothing else makes sense.''

There wasn't anything left to ask. I stood up. ''I'll see you at Tom's funeral tomorrow.''

''What are you going to do?'' he asked.

''I'm going to get my father and go home. There's not much else to do. You seem like you're on the level.'' I turned to leave the study. He trailed after me.

''Do you have any idea now who killed my grandfather or Tom?''

I turned and faced him squarely. ''I haven't a clue.''

TWENTY-THREE

DAD WAS ASLEEP when I returned to the kitchen. I woke him and led him to the van, Jimmy impatiently ushering us along. When the door was shut and Jimmy walked away, Dad asked sleepily, "What did he say?"

"The same thing every other suspect in this case has said," I replied, "that he wasn't guilty. He made a logical case for it. I guess I believe him, but I'm about out of suspects." I put the van in reverse and began to back down the long Iavello driveway, difficult in the dark with only the tail lights to use for a guide.

"That's it?"

"Pretty much," I answered, concentrating on staying on the driveway. When I finally backed onto the county road, I turned to my father and said, "I did find out that Jimmy is staying with Margaret..." but Dad had nodded off.

I guided him to his bedroom when we reached his house. It was a little like putting Stephanie to bed when she was asleep. He had no real idea what he was saying or where he was, he just recognized his bed and fell into it. I took his shoes off and covered him up.

The clock chimed 2:00 a.m., but I wasn't tired yet. Instead of tossing and turning trying to get to sleep, I gathered my notebook and a pen and sat in the family room scribbling some thoughts about my conversation with Jimmy. I wanted to get everything down on paper while it was still fresh in my mind, even though I was discouraged by what

I'd found. Yet another person with an alibi who claimed to have no reason to want Signor Iavello dead. Every suspect I came across logically disqualified himself. I had no idea whom to believe.

When I finished writing, I laid the notebook aside and picked up the remote control to the television, hoping to find something that might lull me to sleep.

Instead, I found myself sitting upright in the chair. On Channel 55, Pastor Carl Young of the Church of the Mystical Jesus worked himself into a pre-recorded frenzy, going on and on about Anna Veloche and the apparitions at St. Mary's. I set the volume up a notch.

"Make no mistake about it, my brothers and sisters, this supposed apparition is nothing less than the work of the devil. The true nature of this organization, Children of the Second Advent, is now revealed. Three murders have been committed, and where are the suspected murderers? In hiding! What does that tell you about Martha Iavello and Anna Veloche? Doesn't it look as though they have been misleading the good people of this community? But rest assured, the police—especially our good brothers Captain Jack Slater and Detective Joe Morini of the Clinton Police—are hunting down these women and will bring them to justice."

There was great applause at this point. Carl Young, resplendent in a pure white suit made even whiter by the intense spotlight on him, held the microphone away from his face as he acknowledged the applause. Cameras panned the audience, focusing every few seconds on enthusiastic faces taken in by what the preacher had to say. When the applause died down, Young began again. He stood on a bare, black stage that seemed enormous.

"Let me just take a moment to express my sorrow to the family of Gregorio and Tom Iavello. In Gregorio's state of depression, he had come to trust his granddaughter too much and she betrayed that trust. Mr. Iavello was truly a godly man, a pillar of the community, and we will miss him. Tom Iavello had developed a dependency on steroids, and his sister took advantage of that weakness to poison him. He never had a chance to experience the healing power of Jesus Christ, and for that we are truly sorry. May God have mercy on his soul.

"To those parishioners of Holy Family church, please accept our words of sympathy on the death of Father Skip Scipiannini. He was a well-meaning colleague too easily taken in by the Devil's work in Diamond. If any of you find yourselves questioning the truth of God because it was fed to you by a false prophet, Anna Veloche, we would welcome a visit from you to our church. Here you will experience the power of the mystical Jesus in true action."

The next few minutes was a pitch for Pastor Carl's upcoming healing service Friday night. The advertisement contained excerpts from previous healings where the lame tossed away their canes and the blind dropped to their knees in thanks as they saw their hands for the first time. I especially liked the special effects, which included flashing rays emanating from the healed.

At the end Channel 55 made a disclaimer, noting that the previous program was paid for by the Church of the Mystical Jesus. The Channel bore no responsibility for its content. Enough said, I thought.

The pastor had talked openly about Iavello's depression and Tom's steroid problem, yet the information hadn't been publicly released as far as I knew. Where had he gotten it? Had to be from the chief of police, Captain Slater. Surely that was a violation of some kind. I needed to talk to Charlie Cammack in the morning.

I shut off the television. In pitching the Friday night healing service, Carl Young had said something about "praying mightily" for the salvation of misled souls who showed up

Saturday morning in Diamond. While he avoided mentioning anything about Anna's promised miracle on that morning, it clearly concerned him. He said he would personally be there to provide his healing touch. I wondered what he had planned.

A yawn stretched my mouth so far it hurt. I stifled the next one. It was two-thirty in the morning. Dad snored loudly, his open-mouthed breathing rumbling through the closed door. I turned off the lights and went to bed.

The maze was back in my dreams. I felt like I needed to climb to the top of the maze's wall to see my way out, but the steep, smooth walls prevented me. I began to yell for help. Instead of help, I got pelted by Miraculous Medals, causing me to run for cover. Then I found myself in St. Mary's church. Tom Iavello was there, even bigger than I remembered him, shooting himself in the arm with anabolic steroids. He turned the syringe toward me and it was filled with a black liquid. He backed me against the wall and advanced with slow, menacing steps, holding the needle as if to jab me. I was relieved to find Dad shaking me awake.

"Nick, it's eight o'clock. We've got to get moving if we're going to make Tom Iavello's funeral at nine. *Ti alzi!*"

"Huh? What?" I mumbled, just awake enough to know what he'd said. I halted him when he tried to repeat it. "Okay, sure, I'll get up."

I rolled out of bed and stumbled to the shower, letting the water wash the night from my face. Unless I missed my guess, Tom's funeral would give me a chance to view all the remaining suspects at once. I needed to be awake. But when I finished showering and stared into the mirror, I saw droopy eyes. Got to look better than this, I thought. I downed a mug of Dad's coffee, strong enough to beat Hulk Hogan two out of three falls. Between that and the charcoal gray suit I'd worn to Gregorio's funeral just four days earlier, I managed to appear presentable.

The parking lot at Holy Family Church was full, and the church was packed. I was surprised because I hadn't thought Tom had many friends, but maybe his death affected the whole community and they felt a need to turn out for the funeral.

Holy Family, built in the 1900s and modeled after an Italian cathedral, has twin bell towers which flank the church entrance. The sanctuary is rectangular with pews down the long sides and an elevated altar at the front so the priest could be seen from all points. From the back of the church a stained glass window of Jesus, Mary and Joseph glowed, lit by the morning sun. Unlike St. Mary's Church where there was an abundance of statues, Holy Family had only two, although they were bigger than life size—one of St. Joseph holding Jesus as a young child, and the other of Mary holding her hands together in prayer. These flanked the altar, above which hung a large crucifix.

Father Vince conducted the funeral Mass, and he was evidently fond of incense. The pungent smell reminded me of my days as an altar boy, and I could smell it even at the back of the church, where Dad and I sat with a good view of all the suspects present. My editor, Dana Rardin, came in just before the funeral started and sat next to me. Dressed in a business suit, she looked ready for the funeral, but I noticed a reporter's note pad sticking out of her purse. As quietly as I could, I filled her in on everything I knew and pointed out the suspects.

Jimmy and his wife were up front on the left side. I wondered when Jimmy's wife had come in. She was an interesting contrast to Margaret, thin where Margaret was big-boned, elegant where Margaret was wholesome. Both had blond hair. Jimmy and his wife were dressed for a New York funeral, with a tailored, gray pinstriped suit on Jimmy and a designer black dress with pearls on his wife. The two of them looked mournful, though I wondered if Jimmy's sorrow was over his brother's death or his own marital predicament.

Bill Blazevich, his wife Ginny, and Margaret and her three children were on the other side of the church about a quarter of the way back, dressed for a Clinton funeral with off-the-rack suits and dresses. Bill looked respectful but not sad. Margaret looked sad and kept glancing over at Jimmy. I could see the eldest boy. He didn't look quite as much like Jimmy as I'd thought the day before. Maybe a lucky guess on my part. Jimmy avoided looking at either of them.

Angelo Ronchi and his wife sat two rows in front of us, dressed in nice clothes that looked like they had been bought years ago and were now slightly out of style. Angelo kept turning around. I wondered if he knew it had been Dad and me at his house last night. Angelo had two facial expressions, the scowl and the suspicious scowl, and he gave me the suspicious scowl before the funeral started. I smiled politely and nodded. He turned around quickly.

The funeral did not drag. Father Vince Kennedy handled the Mass and spoke sparingly about Tom, partly I suspected from ignorance, and partly because there hadn't been a lot of good things to say about him lately.

In any event, Tom must've had some friends, because the four pall bearers were huge men with massive chests and tiny waists crammed into ill-fitting suits. The four big guys effortlessly moved the coffin down the aisle, no doubt a light workout for them.

When the funeral was over, Dad, Dana and I discussed strategy. Dad and Dana went to eavesdrop on the Ronchis and the Blazeviches. I went to the rectory to see if I could get into Father Skip's office. All of us were sure his death had to be related somehow to the two deceased Iavellos.

When I got to the rectory, I found Rose, the blue-haired

church secretary, on the phone. I pantomimed a request to use it, and indicated I would go to Father Skip's office. She waved me back there.

Police tape guarded the door, warning me not to go in, but I slipped under it anyway. Wrapping a handkerchief around the phone handle to avoid leaving fingerprints, I lifted the receiver and pressed the "hold" button so Rose would see the phone was busy.

Looking about the room, I had to sandbag myself against the flood of memories that threatened to swamp my thinking. Father Skip's sturdy oak desk and the crucifix on the wall behind it, the matching bookcase containing tomes about apparitions, the door Martha had leaned against that kept me from bolting—all these reminded me of our Tuesday meeting. Just three days ago Father Skip had been alive, an old friend explaining why he'd called me back to Clinton. And I'd found him... I had to push the image of his dead body from my mind.

To my surprise, nothing in the room was locked. I checked Father Skip's desk drawers and scanned his files. I noticed the desk calendar lay open to Thursday. Odd, since he had disappeared on Wednesday. I paged back to where Wednesday should have been and found Tuesday. Wednesday was missing.

The Tuesday calendar showed the morning Mass listed, followed by my name on the next appointment line. At the bottom of the page was a small notation reminding him of an early meeting the next day.

What meeting? And with whom? And who had torn the page out?

I started toward the bookcase but slowed down when I saw the pregnant Mary statue in front of the books. Second Advent. Was it real or imagined? If imagined, did it necessarily mean Martha and Anna were guilty? I checked the bookcase, but nothing seemed to be missing.

On my way out, I asked Rose if Father had had a meeting Wednesday morning. She checked but didn't have anything listed. I thanked her and left.

By the time I got back, not many people were left at the church. Dana, Dad and a uniformed Charlie Cammack stood together on the steps of the church.

"The only thing I found out," Dana said, "was that everyone agreed we should fire the current high school basketball coach if he doesn't get the team out of its slump. No one mentioned Tom Iavello until I finally fished, asking for a quote. Bill Blazevich said Tom should have stuck to baseball and not gotten involved in bodybuilding. Not much there."

I told Dana, Dad and Charlie about the missing calendar page. Charlie seemed embarrassed the police had missed it, or at least hadn't mentioned it in the report.

Dana turned to me. "I've been looking for some kind of quote to end a short piece on Tom's death," she said, "but no one has had much good to say about Tom. You have any ideas?"

"Did you know Tom worked as a physical therapist at Vigo General in Terre Haute?" I asked.

"He what?"

"Worked as a physical therapist. That's according to Dr. Crowley, the psychiatrist who treated Signor Iavello. Tom helped the *signore* with the exercise program she had prescribed."

"The officer who investigated Tom's death found his license and some check stubs," Charlie said, confirming my information. "Morini's already been to the hospital and talked to them about it."

"You need to get over there and talk to them," Dana said. "You're still working for me, aren't you?"

I nodded.

"Then get over to Vigo General pronto and get me a

story. And here's another lead to follow up on. I was just telling Charlie about it. We called Oregon Bible College. They received a request to reissue Carl Young's diploma, but didn't do it. That's because they found out the Reverend Carl Young is dead."

The word dead startled me, though I'd heard it a lot lately. "Well, whoever the current Pastor Carl is, he's having a healing session tonight. Perhaps I ought to go."

Dana liked the idea, but cautioned me again that the Church of the Mystical Jesus was a paying customer. "Get the information carefully," she said.

Charlie was waiting for the limousine to return from the graveyard with Jimmy Iavello. "Morini wants to talk to him about Tom's death," he explained. Charlie had also said he was off duty after he delivered Jimmy Iavello, and he wanted to accompany me to Vigo General, which I welcomed.

"Is Morini questioning Jimmy about Father Skip's death, too?" I asked.

"No, that's been pretty well pinned on Martha."

"I don't like the evidence they have on Martha. When I was at the Iavello house, she noticed the knife was gone and said she'd used it the day before. It could be she's being framed."

"It's also possible she was planting doubts knowing the knife might turn up later," Charlie said.

I closed my eyes, trying to recall the look on Martha's face when she discovered the knife missing. "Maybe," I said. "She seems pretty good at acting. But something doesn't feel right to me."

Just then the limousine bearing Jimmy Iavello pulled up. Although Charlie assumed a thoroughly professional manner, Jimmy didn't want to get into the police car and Charlie had to resort to a firm grip.

As Jimmy stepped into the car, he flashed me a forbidding look. I hadn't told Charlie anything about my conversation with Jimmy the night before, but Jimmy saw guilt by association.

He mouthed an obscenity and followed it with an expression that chilled me.

"You'll pay for this."

TWENTY-FOUR

I HAD FORGOTTEN to call Joan earlier, so I took care of that when Dad and I returned home. Joan didn't sound resentful that I hadn't called before; in fact, she sounded relieved to hear my voice, which felt good. I promised to be careful and said I would call her again the next day.

Charlie came over after lunch. We left Dad's house together in my van and made the half-hour trip to Vigo County General Hospital in Terre Haute. Though I'd planned to use the time to pry into the details of the case against Martha and Anna, he questioned me first.

"Have you worked out at the Big Sycamore Gym since Tuesday?" he asked.

Just the fact that he asked dredged up some guilt at having slipped off my weight-gaining diet and missed two work-outs. "No, I haven't had much of a chance."

"Really? I figured you worked out pretty regularly. I was hoping you'd have been back to find out if anyone was talking about Tom now that he's dead."

I glanced over at him. "I thought the police interrogated everyone at Big Sycamore the day they found Tom dead."

"True, but that was Morini and Captain Slater, not me. Even if I had been there, though, what people tell the police and what they gossip about later are often two different things."

I should have thought of that. "I'll try and get over there tomorrow," I said.

It didn't take much to get him to open up about the case against Martha and Anna. "Slater and Morini consider the knife with the fingerprints and the syringes found at Anna's house to be nearly conclusive evidence. They have a few loose ends to tie up but expect to turn everything over to the Vermillion County Prosecutor within a few days. They're also looking for evidence to tie the two women to Tom's death."

The Clinton Police had once conclusively decided that Signor Iavello committed suicide, but I didn't say so to Charlie. It didn't help matters that Martha and Anna had vanished. Although everyone is supposed to be innocent until proven guilty, I had to admit the two women made themselves look guilty by running away. But where had they gone?

As Charlie fell silent, I tried to imagine the court case if they were found. I was sure I would be called as a witness for Martha. She had noticed the missing knife in my presence. Her explanation for her fingerprints on the knife, that she had used it at the family reception after the funeral and hadn't had time to wash it, made sense. But Charlie had been right this morning when he said it could be a cover. Was it enough to call the evidence into doubt? She had motive to kill her grandfather, and if Father Skip were thwarting her plans for marketing Second Advent, well, she might have killed him, too.

Anna's defense would be sketchier. She had left her fingerprints on literally hundreds of objects through the blessings of Mary. A defense attorney could argue that someone seeking to frame her had shoved a syringe and the prescription bottle toward her during a prayer session, and that she had touched them, but what would a jury think? A woman who sees a pregnant virgin and predicts the Second Coming of Christ could certainly qualify as being crazy, crazy enough to kill for money that would make her famous. I didn't think Anna was guilty, but I wasn't sure I could be objective.

The one thing I did know was that perception mattered as much as reality. If the women looked guilty, Second Advent—and Martha and Anna—were finished.

Charlie hadn't been told yet what Morini had found out at Vigo General and he seemed as curious as I was. When we got to the hospital, Charlie displayed his badge, which got us in to the cramped office of the assistant personnel director, a petite redheaded woman whose every word sounded smooth and soothing. She identified herself as Melinda Hensley and apologized that her supervisor was on vacation and couldn't answer our questions, since her supervisor had been the one who had talked to Morini yesterday. Charlie asked if Hensley had sat in on the session, and looked relieved to find out she hadn't.

"Let's start at the beginning, then," he said as she opened a door into a small conference room adjoining her office. We sat around a circular table in cushiony, cloth-covered chairs. "Did you know Tom Iavello?"

"Yes, I did. He worked here part-time for several years. He was a huge man, but unexpectedly gentle, particularly with our older patients. They miss him already. He'll be difficult to replace." She leaned on the table. "Oh, we had troubles with him from time to time, particularly a year or so ago when we had to test every employee for drugs. In one so muscular, we expected to find traces of steroids. He fought against taking the tests, which made us suspicious. I hate to say that," she confided. "Everyone has some right to privacy and we shouldn't judge people on looks. Anyway, when he took the tests, he passed them."

I looked at Charlie in surprise, but if he was startled by the information, he didn't show it.

"Did you administer urine tests or blood tests?"

A secretary interrupted, bringing Ms. Hensley a file.

"Both," she said. She consulted her file. "Yes, the results are right here. He was clean."

I turned to Charlie. "How?"

He wrinkled his nose. "I don't know. I've read about masking agents for steroids. They're expensive, though, and I have no idea if they really work."

Ms. Hensley frowned. "You gentlemen don't believe the results."

"It's just that the Vermillion County coroner found traces of several different kinds of steroids in his blood. You surely were told about that when you were contacted about his death."

Ms. Hensley closed the file. "We believe the steroids must be something he started recently. We were sorry to learn of it."

Charlie paused a moment. I could tell he was searching for words that didn't imply the hospital was negligent in its testing. "The liver showed extensive damage," Charlie explained. "He had to have been taking steroids a long time."

Ms. Hensley shrugged. "We stand by our tests. We run them as honestly and as accurately as we can. We can't prove he didn't find a way to fool us, but our procedures are tight."

She let that sink in. "Do you gentlemen have any additional questions?"

"Can we talk to some of his patients?" I asked.

"We don't have any objections to the police talking to them," she said. I didn't think she knew that would exclude me. Charlie hadn't said one way or the other whether I was with the police. "I could pull together a list for you, but it might be easier to see his patients at the time of their physical therapy sessions since some of them are out-patients. Mr. Iavello worked in the evening after 7 o'clock. If you would like to come back then, I can leave word with the night staff and the therapist who replaced him."

"That would be fine," Charlie said. "I can come back then."

I realized I couldn't. Tonight was the healing service at the Church of the Mystical Jesus.

"Fine. I'll let the night staff know," she said.

As we were leaving, Ms. Hensley gave us a final note of caution. "Please remember that Mr. Iavello's patients were elderly. Don't get them agitated about his death. It would be counterproductive to their health."

"How old are his patients?" I asked.

"In their seventies and eighties. Mr. Iavello was remarkably good-natured and caring with them. Many switched to evening physical therapy to work with him."

I could hardly wait to get Charlie out of Ms. Hensley's earshot. "Do you believe that?" I asked him as we left the building.

He shoved his hands in his pockets. "Which one? That he worked well with old people or that he passed his drug test?"

"Either, I guess, although I remember when I saw him the first time at the Big Sycamore gym he helped an older gentlemen without being asked. How could he have passed a drug test, though?"

We arrived back at the van and I unlocked the doors.

"I suppose there could have been several ways," Charlie said, climbing in. "He might have used a masking drug or given them a false urine sample. Then again, he might have done something as simple as bribe a lab technician. It happens. But I can't get over Tom Iavello being a hit with the older crowd," he added. Charlie donned a pair of Oakley sunglasses, very stylish.

I slipped on sunglasses that cost a lot less. "Maybe Tom had a soft spot for older people. Maybe they reminded him of better times with his grandfather. Signor Iavello was old when he raised Tom.''

''I never thought of that. You ought to ask the psychiatrist about it.''

''Have the police sent anyone over yet?''

''Morini, today. But he won't ask any questions that don't convict Anna and Martha.''

I turned into light afternoon traffic and headed toward the highway. ''Why is he so anxious to pin it on Anna and Martha?''

''For one thing, we have a motive. But there might be something else. The crowds coming to the supposed appearances of Mary have been growing. Where do you suppose they've been coming from?''

It hit me where Charlie was going with this. ''The Church of the Mystical Jesus? You think Second Advent has been thinning their crowds?''

Charlie gave a short laugh. ''I don't know, really. But it has occurred to me. Why don't you find out how attendance has been when you visit them tonight?''

''Good idea.''

TWENTY-FIVE

WHEN I RETURNED to Dad's house, Dad was in the family room talking on the phone. He jotted down notes on a pad of lined paper. When he finished, he brought the pad over to where I sat on the couch.

"Just doing a little research on the Church of the Mystical Jesus," he said. "Here's a list of some members."

I looked over the names. "How'd you get this?"

"Called and talked to church secretary, Rose. If anyone's in tune with the grapevine, it's her. She gave me a few names, then told me who might know some more. I followed her trail."

"Wait a minute," I said, putting my finger on one of the names. "Where have I heard this name before?"

Dad leaned over to examine the one I was pointing to. "Daniel Tripp. I thought it was unusual to see his name on there. He's a lawyer."

"Not just any lawyer," I said, thumping the pad with my knuckle. "It's Signor Iavello's lawyer, isn't it?"

"You're right," Dad exclaimed, straightening up. Then he frowned at me. "Does that mean something?"

"Maybe." I started to pace. "Maybe. Tom said Jimmy found out about the will change from the lawyer. He had to have meant Tripp. So Tripp had no qualms about divulging the contents of the will ahead of time. Why? To stir Jimmy to some kind of action?" I stopped pacing. "But that may have nothing to do with the Church of the Mystical Jesus.''

"No," Dad countered. "Didn't you tell me Tom and Jimmy planned to fight the will? That would prevent Martha's group from getting their hands on the money. The Mystical Jesus group would love that.''

"Charlie Cammack thinks some of Reverend Goldentones' church members are becoming intrigued by Second Advent. He thinks that's why Detective Morini is anxious to see the murders pinned on Martha and Anna even though the evidence is weak. He wants me to check on church membership tonight when I visit the healing service.''

"When *we* visit the healing service," he said. I nodded, no objection. I couldn't see any reason he shouldn't go. And I preferred to have moral support.

Since we still had several hours before heading out to the service, Dad suggested we check out the tire prints he'd discovered the day before. We took the van and headed out to the Blazevich property near the Iavello homestead.

In the daylight I could see how difficult it would be to pin down which type of tire had made the tracks. Not only did the tracks overlap in some places where the vehicle had backed out, but any groove pattern had been smeared and washed out by the rain. I stood up and wiped my hands with a rag. "I don't think the police can get much out of it," I told Dad. "I would guess it was a four-wheel-drive vehicle like a truck or a van since it didn't get bogged down." I compared the tires on my van to the messy tracks that had been left. "The tires look to be bigger than normal. Maybe the police can narrow the possibilities, but I don't think it'll be conclusive.''

We followed the tire tracks into the field until they ended. We were still on the Blazevich property but within sight of the *signore*'s house. Muddy indentations that one time might have been boot prints led toward the house, disappearing at the edge of the grassy yard. "These are way past the time they were clues," I said, "but I'll tell Charlie about them."

We had slightly better luck at Holy Family Church. The tire prints had some resemblance to a pattern, though rain had eroded the definition. "The police might be able to do something with these," I said. "There are some grooves left in the mud."

"And it looks wider than normal, like the last one." Dad looked up at the huge, leafless trees that formed a canopy over the area. "The trees must've protected this spot from the rain."

I looked up, too. "I don't think so, Dad. We had a hard rain here on Tuesday and the wind was blowing. It would have gone right through those branches. I think this print must've been made at a different time than the other one, say Tuesday night or Wednesday morning just before the rain stopped."

"You better ask Charlie Cammack to look into it," Dad said.

"Yeah, Morini won't be too interested. Neither Martha nor Anna owns a vehicle that could have made these tracks." I looked at my watch. Four-thirty. Charlie would be napping. "I'll wait until it gets closer to six. Charlie's supposed to question Tom Iavello's patients at seven. He ought to be up by then."

We climbed back into the van and returned to Dad's house. Dad found the pamphlets from the Church of the Mystical Jesus that had been thrown in the van right before Wednesday's prayer meeting at St. Mary's. He poured over those while I channel-surfed, hoping to find more programming by Pastor Carl Young. When I gave up on that, I went to the kitchen.

"Don't make dinner," Dad said. "I'll take you out. Let's go to Miller's again."

"What?" I said, pretending to be offended. "You don't want me to pull out another culinary miracle?"

"Best to conserve miracles," Dad responded dryly. "The minister may need some tonight."

"And Mary will need one tomorrow."

"Right," Dad said.

I called Charlie before we left for dinner. Since it was getting dark, he said he'd stop by and take a look at the tire tracks at Holy Family tomorrow, but he didn't sound like he held much hope in it. I wished him luck in interviewing Tom's patients, and he wished me luck at the healing service. I wondered which of us needed it more.

I appreciated Dad's buying dinner. Since I had promised Charlie I'd work out at the Big Sycamore Gym tomorrow to do a little eavesdropping, I decided to get back on my weight-gaining regimen. I ordered a big plate of chicken cacciatore, only to find I was so nervous about tonight that I left half of it. After Dad paid the bill we drove to the south end of Clinton.

The Church of the Mystical Jesus, the name now emblazoned on a well-lighted sign, was the old Evangelical Wabash Valley Christian Church. I had no idea how long it had stood empty before Pastor Carl's group bought it. They'd done a marvelous job of fixing it up. The stone walls looked smooth and white and freshly painted. They had added four neon blue crosses, one on each side of the church's bell tower. The neon glow could be seen from nearly a mile away.

Taking my cue from Wednesday's prayer service at St. Mary's, we arrived a full half hour early. The parking lot was filling up but there were still empty spaces. As we followed a group toward the entrance, I noticed the team who'd given us the Mystical Jesus literature Wednesday night in Diamond. They stood ready to divert traffic again, but this time away from the main lot into a field across the street. It would be a while before they were busy.

The church was bigger than St. Mary's. From the outside I'd guessed it could hold maybe 200 people, but when we entered the building I raised my estimate to 350. The whole main floor had been gutted so that it no longer looked like any church I had been to. There was no altar, no pulpit, and no organ, just a huge raised platform that resembled a stage. A wide runway led down from the stage and into the middle aisle. The only Christian symbol was a large cross which hung above the stage.

There was room at the back but the ushers were directing people toward the stage, filling up the front row seats first and moving back from there. From the placements of the broadcast cameras, I was sure they wanted to give the illusion of a packed house. They were going to have a good crowd, but I doubted the church would be full.

Dad and I were seated about midway back near the center aisle. Unfortunately, I had about as much arm room as one gets flying coach on a discount airline. Writing was awkward. I wished I'd been smarter and had brought a tape recorder.

The man seated on my right nudged me. He was a short, mousy fellow with a shallow face and nervous, darting eyes. He wore what looked to be second-hand clothes. They hung on his thin frame. "Whatcha doin'?" he asked.

"Making notes," I said stiffly, ignoring him as best I could.

"Why?"

"So I remember what happens."

"What for? You a reporter or somethin'?"

"A freelance writer," I replied. I attempted to look him in the eyes only to find they had shifted. "I'm here to see about doing a story on Reverend Carl."

"Amen and praise the Lord." He patted my arm. I had

to resist the urge to jerk my arm away. "Pastor Carl is devoted to doin' the work of the Lord. This the first time you been here?"

"Yes."

"Well, welcome to the Church of the Mystical Jesus," he said, holding the 'e' sound in Jesus out so long I almost asked if that was 'Jeeeeesus' with six e's or just five.

"Thanks," I replied. Seeing that he'd put his hand out, I shook it. It felt sweaty. I noticed he wore his crystal Jesus pendant outside his shirt.

"How long have you been with the church?" I asked.

"Goin' on about a year now. The reverend saved me from my sinful ways. I thank Jesus every day for sendin' him."

I did not want to imagine what his sins might have been. "I understand quite a number of sinners have been healed here."

"Oh, yes. The reverend has the power of the Holy Spirit in him, he does. Are you here to be healed?"

"No, I'm fine," I said. I heard some music and looked toward the stage. At the center, four men about my age began singing gospel music *a cappella*. While the crowd watched them, a group of stagehands moved an electric piano, two guitars, and a set of drums onto stage left. I looked back at my neighbor. "Do you know anyone personally who has been healed? Physically, I mean?"

The man fiddled with his pendant. "No." His voice dropped. With the loud music and crowd noise, I had to lean my ear toward him to catch his words. "I wish the reverend could've healed my dad," he said, "but I just couldn't raise the money."

"Money? You mean he *charges* for miracles?"

"'Course not. It's my fault. I didn't sacrifice enough, didn't show Jesus how deep my faith was. Pastor Carl can't cure if the Holy Spirit won't work through him. If I just could've gotten enough money, made it onto the "Faith Partner" list, I know Pastor Carl would've been able to cure him. I let my dad down. I didn't show Jesus I was a true believer." He said it mechanically, as though he had thought about it so many times he had come to believe it.

"How much, uh, faith, does the Holy Spirit need to see?" I asked, trying to control my excitement.

The man glanced around. He licked his lips with a quick movement of his tongue. "I shouldn't have said nothin'." He played with his pendant again.

"No, you haven't said anything bad," I assured him. "I'm sure Pastor Carl—I mean, the Holy Spirit—needs to see this kind of faith only because it, uh, helps continue Pastor Carl's work." Whatever work that was, I thought. "What did your father suffer from?"

"He was very sick," the man said, shaking his head. "At first it was his heart. The doctors done by-pass surgery on him to fix it. But he got weaker later. Started talkin' to himself day and night like he was two different people. The doctors said he was depressed."

"I'm sorry," I replied. "When did he pass away?"

"Last week, at Vigo General over 'n Terre Haute."

The mention of Vigo General stopped me. "Did the hospital treat him for his problem?"

"Gave him shots of some drug for his depression after he wouldn't take no more pills for it. But he didn't get no better."

I chewed on the top of the pen in thought. "Just out of curiosity, was your father also taking physical therapy? From a big guy, all muscle?"

"Yeah, he was one big sonofabi—excuse me," he said penitently. "I really didn't mean to say it like that. He was nice to my dad. Dad liked him a lot."

I twisted in my cramped space and smiled at my neighbor. "Your father liked the big guy, the physical therapist?"

"Dad said he talked all the time to him, 'bout the exercises and muscles and how they would help him get stronger." The noise of the crowd rose dramatically. The band and four singers staged a hand-clapping, foot-stomping version of "Down By the Riverside." My neighbor leaned toward my ear and spoke louder. "He kept encouragin' Dad, tellin' him he could do things. And Dad believed him. Dad always seemed better after workin' with him. 'Course it never lasted more than a couple hours. Then Dad'd be right where he started. I was always tellin' Dad, give your life to Jeeeeesus, there's where you get healed."

I nudged Dad. "Are you getting this?" I whispered through gritted teeth.

"Uh-huh."

The band gave an entrance cue. The noise became deafening. "What was your dad's name?" I shouted to my neighbor. "What was his name?"

He wasn't listening to me anymore. His eyes were fixed on the stage, where Pastor Carl, illuminated in spotlight, threw his hands in the air.

"God is alive!" roared the pastor. "God is alive! And His Spirit is alive in us!" The singers sang. The crowd, surging to its feet, yelled, "Be healed, be healed."

"We're going to do some healing tonight, my friends, yes we are, my friends," intoned the pastor. The crowd quieted. He raised his voice. "I haven't felt so alive in Jesus as I do tonight. Satan can't fight us tonight, can he, my friends? Not with so many, many believers here in this house of the Lord." He pointed at the crowd and swept his hand across the stage, indicating the masses. The crowd thundered its approval. Several voices shouted, "Amen."

"Let me tell you a story," he said, holding the microphone with one hand and indicating for the crowd to sit down. "This is a story about my great-grandfather," he began. "His name was Seth, and he was a carpenter, doing very much the same kind of work Our Savior did, but my great-grandfather was not a man of faith. He always put the things of this world ahead of his soul. He didn't get married until he was nearly 40, and the woman he married, Judith, was a widow about the same age. Judith and her husband had never had any children because the doctors told her she was barren.

"Well, she tried hard to persuade Seth, my great-grandfather to start praying with her. He loved her very much, but he didn't believe in God, like she did. He told her that if her God was so mighty, then He should give them a child, and then Seth would pray with her." Pastor Carl began to get louder, and he walked into the audience, lifting his arms for emphasis. "So Judith prayed hard, asking the Lord to give her a child. She told Him she believed in Him, believed he could give her the child she wanted, and in return she would save Seth.

"Well, my brothers and sisters, do you know what happened? She believed." Pastor Carl put his hands together in thanksgiving. "She believed, and she had a baby, who became my grandmother."

"Amen, amen," someone shouted.

"That's right, Amen. Seth, my great-grandfather, became a believer and a follower the day my grandmother was born. Folks, let that be a lesson to us. If we believe, Jeeeeesus will grant us miracles."

A bunch of hogwash, I thought, and not very original. It sounded like a modified version of the story of Abraham and Sarah.

The pastor indicated for a collection to be taken. "All Jesus wants, my friends, is a sign of your love and faith. Then he can work in you, and in me, and heal us."

Reverend Goldentones introduced a sister-in-faith and

disappeared from the stage. Backed by the band, the young, statuesque woman sang a song about the loaves and the fishes and how Jesus had fed the crowds with them. She sang with strength and conviction. Then she gave a personal testimony about Pastor Carl and how he had healed her. She said she had been hopeless and poor, selling her body to men for a living.

"And then I met Pastor Carl, who truly has the gift of healing," she said. "The first time, the very first time I felt him touch me, I knew power had come out of him. I saw what I was doing, how I was sinning. Even more, I knew with his help I could change. My spirit and my hope returned. Jesus gave me the grace to climb out of that poverty-stricken, sinful way of life, and now I do His work and His work only." She paused to acknowledge the cheers of the crowd. "And I owe it all to my friend who was truly heaven-sent, Pastor Carl." She had tears in her eyes. Pastor Carl walked out onto the stage and embraced her. Then they waved to the crowd.

There was long, sustained applause. The collection baskets were nearly overflowing when they reached me. I passed it by without adding anything. My neighbor noticed and handed the basket back. "Won't you help Pastor Carl do the Lord's work?" he whispered.

"I gave at the office," I whispered and winked at him.

He might have been a pushover for Pastor Carl, but he wouldn't give in to me. He held the basket out to me in expectation. "I'm not giving," I stated firmly.

The ushers noticed there was a holdup with the basket but couldn't get to us. Soon everyone within five rows had noticed. Embarrassed, I grabbed the basket from the guy and passed it over his head to the next person. The mousy guy retrieved it and held it out again. The crowd buzzed.

The ushers got the attention of the pastor. He returned to the stage. "My friends, my friends," he intoned. The spotlight followed him as he came down the runway into the center aisle toward our row. "Ah, Brother...Brother...—" someone behind him whispered a name "—Brother Timothy," the reverend said. "The Lord recognizes not all can give to God's work."

Timothy leapt to his feet. "He can give, Pastor Carl. He ain't a believer. He's a newspaper writer."

The pastor smiled radiantly. "Brother Timothy, everyone starts out as a nonbeliever. God works in his own time, in his own way. Let us be thankful God has brought him to us tonight." Pastor Carl turned to me and the expression on his face was one of recognition. "We've met before," he said. "Please come here."

A spotlight hit me. I exhaled in anger. What to do? Dad reached over and gave my hand a squeeze. I made my way toward the center, bringing my notebook with me.

The pastor had now reached our row. He had his black book in his hands and took a quick look into it. "Mr. Bertetto," he said and shut his book. "We are pleased that *The Daily Clintonian* would send someone to cover our little service this evening. Come up front where you can have a better view of all that happens." When I reached him, I saw him hit the switch on the mike that turned it off. He wrapped an arm around my shoulder and gripped me tight. "Don't think I don't know what you're doing here," he said through his teeth, all the while smiling as though we were friends.

"What's that?" I asked, surprised.

"You and your little friends at Second Advent may have been dragged into the mire, but you won't take me down with you. Try anything with me and I'll show you just how powerful I am."

He guided me toward the front. "My friends, let's welcome Mr. Bertetto," he said. There was polite applause. "Does *The Daily Clintonian* have any questions for me?"

I nodded. I couldn't believe the gall of this guy. Time to pull out the big guns. "I understand you graduated from Oregon Bible College, is that correct?"

"Yes, that's true," he exclaimed. "It was the place where I found my true calling, to bring the word of the Lord to everyone."

Someone shouted, "Praise the Lord." Another yelled, "Amen!"

"How do you explain the fact that the only Carl Young who graduated from Oregon Bible College is dead?"

There was a gasp from the crowd. A few booed me. "Tell him it ain't so, Pastor Carl," someone called.

Suddenly there was a distraction. A backstage hand brought out a stool, setting it on the far left side of the stage. The minister walked me over to it, holding up his hand to silence the crowd. A neat trick, I thought, buying him time to think. I stood beside the stool, engulfed in the warm spotlight. I could hear the crowd shifting restlessly in their seats.

"Sit down, please, Mr. Bertetto," the pastor said. The spotlight left me and followed him to center stage. He turned his back to the audience momentarily. When he spun around, there were tears in his eyes. "My brothers and sisters," he began, "it is true what Mr. Bertetto says. The Carl Young who graduated with me died." A ripple of murmurs flowed through the crowd. "He was my friend and a great source of inspiration to me. Let me tell you the story."

The preacher paused expectantly and the noise dissipated. In a choked voice, Carl Young wove his tale. It was lengthy, full of detail. He wept openly at some points, usually when describing the saintly Carl Young and all the great works he did. The last details he gave were of a housing project where the two men had tried to heal the sinners, and how a drug dealer had shot Carl Young, who died in the pastor's arms.

"And that, my brothers and sisters, is why I vowed to him as he breathed his last breath I would take his name and carry on his work."

When he finished, there was a standing ovation. Pastor Carl continued the service, ignoring me.

"My friends, let's welcome a brother who is ready to confess his sins and be cured of his crippling arthritis," he shouted. A man hobbled to the stage. As the service went on, more and more people came up. Each time Reverend Carl wound himself up and smacked them in the head to heal them. Some people he draped with crystal Jesus pendants. Some received spiritual healings. Several were cured on the spot of arthritis and other ailments. I also got to hear the testimonies of several who received jobs or won money after receiving the touch of Carl Young.

I took notes without enthusiasm. This wasn't a story I wanted to write. Reverend Carl came over to me one more time, sharing the spotlight and asking if I had any further questions.

"Yes, I do," I said. "What was your name before you became Carl Young?" I didn't really expect an honest answer, but if he gave me a false one I could at least prove later that he lied. But he was too slippery for that.

"Mr. Bertetto, it doesn't matter what my name was. That's in the past. What matters is the future. Have *you* given any thought to the future? Have you opened your mind and heart to Jeeeesus? Are you ready to admit your sins and be healed?"

I ignored the question. "Isn't it true that the apparitions of Mary in Diamond have been drawing away your congregation and you feel threatened by them?"

There were immediate boos from the audience, and a few shouted, "Devil's work! Devil's work!"

"You might as well know, my friends, that Mr. Bertetto here is a follower of Anna Veloche." This practically turned the crowd into a lynch mob. But Pastor Carl had them in his hand. "My friends, let's not be angry at any of those that have followed the false prophet. Let's pray for their salvation."

He then said he and his faithful followers would be in Diamond tomorrow to save any misguided souls. It was much the same speech I'd heard on the Channel 55 broadcast.

Dad, bless him, stood up and shouted in a surprisingly loud voice that if Pastor Carl would spend more time saving those who didn't attend church instead of those who already do, he'd do more for God. Dad was shouted down by people praying for him.

A little later Carl Young had the band playing again, and he made his way over to me without the spotlight. "This would be a good time for you to leave, before the service ends and my faithful followers are outside my influence. And I enjoyed your questions. I look forward to seeing your article." I burned inside.

Dad had been watching and saw me leave the stage. We met up outside at the van just as the service let out. As we drove away we passed people hawking copies of Reverend Carl's latest video and crystal Jesus pendants. I got in the van angry at myself for letting Carl Young get away from me and turn me into a chump. I hadn't felt so discouraged in a long time.

It was nearly 10:00 p.m. We drove by Charlie Cammack's house. I wanted to tell him about Brother Timothy's father who'd received drug injections for mental illness and had had Tom Iavello as a physical therapist, the only interesting connection I'd uncovered.

Charlie's house was dark. I rang the doorbell but got no

answer. "He must still be at the hospital," I told Dad. We returned home.

Dad went to bed. I was still too keyed up to go to sleep. If there was a fallout from the service over what I'd done and Carl Young dropped his advertising, so be it. Dana could just fire me.

Hoping she wouldn't, though, I wrote a quick article about Tom Iavello's seemingly secret occupation as a physical therapist. It flowed smoothly but I couldn't find a concluding paragraph for it. Finally discouraged, I turned off the computer and went to my room.

I kept thinking about Mary's message to me. It told me to go forward, and I presumed it was to understand something that wasn't understood and reveal it. Well, I didn't understand anything. The message was cryptic, the miracle was cryptic, and all I had was a couple of Bible verses. It would be interesting to see if this mysterious miracle took place in the morning. As for Mary's Immaculate Heart protecting me, nothing had saved me from being humiliated in Reverend Goldentones' service. I tried to unclasp the Miraculous Medal, but I was all thumbs and it wouldn't come off. I decided to use wire clippers in the morning.

Sleep came upon me, but it was an uneasy sleep.

TWENTY-SIX

I WAS BACK IN the maze, but this time as a child. I turned a corner in the maze and found my brother John and my cousins playing tag around the trees surrounding St. Mary's Church. I ran to join them. From the open windows of the kitchen at St. Mary's, the delicious aroma of ham and beans escaped into the outside air. Mom was up there, I knew, working on the food with my grandmother and the other women. Dad and the rest of the men set up tables. My brother and I called to Dad. He told us it was still a half hour before dinner started. "Find something to do," he said.

The day was warm and sunny and we were thirsty. The downhill door to the basement was open, and we headed there to get a drink from the coolers filled with lemonade, iced tea and ice water for dinner. We weren't supposed to drink them and we knew it. But where we disposed of the cups, no one would know. I played lookout while John ducked behind the furnace, opened the door to the old coal bin, and threw the cups. The bin was completely hidden by the new oil furnace.

I stirred in bed. It wasn't day and it wasn't sunny or warm. Groggily I tried to push the thought from my mind and return to sleep, to the happier times of my youth. Even in the maze, I wanted to go back to the St. Mary's I had known as a kid.

But I sat up suddenly in bed. The solution to getting out

of the maze wasn't to go over as I had tried in earlier dreams, it was to go under! The police couldn't find Anna and Martha because they weren't looking in the right place. Even if they had checked St. Mary's, they wouldn't have found the old coal bin in the basement. It was well-hidden behind the new furnace, and getting into it was a squeeze. Only a child, or someone thin, like Anna or Martha, would fit through the door. I knew where they were.

I pulled on jeans and a heavy wool sweater, leaving a note for Dad that I'd gone to St. Mary's and would be back soon. I strapped on my watch; it was 3:00 a.m. I yawned but didn't feel tired. Though I'd only found one piece, I felt the puzzle was finally coming together.

The moon was just a sliver. The night was moist, clammy, and dark. The sweater felt scratchy and I wished I'd put a shirt underneath it, but I couldn't turn around now. I had to get to the church. Not willing to chance the back roads at night, I took the long way at a fast clip.

Just before I reached the church, a roadblock showed up in my headlights. I slowed quickly. A county deputy came toward me with a flashlight. I rolled down the window.

"Hello, officer," I said, "is there a problem?"

"We're blocking off the road to keep people away from St. Mary's. We think there may be trouble later, and we're trying to keep civilians away."

"What kind of trouble?" I asked innocently.

"We think two people who are wanted for questioning in a murder case may try to show up around here early this morning, trying to get to that church up ahead. I'm surprised you haven't heard, but somebody's been claiming some kind of miracle will take place this morning, and between the suspects, the people who believe in this miracle and the people protesting this miracle, it could turn out to be dangerous. We think it's best to block the roads and keep everyone away from the church."

"I guess I have heard about that," I said, "but I really need to get through to Diamond," I said, thinking fast. "I'm trying to get to my aunt's house, down the road. She called me just ten minutes ago, sounding frantic. She said she forgot to take her pills last night before bed and now she can't find them." The deputy squinted at me suspiciously. "I make this trip once a week," I confided. "She's always forgetting to take her medicine. I wish I could persuade her to live in Clinton with me, but you know how stubborn older people can be. She just won't hear of moving." I gave him the sincerest look I could muster.

The deputy nodded his head. "My mother is exactly the same way. Well, let me move this sawhorse and I'll let you get by. But do your best to get your aunt away from here. Security'll be a lot tighter in a few hours. We wouldn't want her or you to get hurt."

He moved the blockade and motioned me forward. I rolled past, waving. "Thanks again." I drove past the church and went well beyond it to the next county road and turned right. There I found a field that wound back to the wooded area behind the church. I didn't want my car to be seen. Shutting off the headlights, I eased into the field and bumpily made my way toward the woods behind St. Mary's. At the woods, I pulled to a stop. I removed a flashlight from the glove box and got out.

The woods weren't thick, and I soon made my way to the church. The lone deputy must've been the only person standing guard that early. I stood absolutely still for several minutes just to be sure, but I saw no movement. I sprinted to the downhill basement door leading directly into the basement. It was locked.

"Damn," I muttered. I ran uphill to see if I could get in the back door, but it, too, was locked. Thinking I might be able to find something in the church's shed to wrench the door open, I started toward it. Then I realized I had Father

Skip's keys in my windbreaker. Martha had given them to me. I dug through the pockets and found them.

The basement door squeaked, though I opened it as carefully as I could. Holding my breath, I looked through the darkness. Nothing stirred. I exhaled in relief and slipped through the door.

The basement was darker than the night. I dared not turn on the overhead light in case I attracted the attention of someone other than Martha or Anna. Instead I used the flashlight, remembering how easily I'd stumbled into things when I had been there with Anna. I threaded my way carefully back to the furnace. When I got there, I wedged myself into the opening and knocked gently on coal bin door. "Martha, Anna, it's Nick," I whispered. No response. "Martha," I repeated, this time tersely. I heard the sound of someone shifting inside. I slid the flashlight to the hand by the door. Prying the door open with my fingers, I shoved my arm in and let the flashlight illuminate the room. I deflated my chest and somehow wriggled through.

"Hi," said Anna, pushing a lock of damp hair behind her ear, looking unkempt and nothing like the visionary who'd announced a miracle three days ago. "You found us."

I stood up and dusted myself off. The bin was not large, maybe six feet on each side. There was a coal chute, but it had been covered over with plywood. Martha leaned against the wall, her head propped up by a pillow, asleep. Both women wore jeans and thick cotton sweaters. Blankets were pulled up around them for warmth.

"How long have you been here?" I asked.

"Since early Thursday morning. It was Martha's idea. She says we're being framed."

Anna raised Father Skip's chalice to her lips and took a sip of something. Then she ate a few hosts out of a plastic sack. "Sacramental wine," she said as I stared at the chalice curiously. "We brought water with us, but we've run out and the water here is pretty rusty. The food is gone, so we're working on these hosts. Don't worry, they aren't consecrated yet."

She sounded as if she'd had a bit too much sacramental wine. "Are you being framed, or did one of you really do it?" I asked.

Anna pouted the way Stephanie had a million times. It didn't work any better for her than it did for Stephanie. "You don't really believe I did it, do you?" Anna asked.

"I don't know what to believe anymore." I sat down next to Martha and nudged her. She yawned and stretched, apparently unaware of me. She opened an eye and sat up straight.

"What are you doing here?" she whispered, eyes wide open.

"That's my exact question to you. What are you doing here? Who are you hiding from?"

Martha fidgeted. "From the police. They want to arrest us for Papá's murder and for Father Skip's. We didn't do it!"

"Why are you so afraid of them?"

"They have evidence, don't you see? We're being framed. They'll throw us in jail."

Anna offered the chalice to Martha, who took a sip. Martha rubbed her eyes, then turned to an oil lamp and lit it. The room lit up, and I could see tears in Martha's eyes. She scooted close to me. "Nick, you believe me, don't you?" she pleaded. "I know you can solve this thing. Mary said so."

I sighed and looked away.

"I'll pay you more than $25,000 if that's what it takes," she whispered sharply.

"Twenty-five thousand dollars'll buy you a good lawyer, Martha. One that'll keep you out of jail, I bet."

Martha gritted her teeth. "But we're not guilty, and we want to see the miracle!"

Anna nodded in agreement. "Nine a.m.," she said. She held her index finger in the air, pointing toward the ceiling. "Right up there in church."

"I wish I could believe it was going to happen."

Anna became indignant. "You don't? But you have to. Mary even gave you a message. I wrote it exactly as she said it. I asked her to repeat it to be sure. It's a clue."

"Right." I closed my eyes. Isaiah. Luke. Go forward. Just what was that supposed to mean?

I opened my eyes. The two women stared at me. I studied Anna's face first, then Martha's. They trusted me. They expected me to come up with something. I bit my lower lip. "All right. You're not guilty. I can see that."

I pulled my knees up. We remained in silence for a few minutes. "Martha," I asked, "did you know Tom worked as a physical therapist at Vigo General Hospital?"

"No," she replied. She registered only mild surprise.

"You don't find it unusual?"

"Only a little. Papá told me once that Tom was a physical therapist. He said Tom came by sometimes at night to work with him. I didn't believe him. Papá was really low at the time. I wrote it off as fantasy. Maybe it wasn't."

"Why do you think Tom would do that?"

"Money. I can't think of any other reason." Martha shrugged.

Anna reached over and took the cup from Martha. "We need more wine. I'll head up to the altar."

"No, you won't," Martha commanded. "You'll stay here."

"Mary will protect us, here in the church," Anna answered.

"I wouldn't leave the basement," I advised. "There's a deputy standing guard down the hill and more police will be here by daybreak. They plan to arrest you if you show up.''

The two women looked at each other. ''Then I guess they'll have to arrest us at nine,'' said Martha. ''We intend to see the miracle.''

I tried to dissuade them. They wouldn't listen. They begged me again to help. Finally I agreed to try to come up with some way to help them.

I worked my way back out of the coal bin. Isaiah, Luke, go forward. Was it really a clue? Even Father Vince hadn't known what it was about.

Except, I thought, suddenly excited, he had told me Jesus had quoted the same passage from Isaiah in the same chapter as the Luke passage. I hadn't looked it up. Maybe it was a clue. I needed a Bible; fortunately I was in a church.

Using the flashlight, I made my way up the basement steps to the sanctuary. I found the Bible on the lectern and flipped to the beginning of Luke 8. It didn't take long to find the passage Father Vince had mentioned.

''He replied, 'To you the mysteries of the reign of God have been confided, but to the rest in parables that ''Seeing they may not perceive, and hearing they may not understand.''' ''

I still didn't understand. I closed the Bible and felt the weight of failure. Passing by the statue of Mary, I knelt impulsively and turned the flashlight to her face. Kindly blue eyes looked down on me. ''Help me,'' I whispered. I heard only the faint echo of my voice.

I retraced my steps to the basement door and slipped out. There were no signs I was being watched. I rushed to the woods and picked my way back to the van.

The black sky had lightened a bit. Soon it would be morning. I checked my watch. Five-thirty. I had so little time.

I climbed into the van and sat there, despondent. In my

mind I could see the women climbing the stairs at nine o'clock, looking for a miracle and delivering themselves into the waiting handcuffs of the police. What could I do? I pounded the steering wheel in frustration.

"They're as good as dead," I said aloud.

The words echoed. I stopped and thought about what I'd said. "As good as dead," I repeated. "But not dead. Like a parable. 'Someone thought to be dead.' But maybe not thought to be physically dead."

I thought a moment. "Spiritually dead? 'Someone thought to be dead will be brought to life.' If it were Anna who was spiritually dead, then who's spiritually…?"

"Oh, yes," I said, laughing, "it makes sense." I laughed some more. "It makes complete sense."

I climbed into the back of the van, looking inside the box of papers and books I'd accumulated on the case. Digging around, I found the bill from Dr. Crowley's office. I tore it open and read it. "Just as I thought," I mumbled to myself. Sorting the mess again, I dug out my notes on Gregorio Iavello's schedule. I checked the dates. Then, just to be sure, I looked over the list Martha had made of people who had brought food after the funeral. I found the name I was looking for.

PC wasn't Patricia Crowley, Iavello's psychiatrist.

But I knew who PC was. I knew who was behind the deaths of Signor Iavello and Father Skip, too. Now I just had to prove it.

TWENTY-SEVEN

ON MY WAY OUT of Diamond I slowed for the roadblock. I rolled down the window and made the courtesy effort of lying to the deputy. "My aunt won't leave," I called, "but she's asleep now. I don't think she'll surface before this afternoon." The deputy removed the sawhorses. I waved and moved on.

It was almost six thirty by the time I reached Vigo General in Terre Haute. I flew through the revolving doors and accosted the receptionist. "Officer Cammack from the Clinton Police sent me to ask the patients he saw last night a few more questions. They were Tom Iavello's patients. Do you remember their names?"

The receptionist, a fiftyish woman with green eyeshadow, gave me a puzzled look. She put on her reading glasses and unhurriedly read through the sign-in sheet. "Don't see any Officer Cammack here," she said.

"Well, he must be there," I replied, flustered. I yanked the chart out of her hand and glanced over it. She was right. His name wasn't there. Neither was anyone else from the Clinton Police Department.

"Can I use your phone?"

She looked down her nose. "You can use the public phones over there along that wall." She pointed.

I dug through my pockets for change and inserted it. Information gave me the number for the Clinton Police Department. After what seemed a lifetime, I was connected.

"This is Nick Bertetto," I told the dispatcher. "I'm a friend of Charlie Cammack's and I need to talk to him right away. I know he's on duty. Can you get a message to him?"

The dispatcher hesitated. "Is this an emergency?"

"Very much," I said.

"Can another officer help you?"

I clenched my fist. "No, it's a personal emergency. I need to talk to him right away."

"You need to try him at home. He didn't come in for his shift."

"He didn't?" My heart started to pound.

"No."

I slammed the phone back on the hook and dialed my father. *"Ti sveglia, Papá!"* I exclaimed, when he muttered a nearly incoherent hello. "You've got to wake up. Get over to Charlie Cammack's house. Break in if you have to. I think something's happened to him."

"Huh, what?" Dad blurted. I could picture him sitting up in bed, rubbing his eyes, trying to wake up and understand what his son was shouting about.

"Ti alzi! Dad, are you there? Are you with me?"

"Yeah," he said, suddenly alert. "What's going on?"

"I know who killed the *signore.* But I have to get proof. Charlie was getting close. I think something's happened to him. You have to get over there and make sure he's okay. And don't call the police, you can't trust them."

"I can do that," Dad agreed. "I can do it."

"Good. I've got to go."

I dashed back to the receptionist. "Is Ms. Hensley in?" I asked, remembering the name of the assistant personnel director. "She said she would get me a list of Tom Iavello's patients I could talk to." I stared at her hopefully.

She hadn't gotten any faster since I left. She looked me over. "Ms. Hensley is not in. Are you with the police?"

"Yes."

"I'll need to see some kind of ID," she replied.

"I don't have it with me. Look, can I maybe talk to someone in personnel?"

It took ten agonizing minutes, but I did get someone, a young man cutting his teeth on the night shift. I explained the situation. He insisted that I had to have identification. "Surely you have something that shows you're a police-man."

"I don't," I answered quickly. "Look, can I at least see the list Ms. Hensley left? How can that possibly hurt any-thing?"

With continued badgering he finally came around. I read each name on the list, looking for one that would stand out in my mind. None of them hit me.

"Can you tell me if any of your patients who had Tom Iavello for physical therapy died in the last month?"

He gave me three names. Maybe he just wanted to get rid of me.

When I asked to see their medical records, the momentum stopped. "Sorry," he said. "I can't do that."

After more pestering, he paged a resident, Dr. Tomarchio, who treated elderly patients. It took a foot-tapping half-hour for the doctor to fit me in.

He met me in the narrow, tiled hallway near the psychiatric ward. The tall resident looked amused as I rattled off everything I knew. I ended with my guess that all three patients took an injectable form of amitriptyline and none had responded to the treatment.

He tapped the folders containing patient information but didn't look at them. "Two of them took amitriptyline," he said. "And no, they weren't doing well on it. We were getting ready to switch them to another antidepressant. But," he added with emphasis, "they were given two daily doses, none of them near the time of Mr. Iavello's physical therapy sessions.''

I leaned against the wall. The coldness of the tile seeped through my sweater.

"If there are no other questions…"

"Did Tom ever visit his patients during the day?" I asked, virtually sure of the answer.

"I don't ever recall seeing him here during the day."

There was a clicky-clack sound and I looked up to see a pharmacy cart being wheeled into a room. Across the hall, a white-collared minister emerged from another room. "Of course," I announced, catching Dr. Tomarchio off guard.

"Of course, what?" he asked, startled.

"Did Reverend Carl Young ever visit those patients during the day, maybe during the time they were supposed to get their medication?"

"Who?"

"Pastor Carl, from the Church of the Mystical Jesus, youthful, white-haired guy, good-looking? Probably wearing a crystal pendant with a picture of Christ in it?"

There was a smile of recognition. "Oh, yes, he's here frequently." Then the resident frowned. "But there's no way he could have obtained the amitriptyline."

"Trust me, if the man can get away with his phony healing," I said, "he could find a way to get that medication." I grasped his hand and shook it. "Thanks, you've been a big help."

I dashed out of the hospital, waving at the receptionist with a spirited good-bye. Tom Iavello, steroid junkie, was handy enough with the needle to inject his grandfather with the overdose. He'd done it for the pastor, but I hadn't thought the pastor would be bold enough to obtain the stuff himself. Obviously he had.

It was 7:30 and the sun was up. I had wasted too much time at the hospital. I had enough information to piece together a story but no hard evidence to support it. I drove like a maniac out of Terre Haute and back to Clinton, to the Church of the Mystical Jesus. It took twenty minutes.

Leaving the van running, I jumped out of the car and thumped the church's front doors. No one was there. I circled the building, rattling the doors. Locked tight.

I shoved my hands in my pockets and started back to the van but changed my mind. It was now or never. I dashed to an ornate office I'd seen in back—it had to be Pastor Carl's. Swiping a stone from a flower bed, I shattered the window. I cringed, but no alarm sounded. The pastor had been too smug to buy a security system.

I pulled fragments of glass from the window until I could climb through it. Searching his desk, I looked for something that would connect him to Father Skip or Gregorio Iavello. Nothing there, not even a desk calendar. Then I remembered Pastor Carl's black book. That was his calendar. But it wasn't in the room. I jumped out the window and ran for the van. The critical thing was to get to that black book. With his bad memory, Pastor Carl depended on it. It had to have the entry I was looking for.

I checked my watch. Pastor Carl had said he'd be at St. Mary's on Saturday trying to save the souls being misled by Anna. It was nearly 8:00 a.m. I guessed he'd be there. With no time to waste, I put the car in gear and took the short cut through the back roads to Diamond.

Going the back way gave me the advantage I hoped for. I entered Diamond on the west side of town, the opposite side from where the main road entered. The little road I was on was far enough away from the church that the police hadn't set up a roadblock there. I was able to get close to St. Mary's Church before I saw where they had placed the roadblock. I was in no danger yet of being stopped by the blue-uniformed policemen.

Wait a minute, I thought. The uniforms shouldn't be

blue. They should be brown, county sheriff brown. This roadblock was being handled by the Clinton Police Department, and I knew I couldn't trust them. They were tied too close to Carl Young.

Avoiding the roadblocks, I cut across the fields, bumping and bucking my way cross country until I reached the woods behind St. Mary's, the ones I'd used earlier to access the basement door.

I left the van and crept into the woods, using the huge trunks of the trees as cover. I hoped the basement door would still be clear. I could hear my own shallow, excited breathing as I picked my way closer to the church and I worried I was making too much noise. When I got close enough to see the back of the church, I could see a figure circling the grounds. I ducked behind a large sycamore.

Squinting into the sunlight, I tried to identify the figure. Dressed in the navy blue of the Clinton Police Force, he had a large body and walked with a swagger. That was all I needed to know. Detective Morini. Definitely not a man to be trusted.

Morini moved around to the side of the church where I couldn't see him. I crept forward again, advancing a few more feet toward the clearing. Every little step on the leaf-encrusted ground sounded to my ears like pop guns going off. I halted, crouching in shadow, and waited. Morini vanished around the side.

My heart pounded. I remained still for what seemed an eternity. Morini did not return. I stepped into the clearing, aware of even the tiniest sound I made. Once in the open, I sprinted for the church shed and hid behind it, wondering if I'd made any noise. I peeked around the corner.

Morini hurried out from the side of the church, advancing toward the woods with his gun drawn. He went close, no more than three feet from where I'd been minutes ago. I slowly pulled back.

I dropped to my hands and knees. My arms shook. I could hear my heart in my ears. I hoped Morini couldn't hear it.

When I finally peeked out again, I didn't see him. I crawled to the other end of the shed and checked. Now he was standing guard at the downhill basement door. He'd tucked his gun back in his holster.

I ducked my head and changed to a sitting position, my back braced against the shed. The Miraculous Medal jingled when I moved. I grabbed it in anger.

A lot of good Mary was doing me, if she were really here. Anna and Martha had convinced me they were sincere, but that didn't mean Anna wasn't sincerely crazy. Maybe I was going crazy, too. I wanted to believe them.

Do something, I whispered into the air. I heard an engine. Crouching, I peeked around the corner.

PC himself, Pastor Carl, pulled up in his Ford Explorer, parking only two feet from the shed. I yanked my head back, praying he hadn't seen me. A door slammed. A minute went by. I stuck my head out again. The vehicle blocked my view of the basement door. I stared at the tires.

They were bigger than those on my van. I thought about the undefined tracks I'd seen at the rectory and the Blazevich property. The tires were about the right size. It wasn't proof, though, just circumstantial evidence. I sucked in some air.

Where had Morini and Pastor Carl gone? I tried to see around the vehicle but it loomed large. I checked my watch. Ten minutes before nine. The roadblocks must be effectively keeping the crowds back. Morini obviously had reserved church duty for himself. I had to get in the church and stop the women from revealing themselves.

I crept out from behind the shed, sneaking up to the Explorer and using it as cover. Slowly I raised my head until I could see through the driver's side window. The basement door opened and I dropped my head again, but not before something on the passenger's seat caught my attention: the pastor's black book. His calendar and memory jogger. It had to contain the evidence I needed.

Morini stood by the door for a short while. I watched his feet from under the Explorer. Then he disappeared around the side. I shook off my nervousness and slowly, painstakingly lifted the Explorer's door handle, wincing when I heard the click of the latch.

I swung the door open. Reaching inside, I snatched the book, crouched again and thumbed to the date six weeks ago. The name I'd expected to see was there. Gregorio Iavello, on the four consecutive Wednesdays after his last session with Patricia Crowley. I was right. In my excitement I shook out a page which had been tucked in the book. I picked it up and unfolded it. It was the missing page from Father Skip's calendar. Carl Young's name was scribbled prominently in an early morning slot with the notation: "To discuss if I should appear on PC's radio program." I slipped it into my pocket.

My victory was short-lived. "Raise your hands, Bertetto."

I looked up. Morini pointed his gun at me. "Sure," I said. I held my hands in the air, still gripping Young's book.

"I'll take that," Morini said. He grabbed the book, marched me down to the basement door, told me to open it and we went in.

TWENTY-EIGHT

ONLY A LITTLE DAYLIGHT filtered into the basement from a couple of dirty windows. I slowed my pace, stepping carefully as Morini forced me up the stairs.

"Where are we going, Morini?" I asked loudly. My words echoed in the big room. I hoped Anna and Martha were listening.

"Upstairs." He pushed the gun into my back.

"Was this a trap for me or for someone else?" I half-turned to him as I said it, sending my voice toward the basement as much as I could.

"Don't flatter yourself. This wasn't for you," he replied. He nudged my shoulder with the gun. I straightened, my hands still in the air.

"Then who?"

"If you can't figure it out, I'm not going to tell you."

"It's for Martha and Anna, isn't it? You're hoping they'll walk right in so you can arrest them." I kept my volume up but began to worry that it might alert him to the women being in the basement if I continued it much longer.

"Let's just say we're taking precautions to make sure there isn't any bogus miracle."

We advanced a few more steps. "Or that if there's a real one, no one sees it?" I asked.

Morini laughed. It was an ugly, harsh sound. "There's no such things as miracles. Don't you know that?"

"I was at the pastor's church last night. If there aren't such things, you're misleading a lot of people."

"People believe what they want. Get going."

I tripped when we reached the landing. With my hands up, I didn't catch myself in time. I braced myself just before my chin hit, lessening the collision, but not by much. My knees also banged the hard floor. I struggled to my feet with my chin in pain, my kneecaps sore, and my wrists aching. "Can I put my hands down, Morini? I'm not armed."

"Get into the light," he ordered. We were in the room with the hidden door that opened behind the altar. A small window let in faint light. Morini grabbed my shoulder and told me to stand still. He patted me down for weapons with one hand and steadied the gun in my back with the other. Satisfied I was unarmed, he pushed me through the door.

As I came out from behind the altar, Pastor Carl and Captain Jack Slater of the Clinton Police snapped their heads toward me.

"Found him outside," Morini reported. "He's unarmed."

Slater's thin lips curled into a smile. "Welcome, Mr. Bertetto," he sneered. "You're better than I thought. How did you get past our roadblocks?"

"These are my old stomping grounds," I answered. "I know my way around." I hoped they hadn't heard the quiver in my voice.

"He had this," Morini told Pastor Carl, holding the black book out to him. Carl took it.

"What was so interesting about that book?" Slater asked.

I didn't reply. Morini prompted me with the gun. "Answer him."

"I thought it might have some evidence, but it doesn't," I lied.

Slater advanced toward me. "Evidence of what?"

Again I didn't answer, and again Morini dug the gun into my ribs. I put my hands down in defiance. "Cut it out with the gun. I know you've got it."

Slater nodded his head at Morini. "Better get back outside. If Veloche or Iavello shows up, hold them for me out there."

I thought about what he'd said. "Why not bring them in here?" I asked. "Or is there something you're worried about?"

Slater pulled out his gun and held it on me. "We're not worried about anything," he replied. He kept one eye on me, walked over to the pastor and snatched the book out of his hands. "What are you keeping in here, Carl, that he would find so interesting?"

Pastor Carl looked away. "I can't imagine."

Slater flipped through the book. I must've bent the page I was looking at when I closed the book because he saw it right away. "Ahhh," he said. "He found the spot in the book where you had your appointments with Gregorio Iavello, Carl. Not that it necessarily means anything." He closed the book and shoved it back at the pastor, then regarded me again. "What do you know?" he demanded.

"I don't know anything."

"Of course you don't. You only knew to go looking for Carl's book and managed to find a reference to Gregorio Iavello. Let's stop playing games. I want to know what you know and who else knows it, and if you don't tell me I will kill you now." He pointed the gun at my face.

I wondered what time it was. If I could keep talking long enough, Martha and Anna would hear me at 9:00 and know not to come into the sanctuary. I couldn't do anybody any good if I was dead before 9:00 a.m. "I know you killed Signor Iavello."

"Oh? And how did we do that?"

"You tried to kill him with an amitriptyline overdose Pastor Carl stole from Vigo General. I think Tom Iavello did the injection for you, though that's probably not important now. When the overdose didn't kill him, you shot him in the head and made it look like suicide." I took a breath and tried to look unworried. "How am I doing so far?"

"Not very well. You see, it was Martha and Anna…" Pastor Carl began.

"Please," I said, focusing on him, "don't take me for a fool like you did last night. You're not so glib when you don't have a mob of supporters behind you. Your black book shows Signor Iavello came to you for one of your famous miracles four weeks in a row. It corroborates with the 'PC,' 'Pastor Carl,' found in the *signore*'s schedule." Carl Young's tanned face began to pale.

I glanced down, I hoped inconspicuously, at my watch. Five minutes before 9:00. A lot of time to eat up. "I had it all wrong in the beginning," I said. "This was never about who was going to get the money. It was about who *wasn't* going to get the money. You fully expected to keep shaving Signor Iavello of money, promising him a cure week after week, promising him if he showed enough faith by donating lots of money—God would let you cure him. Instead, he got fed up and went to Anna. That was a problem because you had had enough defections to Second Advent. So you killed him after he was cured, even though he'd changed his will. You knew with a little prodding from your lawyer friend, Tom and Jimmy would challenge it and likely win. The important thing was not letting Martha's group get hold of all that money."

Carl Young's mouth hung open. The police chief laughed. "You're right, of course. We couldn't let Iavello live and blab about his supposed cure to everyone. If word had gotten around, it would have made his changing the will seem logical. And we didn't want any more of our faithful followers throwing money at Second Advent.''

"To get rid of Second Advent," I continued, "you killed off Father Skip and tried to frame Anna and Martha for it…''

"Tried? Tried?" he echoed. "I think we did a pretty effective job. Especially since it wasn't part of the original plan and we had to scramble to get it done.''

I couldn't think of anything else to do but keep them busy talking. And there were a few facts I wanted to be sure of. "Carl was at the *signore*'s house after the funeral offering condolences. His name was on Martha's list of people who stopped by to offer food." The pastor watched me guardedly, his hands twitching. He was nervous. That was good. I wanted him to be nervous. "He saw her using the knife. That's when he took it.''

"He was pissed off to hear them arguing about the money they were going to get from Iavello's estate," Slater said, "and it came to him. It was an inspired idea.''

I thought back on my initial trip to police headquarters. "Carl suggested it to you the day I first met you at the station. You saw the possibilities, so you conveniently lost the prescription bottle and bathroom glass. Then you lured Father Skip to his office early one morning with the promise of putting him on Carl's radio show, and killed him using the knife with Martha's fingerprints. Someone held the syringe, bottle and glass up to Anna in the crowds at her prayer meeting and boom, you had her fingerprints on them. Then you dumped Father Skip in Martha's back yard with the knife still in him, and let the drama play itself out.''

The pastor's eyes got wide. "How does he know about the radio show?''

Slater cocked an eyebrow. "Good question. How do you know?''

I tried to sound brave. "An even better question is, who else knows?"

"Okay," Slater said. "Who else knows?"

"Someone who's been gathering evidence. Who knows everything I know, and won't hesitate to use it, especially if you kill me." For a bluff, I thought it sounded pretty good.

Slater winked at Pastor Carl. "I think he might be referring to Charlie Cammack, our former police officer." A large smile came over Slater's face, chilling me. "Oh, I'm afraid you didn't hear about poor Charlie," he said to me. "We found he deliberately disobeyed my order to stay off the Iavello case. When Morini caught him outside Vigo General last evening, I'm afraid we had to fire him. The poor guy was so distraught, he took some sedatives just so he could sleep. At least, that's what we'll say. Actually, he wouldn't take them so we had to shoot them into his system. And he was so sleepy he didn't wake up when his gas furnace exploded this morning. That was about half an hour ago."

"No," I whispered. Had Dad gotten to Charlie in time? What if Dad was there when…? I choked back the urge to vomit.

"No one will find out what we've done," Slater stated confidently. "Not after we burn that black book of Carl's." He walked up to me and held the gun at my heart. "Not after we burn you, too."

The barrel of the gun pressed against my chest, a troubling reminder of my fragile mortality. I closed my eyes to think. "Martha's got enough money to hire a smart lawyer," I said, "and all you've got is circumstantial evidence. She'll get off. Anna, too."

Pastor Carl checked the time on his watch. He was trembling now, but my words didn't faze Slater. "Doesn't matter if she does. By that time, Second Advent will be out of business.''

I could see Carl's watch. If it was correct, the time was three minutes until 9:00. Three minutes to try something. If I could only think of what. Had to keep them talking. "How did you get hooked up with him?" I nodded at the pastor.

"Once I figured out what Carl's game was, I not only wanted to get in on it, I wanted to make it bigger and better. Carl graciously consented, considering the alternative was jail. You were right—he didn't graduate from Oregon Bible College. Or anywhere else, for that matter.''

Keeping the gun pointed at me, Slater sauntered back to Young and put his arm around him. "Just a con man with Hollywood good looks and a slick style. But he was effective. My contribution was hooking him up to the rich folks. We were doing well.'' He patted the pastor on the back, which didn't seem to have a reassuring effect.

"But you wanted to land Iavello," I interjected.

"Yes, absolutely. The big fish. But he was too Catholic. He wouldn't talk to us. We needed to find a weakness. Martha was unapproachable but Tom wasn't, especially when we cleared out his former steroid supplier and fixed his drug tests for him at the hospital. He told us about the severe depression his grandfather had. Tom was also good at handling a needle. He was the one who gave Iavello the overdose.''

"Did Tom shoot him, too?"

"No, he did," the pastor said, pointing to the captain. "He put the gun in Gregorio's hand, held it to his head and shot him. He's been behind all the killings.''

"Don't try to sound so innocent, Carl. It was your idea to off Gregorio. And you planted the evidence in Veloche's house and put the poison in Tom's steroids after he started having second thoughts.''

"I never meant for so many people to be murdered," Young said to me. "You have to believe me."

"You don't need to plead to him," Slater told Young. "He's not going to be alive much longer."

"Barring a miracle," I said. I didn't have a plan yet, but I was searching for one. I began to walk around, just to see if I could get away with it. Slater kept the gun on me, but he didn't try to confine me to one space. "And there may yet be a miracle," I added. I took calm, measured steps toward Pastor Carl. "Admit it, you're afraid, afraid there might be something to Second Advent. It might be supernatural. Mary might really be here..." I let my voice go raspy on the last word. It hung in the air.

"Stop it," Young said, sounding more whiny than commanding.

I continued to pace. The two men were between me and the altar. I smiled at Pastor Carl. He glanced at his watch.

"Time to end this right now," Slater said, arms extended. He pointed the gun directly at my head.

"The noise'll bring the county deputies in here," I warned. "You can't have them in your pocket, too."

"Oh, you misunderstand. You see, you jumped me and grabbed the gun. I managed to get it away from you, but the gun went off. Carl here will back me up. Won't you, Carl?" No response. "Won't you?" he repeated forcefully.

Someone's watch beeped nine o'clock. There was a gasp from the altar. I saw immediately it was Martha and Anna, but Slater and the pastor had to turn. When Slater took his eyes off me, I grabbed at the gun, knocking it out of his hands. It clattered across the floor toward the Immaculate Heart statue.

We both dove for it. Slater landed on the gun, but before he could maneuver his body in position to grab it, I whacked him in the head with my elbow. We grappled on the floor. I threw punches wildly, struggling to keep the gun away from his hand.

When I felt myself losing the battle, I scrambled for the statue, seeking cover. Before I got there, I heard a shot. I felt something graze my waist, then hot pain knifed me. I looked down. My sweater was becoming darkened with blood, the stain moving up from my side. Staggering, I put the statue between Slater and me.

"You're dead," Slater said.

"Not yet," I answered.

We rounded the statue. I put my hand on it to steady myself but felt it wobble and remembered it wasn't very steady. An idea came to me, but to make it work I needed a distraction. I needed it soon.

Martha's voice rang out, a mixture of awe and fear. "The…the statue. It's bleeding!"

We all stared up at the heart. Sure enough, it was bleeding, and not in little droplets but in a thin stream. I slipped my hand, covered with blood, away from the statue and held it out to Martha. She screamed and tore down the middle of the church toward the back doors, yelling as loud as she could all the way.

"Shit," Slater said. He went into a crouch and aimed the gun at her. I placed my hands on Mary's narrow back between her shoulders. Far from feeling as if it had any sense of life, the statue felt cold and rough and heavy as I gave it a big heave. The statue rocked on its pedestal, scraping the wood mount. Slater turned at the noise. He swung the gun away from Martha and started to take aim at me. Giving the statue a final shove, I watched it spin in the air as it left the pedestal and slammed Slater in the head, coming to rest on top of his body with Mary facing toward me. There was a thud, but no gunshot.

My side ached, the wound aggravated by the pushing. I stumbled over to the statue which continued to bleed on top of the unconscious Slater. Suddenly the Miraculous Medal felt heavy. I grasped at it, but it wasn't caught on anything. It just hung from the chain, pulling me down, down toward the statue. I fell onto Mary, the blood of my side mixing with the blood of her Immaculate Heart.

Out of the corner of my eye I saw Anna kneel and make the Sign of the Cross. "The Immaculate Heart saved him," she said.

It was the last sight and sound my body registered for several hours.

EPILOGUE

I FELT SOMEONE staring at me and awoke to find Father Vince looking into my eyes.

"How does it feel to be touched by heaven?" he asked.

"I'm not sure that I have been. Where am I?" I rubbed my eyes and looked around. Green cloth curtains on four sides surrounded the small bed I was lying in.

Father Vince sat down in a small, white vinyl chair, the only chair in my "room." "You're in the Vermillion County Hospital E.R. You've been here about three hours. The doctors don't know why you've been unconscious all this time, so they've kept you under observation. How does it feel to have been part of a miracle?"

"Quit asking me that."

Father Vince frowned. "Surely you don't disbelieve the miracle. You made it come true."

The events at St. Mary's seemed hazy. "What are you talking about?"

"Don't be modest. You figured out Mary's prophecy. The key was to look at it as Mary would, in a spiritual way. 'Someone thought to be dead' was Anna, because, having been framed for murder, she looked like a fraud—dead in a spiritual sense. 'Someone thought to be alive' was Carl Young, because, from appearances, he was alive with the Holy Spirit. But Mary worked through you to bring the dead to life and the living to justice. And she protected you with her Immaculate Heart—literally, in the form of the statue. All it took was understanding her message, the one you showed me at St. Mary's College."

I rubbed my temples. Another theologically induced headache. Or maybe it was just my side. "My side hurts," I said. I touched it through the sheet that covered me.

"Your right side?" Father Vince asked. "You've been saying that, even while you were unconscious." He pulled the sheet down to my waist. "But the doctors have been over it and they can't find anything wrong."

I stared at the right side of my waist. It was perfectly normal. No blood, no wound. No evidence a bullet had ever grazed me. I reached down and ran my hands over the spot that hurt. "Slater shot me. Didn't Martha or Anna say anything about my being hurt?"

"They were worried about you falling on the hard statue, but that was it. They thought that's why you were complaining."

"No, I was hit," I insisted. I paused. "I think I was hit. What about the blood at the scene? Wasn't there blood?"

"Oh, that," Father Vince said. "There was blood from the statue. The doctors ran a preliminary check on it. O positive, just like all the other times it bled."

"My blood is O positive."

"Is it?" the priest said. He seemed uninterested. Was it possible I had imagined the bullet wound?

"Where's my sweater?"

"In this bag." Father Vince pulled out the blood-stained heavy wool sweater and handed it to me. I looked for a bullet hole, but the sweater was so bulky and loosely knit that the bullet could have passed anywhere through the knitting. The blood, now dried, would have pulled it back in place. But I couldn't have dreamed this.

"I fell on the statue after I was shot..." I said.

"Well, you fell on the statue at any rate," he corrected. "Now that you've tipped it over, I'd like to get a look at that statue, but the archdiocese has spirited it away." He sounded disheartened. "I don't know where they're keeping it, and I may never get to examine it now. They have reason to protect it, I guess. But after this miracle, perhaps it doesn't matter whether I get to see it."

"Anna's prophecy still could have been made up," I said, getting back to the miracle Father wanted to talk about. "It was nebulous enough to seem true given the proper interpretation.

"You're right, I did think about the prophecy in the spiritual sense. I laughed at the time because it seemed to point to Carl Young. But when I worked it backwards, I figured out it was possible Young did it. And he had, he and Slater. But I'm not sure that validates Anna."

Father Vince gazed at me with the same frustrated gaze I'd seen in Father Skip's eyes just a few days ago. Remembering Father Skip hurt. I cleared my throat.

"What happened at St. Mary's after I passed out?" I asked.

"You knocked out Slater with the statue, so Martha was able to get out the front door and bring help. With three witnesses to Slater's confession, Carl Young was ready to tell everything. He plea-bargained testimony against Slater and Morini for reduced charges. The three of them are being held in the Parke County Jail.

"In the meantime, a legion of press people have showed up to talk to you. They think you worked a miracle, even if you don't. The doctors and your father have kept them at bay."

"My dad!" I tried to sit up but felt pain in my side. I winced. "Where is he?"

"He's in the lobby waiting for your wife and Stephanie to show up," Father Vince said with a grin, "and all the while regaling the press with how wonderful his son is." He looked at his watch. "Your wife should be here soon.

Your father called them the minute you were admitted. Let me go get him. I told him I would watch over you. He wouldn't have left otherwise."

"Did he find Charlie in time? Is Charlie…"

Father Vince put his hand on mine. "Charlie has been admitted for an overdose of sedatives. But he will be fine. Your father found him when he broke into the house. And because he smelled gas and got the fire department over there, nothing happened."

"Is Dad okay?"

"Exhilarated. He said this is the most excitement he's had in a long time. If you go back to investigative reporting, you may have a tough time keeping him at bay."

A nurse came in to check on me. I told her about the pain in my side and asked if I could have a painkiller. She went off to find a doctor.

Father Vince left to find my dad. Martha and Anna, having showered and dressed properly and looking nothing like the women who'd spent two days in a coal bin, stepped into my little cubicle.

"Well, Nick, you've certainly earned your $25,000," Martha said. "Thank you." She held my hand warmly. "I'll have a check for you by morning. And don't worry about any of these hospital charges. I've arranged for Second Advent to cover them."

Anna came over and kissed me on the cheek. "I've seen Mary twice since you saved us. Once, right after you collapsed on the statue, she appeared and stood over you. She gave you a special blessing." I knew Anna expected me to react, but feeling confused about this "miracle," I just laid there looking at her, wondering.

Anna continued. "A half hour ago she appeared with another message for you. I've written it down." She handed me the note, written on the same blue stationary as the previous message.

I didn't open it right then. "What about 'Second Advent'? Is she going to keep giving you messages?"

"The messages will continue but not as frequently. She says this morning's miracle has proved the validity of what she says. She still looks pregnant. The Second Coming is still coming."

It has been for 2000 years, I thought. But maybe it's closer than we think. Who knows?

Martha and Anna left, and I opened Mary's new message. It was written in Anna's flowery script. "Thank you for bearing my lamp. Because you have been wise in understanding the ways of God and can be trusted to exercise discernment, my Son has acceded to my wish to give you a unique favor. Whenever you require special help, ask for it in His Mother's name, and He will give it to you. From now until He calls for you."

I refolded the note. The one thing I really, really wanted to do was to believe. I wanted to believe a miracle had saved Anna. I wanted to believe a miracle healed my gunshot wound. I wanted to believe God was so gracious, he'd give me special help if I needed it. Perhaps if I asked in Mary's name for proof that it hadn't been just some amazing conglomeration of events... No, if the gift were real I wouldn't waste it on something like that.

I rummaged through the bag to find my jeans, then reached into the pockets and pulled out the calendar page I'd stuffed in there before Morini took Pastor Carl's book away from me. The page belonged to Father Skip and connected Pastor Carl to the meeting at which he and Slater killed the priest. To my surprise, it was completely untouched by blood, although blood had soaked my jeans. Was that another miracle? Proof for the skeptic? Or just happenstance?

I found the Miraculous Medal Anna had given me and fastened it around my neck.

But whether I completely believed, or just wanted to believe, I didn't know.

ARE YOUR MYSTERIES DISAPPEARING?

As of January 2005, your Mystery Library™ books will no longer be available at retail locations. The good news is, you can still get them delivered right to your door! Fill out the form below to guarantee you'll keep getting these great books each month.

Witness
in Bishop Hill

Sara Hoskinson Frommer
A JOAN SPENCER MYSTERY

A Christmas sojourn to the scenic hamlet of Bishop Hill turns out to be murder for Joan Spencer and her new husband, Lieutenant Fred Lundquist, when Fred's mother witnesses the vicious murder of a local.

Disoriented by Alzheimer's, Mrs. Lundquist cannot clearly identify the killer, but she's still a threat. With her mother-in-law's life depending on it, Joan must sort out which secrets are worth killing for in peaceful Bishop Hill.

"Frommer is a brisk and clean writer, she handles the rueful ambivalence of middle age very well indeed."
—*Booklist*

Available November 2004
at your favorite retail outlet.

W⊕RLDWIDE LIBRARY®

WSHF510

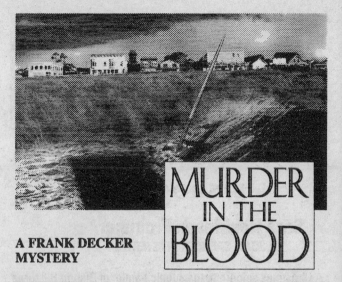

MURDER IN THE BLOOD

A FRANK DECKER MYSTERY

When local history teacher Lou Cameron disappears, Farrell County sheriff Frank Decker is puzzled by accusations of embezzlement from wealthy Nathaniel Wetherston. Was the history teacher really stealing money from Wetherston's company?

Unconvinced, Decker sets out on a bizarre case where the only answers lead to a twisted trail ending in a face-off with a killer....

GENE DeWEESE

"A highly professional dip into moldering Americana."
—*Kirkus Reviews*

"...fabulous police procedural."
—Harriet Klausner

Available December 2004 at your favorite retail outlet.

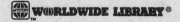